I0680689

Up on the Farm

BEWITCHED BY THE BARISTA

JASON WRENCH

Bewitched by the Barista

ISBN # 978-1-80250-984-7

©Copyright Jason Wrench 2022

Cover Art by Kelly Martin ©Copyright September 2022

Interior text design by Claire Siemaszkiewicz

Pride Publishing

Published in 2022 by Pride Publishing, United Kingdom.

Pride Publishing is an imprint of Totally Entwined Group Limited.

BEWITCHED BY THE BARISTA

Dedication

This book is dedicated to all the professional
online sex workers.

Acknowledgements

First, I want to thank the individuals willing to talk to me about their reasons and motivations for engaging in online sex work. Their stories and voices are heard throughout this book. Second, I want to continue to thank Jamie Rose for her continued support as my editor at Pride Publishing. Last, I want to thank my Ninja Writers family for their comments on early drafts of this work.

Definition of Terms

Camming - slang for web-camming — The art of sexually stimulating oneself or another over the Internet for people to watch.

CammBoy — A young twink who engages in camming to earn an income.

Chapter One

Roger

Christmas music filled the elevator as I rode in silence up to our apartment, thankful my new client had signed on the dotted line with little fuss. I think we had both been trying to get home for the holidays. Nothing sped up the process like a late afternoon meeting on the day before Christmas, I guessed.

The elevator doors opened, and I stepped out into the empty hallway. Even on busy days, people in our building were quiet, respectful and kept to themselves, which was how I liked it. My fiancé, Jeremy, wasn't expecting me for at least another couple of hours. I kind of looked forward to surprising him. We had reservations at nine for dinner, so it would be nice to chill out, maybe throw on some news before we headed into the frosty night. Well, for New York City, it wasn't the coldest Christmas I'd seen. In fact, it was downright seasonal.

I pulled my keys out of my pocket and slipped the right one into the lock before turning it clockwise and pushing open the door. I stepped in and was immediately surprised by the dimmed lights and a handful of lit candles glowing inside. Sometimes, Jeremy takes relaxing baths. I opted not to yell out and didn't want to break his mood. *Hell, if I'm lucky, maybe I'll slip into the tub and join him.*

I hung up my coat on the hook near the door and set my briefcase down on the counter. I walked into the living room and immediately saw clothes strewn about the apartment. *Well then,* I thought to myself. *If that's how he wants this evening, I don't want to disappoint him.* We'd played this little game before. I'd come home, Jeremy would have stripped and had been waiting for me on our bed. Once, for Valentine's Day, he'd had a trail of rose petals leading me into the bedroom.

Without thinking, I shrugged out of my suit coat, laying it over the back of the sofa. I kicked off my loafers and made quick work of my tie. Before long, I was naked as the day I'd been born. I stared down at my washboard stomach. Not as flat as when I'd been a teenager, but I still looked pretty damn hot. Just staring at my nude body and its tightly manscaped features had me growing in anticipation.

The bedroom door was closed. I reached out, grabbed the handle and twisted it. I pushed it open quietly, just in case Jeremy had fallen asleep while he was waiting for me. The thought of walking in on a nude Jeremy lying on our bed facedown definitely caused my cock to twitch. I looked down at all eight inches of me standing as straight and hard as a ship's mast.

It took a second for my eyes to adjust.

"What the fuck!" I yelled.

Jeremy was mid-thrust into some young twink's ass.

He whipped his head in my direction. "Roger," Jeremy started, his voice trailing off.

I stared in disbelief as Jeremy's cock sat nestled in the guy. The twink, whose face was shoved into the mattress, lifted his head and looked at me.

"Oh…hey, Roger," Avery said. "Wanna join?" He winked at me and licked the top of his lip.

Part of me wanted to go over and shove something between those lips to see if he'd choke on it. But with my luck, he'd have no gag reflex. Instead, I narrowed my eyes and said, "Avery Addington." I sounded like a principal who wasn't too surprised to see a pupil in the main office. "What the fuck are you doing here?"

Avery looked at me with a 'are you fucking kidding me' look, before he said, "Uh…having a good time."

My nails bit into my palms in clenched fists. Jeremy sat there with his cock still sitting inside the kid. Then he slowly slid out.

"And you're not wearing a condom!" I was pretty sure neighbors up and down the hall heard that one.

"Don't worry, daddy," Avery said, drawing out the word 'daddy' like it was some kind of badge of honor for reaching the ancient age of forty. "I'm totally on PrEP."

"I'm. No. One's. Father."

I knew if I didn't get out of there, I was going to say a few things I wouldn't want to repeat in polite company, not that Avery was polite. Avery was one of those kids who had a reputation, and now I saw the reputation in all its glory splayed out on my bed…and on the sheets I'd bought!

I shut the door.

I looked out at the living room. Only then did I notice that there'd been two pairs of pants on the floor. *How had I been so blind?*

I walked over to where I'd discarded my clothes and heard the bedroom door open.

"You don't get the right to be angry with me," Jeremy said.

"What?" I spun around and looked at Jeremy. "I'm not the one who was fucking around on my fiancé…on Christmas Eve!"

"Well, if you weren't working all the time…"

"I work all the time so we can afford to live here, so we can afford that dream wedding you've been wanting."

"Hey! It's not my fault I'm having a problem landing a job."

"Jeremy," I said, trying to keep the venom out of my voice as much as possible, "you've been having a problem landing work for years. When are you going to realize that you're a two-bit hack of an actor who will never make it big? Sure, you're hot, but you don't have any fucking talent." As soon as the words were out of my mouth, I kind of regretted them — but not really.

"Well… How long have you been holding that in?"

I breathed in through my nose and let it out. "This is neither the time nor the place to have this conversation."

"Oh, and why not?"

"You're naked. I'm naked. And that two-bit hustling twink is in *my* bedroom."

"*Our* bedroom."

"As if that makes it better?" I groused.

Avery chose that moment to make his appearance. He reached up and rested his arm on Jeremy's shoulder as he draped himself around my fiancé. I couldn't help but focus downward, seeing that Avery was the only one in the room who was on full alert.

"I am not a hustler," Avery said.

"You're what? Twelve—?"

"I'm twenty-five, I'll have you know."

"And yet you act like you're a child. You're the fucking gay version of Peter Pan. All the rumors about you are true, aren't they?"

"I don't pay attention to rumors. Anyone who has a problem with me isn't my problem."

"What the fuck ever," I said. "I just can't—"

"We need to talk about this," Jeremy said, cutting into my dressing down of Avery.

"Talk about *what*?" I asked. In the flickering candlelight, I realized that all three of us were standing there stark naked. I was so mad at Jeremy that I hadn't thought about the fact that I was letting an absolute stranger stare at my naked body. "I can't talk to you now...not like this—"

"Roger—"

"Don't, *Roger*, me." I found my underwear on the ground, reached down, grabbed them and pulled them up. When I was finally covered, I looked back up at Avery and Jeremy. "I hope you two are happy together."

"Oh, I'm not looking for a relationship," Avery said, with almost a hint of disgust at the thought of it. "I found him on Grindr and thought he looked like fun."

"Grindr!" I yelled again. "You're on Grindr?"

"It's not like that—"

"Like *what*? Like you created a profile on a dating app behind my back." Only then did I realize what other implications this had. "Is Avery even the first?"

The look on Jeremy's face was all I needed to see. Avery clearly wasn't the first. My face went slack.

"Roger…"

I couldn't say anything. I didn't know what to say. I'd never felt more betrayed by anyone in my entire life.

"Roger!"

I got dressed. I heard Jeremy's voice in the background, but I'd honestly stopped listening. At some point, Avery had slunk back into the bedroom. I looked up at one point and could see the kid acting like he owned the place. Avery was propped up with his arms crossed behind his head. The light from the living room provided me enough to see the smug look on the little prick's face.

I laced up my shoes, stood, walked to the front door, grabbed my briefcase, pulled down my coat and left.

Even as I shut the door behind myself, I could hear Jeremy calling after me. I walked in a haze to the elevator. A happy, smiling couple stood in the small box hand-in-hand when the doors opened. *That should have been me.* As much as I wanted to make a snide comment about how love was fake, I plastered on a smile and turned my back to the couple. On the ride down, a tear fell down my cheek.

I walked through the lobby and quickly realized I did not know where I was going. Out in the cold air, I pulled out my phone and pulled up my favorite hotel app. On Christmas Eve, there wasn't exactly much availability, and the prices for booking this late made my eyes bulge. I found a hotel I'd always wanted to stay at and booked it. I had the money in my savings, so I might as well enjoy the stay. I booked for three nights. I needed distance. I needed to figure out what my next move was.

Fuck! I have nothing with me. Thankfully, Duane Reade was always open, so I could get my necessities there. If I hurried, I could buy some new clothes for a few days. At least, I hoped I could find a department store still open. I hailed the first cab I saw and said, "Take me to Macy's Harold Square."

The guy got a weary look on his face before saying, "Whatever. It's your funeral."

I leaned back and stared at my reflection in the cab's window as we passed the familiar sights of the city. *What am I going to do now?*

* * * *

I got out of the cab at Macy's Harold Square. I looked down at my watch and saw I had about twenty-five minutes to get inside, make purchases and get out before the place closed at six p.m. I looked at the throngs of people through the windows, took a deep breath and walked in.

I hadn't stepped foot inside a department store in years. Jeremy always shopped for me. I never quite trusted my style choices, so it was nice to have a boyfriend, then fiancé, who enjoyed doing that. I looked at the map and realized I had to get to five floors. I wouldn't have time to try on anything. *This should be fun.* I rode the escalator up to the mezzanine and grabbed some sportswear, so I could still hit the gym. I dashed up to the second floor for casual pants, then to the third for a couple of pairs of jeans. On to the fourth, I stocked up on underwear. Last, I ended up on the fifth floor and picked out three dress shirts, a sports coat, two pairs of slacks and two ties. I looked at my now-overflowing bag of stuff and tried to figure out how much this crazy shopping spree was going to set me back.

I found a checkout line and stood in it with the rest of the impatient holiday shoppers. I let out a breath. The intercom system warned shoppers that the store would close in five minutes, so people needed to make their final selections. The queue was already long, but more and more people seemed to pile in behind me. I guess there were a lot of last-minute Christmas shoppers in the world. Thankfully, the people behind the counter clearly wanted to get out of work as much as the holiday shoppers wanted to make their purchases and be on their way.

A mother in front of me was trying to juggle a bag of stuff, two kids and a baby. I did my best to keep the baby entertained by making faces at it, which made the time fly by faster.

"Next customer," a chipper voice said when it was my turn. I was directed to a clerk in the middle who wore a pair of reindeer antlers with twinkling Christmas lights.

I hoisted my bag of purchases onto the counter.

"Oh dear," the clerk said, "did an airline lose your luggage? I hate it when that happens. You'd be amazed at how many people I see come through here in a hurry, needing to purchase a new wardrobe like this." She kept chatting away as she scanned the barcodes and removed the RFID anti-theft security tags from my purchases. "That'll be thirteen-hundred, seventy-nine dollars and twenty-seven cents. I sure hope the airline is paying for all this. Can I charge this to your Macy's card?"

"I don't have one," I responded.

"Would you like to open one today?" the clerk asked.

"Probably not today. You are busy," I said, looking back at the long line of people still waiting to check out. I pulled out my wallet from my back pocket, flipped through the cards and laid down my platinum American Express Card.

"Thank you," the clerk said as she swiped the card, handed me my receipt and asked me to sign the store copy. Once I had put my John Hancock on the bottom line, she packaged all my new purchases into giant Macy's bags and handed them to me. "Have a Merry Christmas," she said with a huge smile.

"Thanks. You, too," I replied almost automatically.

I grabbed my purchases and followed the path to the nearest exit. A security guard stood next to the door. I wasn't sure if he was there to make sure no one was shoplifting or keep any other customers from sneaking in. I nodded as I walked up. The guard opened the door for me, and I stepped back into the cold air.

With clothing in hand, I knew I needed to go buy the rest of my essentials. I shifted my bags into one hand so I could pull out my phone. I quickly searched for the nearest Duane Reade's and headed off in that direction.

The streets were quieter than they would have been on an ordinary evening. I followed the map to the closest store, which was less than a block north of Macy's, right on Sixth Avenue. I walked in and found it busy, but not nearly the chaos I'd just gotten out of. I grabbed a basket and made my way through the store. I picked up shaving cream and a razor, toothpaste and a toothbrush, gel and a comb, deodorant, bodywash and a small bottle of cologne that I hoped wouldn't make me smell like a teenager going on his first date. I also picked up some food essentials — and by essentials, I mean I bought a shit-ton of comfort food. By the time I got out of Duane Reade's, I had spent almost one hundred and twenty dollars. I looked down at all my bags and made my way to the hotel.

I'd never stayed at The Time New York before, but I'd heard good things about the upscale hotel. I thought about hailing a cab but ended up walking the twenty minutes to West Forty-Ninth Street — quite the feat with the load I was juggling.

My mind was a jumble of thoughts. I wanted to talk to someone, but the last thing I wanted to do was bring my drama into someone's life on Christmas Eve. It wasn't anyone else's fault that Jeremy had imploded my life with one trick.

The snow crunched beneath my loafers as I walked. Along the way, I passed a few restaurants that were still open, serving customers who either didn't want to stay at home on Christmas Eve or didn't celebrate the holiday at all. That's one thing I can say about New York City. There is always something open, since we have so many faiths represented. Many years ago, before I'd met Jeremy, I remembered hanging out with my Jewish friends on Christmas Day. Their tradition was to go to a nice Chinese restaurant then to a movie. Maybe I'd drag myself out of the hotel tomorrow and find a Chinese place…or at least get delivery.

I made it to the hotel, got checked in with no problems and took the elevator up to my room. It was modern but small. There was a king-sized bed and a small writing table, but that was about it for the main part. The bathroom was also pretty small, but it had all the necessities.

I took a shower then pulled the tags off the new pajamas I'd bought and lay down on the bed. For the first time since I'd walked in on Jeremy, I let myself soak in everything that had happened to me that evening. I was numb. Trying to think made me a little lightheaded. I sat cross-legged and let myself cry. At first, the tears came one at a time. But once the flood works opened, I was a waterfall of pain. After I finished my first emotional catharsis of the weekend—I was sure there would be more—I washed my face to take some of the puffiness out. I called down to the hotel restaurant, Serafina, and ordered lasagna al forno. I wanted carbs, carbs and nothing but carbs. I also ordered a bottle of Seravino, Malbec, Antigal Uno, Mendoza. I'd learned a long time ago that I love a good Malbec wine, and the only good Malbecs were the ones straight from Argentina. None of those fake American Malbecs for me. I didn't need to order dessert, since I'd already splurged on comfort food at Duane Reade's, but I ordered the tiramisu, anyway.

I grabbed the remote control from the bedside table and turned on the TV. I flipped around a few channels but wasn't paying attention to what was on the screen. The simple act of flipping channels was enough to occupy my mind for the moment. Part of me wanted to roll up into a little ball and go to sleep, but I knew that would be a bad idea with my room service heading up. I kept channel surfing.

The sudden knocking on the door drew me out of my weird zombie-like funk. I forced myself off the bed and answered the door. The guy on the other side saw my shadow because he said, "Room service," right as I looked out of the peephole. I opened the door.

"Good evening, sir," a handsome young Italian man said in a thick Brooklyn accent. He may have had all the Italian genes in the world, but he was clearly a New Yorker. "Want me to put this on the desk?" he asked, motioning with his head down toward the tray he was holding.

I stared into the man's chiseled face and into the dark brown, almost black, eyes. "Huh?" I heard myself ask in a dazed and confused voice.

"Your food? Would you like me to put it on the desk, then open your bottle of wine?"

"Yes," I said, snapping out of it. "Thanks. Sorry, just a bit slow tonight," I said with a thousand-watt smile. I'd learned years ago how to put on the fake show-smile for clients, so it came almost second nature. I stood out of the way and held the door open for the young man, who quickly entered the room and set down the tray. He made quick work with the wine opener.

"One glass or two?" the guy asked.

Such a simple question with such huge implications. "Just one," I said, casting my eyes down to avoid breaking down in front of this guy—not that it mattered, because it wasn't like I was ever going to see him again. He poured a small amount into one glass and handed it to me to smell and taste. I swirled the wine around in the glass. I noticed the legs sticking to the top of the wine glass before slowly sliding back down, indicating a fuller, richer wine experience with a higher alcohol proof. The Malbec had a bold and spicy aroma with hints of blackberries and plum. I lifted the glass to my lips and took a sip. *Damn! This is good.* But at seventy dollars a bottle, it should have been pretty decent.

"Thanks," I said. The server filled the rest of my glass, then recorked the bottle before setting it back on the desk.

While he did that, I pulled out my wallet and found I had no cash on me but a couple of fifties and a one-hundred-dollar bill. *Oh well, at least someone will have a nice Christmas.* I pulled out the hundred and handed it over to the man.

"I can't," the man said.

I waved him off with a "Merry Christmas."

He thanked me again before letting me know to call down if I needed anything else. I assured him I wouldn't, but I promised to call if I did. I showed him out of the room and turned on the 'Do not disturb' sign when he left.

Once the waiter was gone, I grabbed the tray and moved it from the desk to the middle of the bed. I decided dinner in bed was just what the doctor ordered. Before I dug into the food, I drank my first glass of wine, then topped it off while I tried to once again find something to watch on television. I finally settled in on *A Diva's Christmas Carol*. It was a two-thousand film starring Vanessa Williams as Ebony Scrooge. Part of me preferred the nineteen-thirty-eight black-and-white film, but I never pass up an opportunity to watch Vanessa Williams.

With Vanessa on the television, I dove into my lasagna and enjoyed every carb-alicious, cheesy-drenched morsel. I also finished a couple more glasses of wine. By the time I'd finished dinner, I only had enough wine for half a glass of the tasty red stuff. *Too bad you can't lick inside a wine bottle*, I thought to myself. I also considered ordering another bottle but thought that would probably be a bad idea.

Instead, I made the insta-coffee in the hotel room and served it up with my tiramisu. During all this, Vanessa Williams was replaced with a more recent remake of Dickens' classic novel, where Ebenezer Scrooge was played by Sir Patrick Stewart. When I finished my dessert, I left the dishes in the hall outside my door. The movie played on in the background as I brushed my teeth. I curled back up on the bed and sighed. I can't even remember which Ghost of Christmas Past, Present or Future I'd gotten to before I passed out from emotional exhaustion.

Chapter Two

Light from the corner of the window poked into my room and crossed my face. I'd shut the blackout curtains, but a sliver of sun poked through and hit me right in the eyes. I groaned a little. I wasn't exactly hungover, but that didn't mean I was in a good place. It's moments like these — as I threw back the covers and slung my legs over the edge of the bed — when I realize how old I feel. My lower back aches, my neck aches and my mind is screaming to dive back under the covers. I forced myself to stand, then walked the few short steps into the bathroom as my bladder called.

After washing my hands, I headed back into the room. Walking over to the window, I pulled back the curtain to peek outside and see what the morning looked like. There was a nice coat of white covering the city outside — not enough to make it dangerous, but just enough to make it look pretty. I hoped it would all be gone by noon. I wasn't in the mood for pretty. I knew I sounded like a jaded old Scrooge, but since three Christmas spirits hadn't visited me in the night, I figured I could be cantankerous today. I closed the curtain, slipped back into bed and went back to sleep. It wasn't exactly like I had plans.

I woke up again around eleven and felt even sorer than I had the first time. This time when I got out of bed, relieved myself and looked out of the window, most of the snow had already melted. It was still quiet outside. I did the healthy thing and decided to go for a run. I'm not what you would call an avid runner. I'm not one of those guys who's like 'look at me and my runner's high'. I'm one of those guys who goes for a run only because I know that without them, my body will call it kaput when I turn sixty.

I put on my new jogging attire, a sleek Under Armour number from head to toe. I grabbed my iPhone and AirPods. Thankfully, I'd plugged in the phone the past night when I'd gotten to my hotel room. I slipped a single credit card and my hotel key into the zip-up pocket inside my shorts before stepping out into the hall. I walked to the elevator and was glad no one was out and about on my floor, because I wasn't yet in the mood to plaster on the fake smile.

The elevator dinged as the door slid open. There was a lone guy, who looked like he might be a custodian, standing in the back corner. He looked up, nodded his head and went back to playing with his phone. I stood in the opposite corner and did the same.

I had several text messages from Jeremy. They had started off apologetic.

I'm so sorry. I love you. I won't ever do it again.

That one had been sent almost immediately after I'd left the apartment. As the evening had gone on, the messages had turned to denial.

I have nothing to be sorry about. I'm a gay man with needs. Anyway, let me know you're okay.

By the time I'd already passed out, the texts had become belligerent.

Go fuck your sanctimonious self. If there's anyone to blame for all this, it's you.

The last text was from twenty minutes before.

Heading over to my parents for Christmas. You still joining me?

"Are you fucking kidding me?" I grumbled.
"Excuse me?" the custodian asked, glancing in my direction.
"Sorry," I stammered. "Dealing with the idiocy of my soon-to-be-ex."
"Oh," the guy said as he raised his eyebrows. Apparently, that's all he needed to hear.
The elevator door dinged again, and I exited the elevator into the lobby. I took the stairs to the street level, where the doorman on duty stood wearing a cap and a full-length black wool coat. He looked at me in my jogger's getup and shook his head.
I nodded and gave him a half-smile as I headed outside. I fiddled with my iPhone for a second before turning on my exercise playlist. I was questioning the sanity of wearing jogging shorts in this cold weather. It

wasn't crazy cold or anything, but it was definitely cold enough to not be shorts weather.

My new pair had a cell phone pocket in the back of them, so once the music was pumping in my ears, I zipped up my cell phone and jogged. I turned left and headed toward Eighth Avenue, figuring there would be less pedestrian traffic in that direction. Once there, I turned north and started running toward Central Park. Before I knew it, I'd passed Columbus Circle and kept going north. When I finally hit One-Hundred-and-Tenth Street, I crossed the backside of the park and headed back toward The Time on Fifth Avenue.

I liked the steady feeling of the concrete sidewalk beneath my feet with each stride. I wasn't trying to win a marathon or anything, but I wanted to keep moving. It was as if I knew that when I stopped, I would have to face my life. I wasn't ready for that yet. Some three-and-a-half hours and ten-plus miles later, I got back to the hotel door. The same doorman let me inside. Of course, by this point, I was a dripping, soppy mess. I headed upstairs to the lobby, caught the elevator up to my room and got inside without interacting with anyone else. I pulled my iPhone out of its pocket and hooked it back up to the charger. I made sure I stretched a bit, because the last thing I wanted was for my muscles to tense after that amount of exertion. Once I was sufficiently cooled down, I headed into the shower.

At some point, I ended up sitting in the shower with the water raining down on me as I cried again. When I thought I'd spent every tear imaginable from my body, another bout of sobs seemed to take over. And the worst part? I wasn't sure what I was crying about anymore. Sure, I was crying about the death of a relationship, but it felt larger than that. I'd wrapped up my identity in my relationship with Jeremy for so long that I wasn't entirely sure who I was without him anymore. The more I thought about it, the more pathetic I found it.

It was about four by the time I found myself back in a pair of shorts and a T-shirt, lounging around the hotel room. I decided it was time to call my brother out in California. He lived in Los Angeles and worked in the entertainment industry. I honestly didn't get what he did. I know it involved reading scripts, because he always complained about the pile of them he needed to read. Beyond that, I knew he worked for one of the big production houses and had some kind of authority to green-light projects.

I picked up my phone from the charger and connected it to my Bluetooth headset. I searched for his information and hit the call button.

"Merry Christmas," my brother's wife said as she answered the phone.

"Merry Christmas to you too, Penny."

"Oh…hey, Roger," she said, taking a second to recognize my voice. She then yelled into her house, "Honey, it's Roger."

There was a quick moment of silence before Peter picked up the phone. "Hey, buddy, Merry Christmas."

"Merry Christmas, Peter. What's going on in California?"

Peter told me about what the family was up to. I could hear the kids in the background. Peter had Carly and Katie, the eleven-year-old twins, and Cameron, the sixteen-year-old boy. Peter was only a couple years younger than me, but he'd settled quickly after college. Within a year after they were married, they'd had Cameron. When Peter had first called me and told me

Penny was expecting, I hadn't believed Peter would be a dad. *But he's only twenty-three*, I remembered thinking.

"So, what are your plans for the day?" Peter asked.

"I have no plans," I said.

"That's surprising," Penny added. "I always thought you and Jeremy went to his family's out in Queens."

And there it was. I'd gone through almost twenty minutes of a conversation without having to break the news.

"We're... We're no longer together," I said hesitantly. I did my best not to let any venom and animosity into my voice.

"What?" Penny exclaimed. "I can't believe it. You two were such a perfect match."

"Want to talk about it?" Peter asked. I could tell he was making sure I was ready to have this conversation. He'd always been more empathic than I was.

"Not really," I admitted. "It's still new." I hesitated for a moment, not sure what to say next. I finally added, "But before you ask, I don't think we can patch this one up. He... I caught him cheating on me."

I heard a sharp intake of breath from Penny while my brother said "Dude" in a low, drawn-out voice.

"Yep. So, not exactly the merriest Christmas for me, which is why I need all the Christmas spirit your family can spare."

"Oh, Roger..." Penny said.

"Hey bro, that sucks. I'm sorry to hear it."

I shook my head, trying to wipe the negative thoughts from my head. "So, where are my nieces and nephew?" I asked, trying to change the subject.

"Kids!" Penny yelled into the void of their house. "Your uncle Roger's on the phone."

Within a few seconds, there were a series of phone clicks, and I had the whole family on the line. We talked for a good hour. The kids caught me up on their lives, and I did my best to deflect questions they had about Jeremy. Even though I knew they weren't exactly sheltered, I didn't feel like having a conversation about the pathetic state of my relationship with a couple of pre-teens and a kid who'd just gotten his driver's license.

After about an hour, we hung up, and I was left, once again, alone in my hotel room, not sure what I should do next. I pulled up Google and typed in "What to do in Manhattan on Christmas Day?" I was surprised by the list of options I had at my disposal. One caught my attention. There were a handful of Broadway shows that had evening performances. A new holiday musical, *The Naughty List*, had gotten excellent reviews. I called up the box office and bought a ticket with no problem.

With something to keep me busy that evening, I dove into my treasure trove of junk food then took a quick nap. I got up about six-forty-five. I threw on my new slacks, button-down shirt, tie and blazer and headed over to the Maurer Theater. By the time I got there, the queue into the theater was wrapped around the block. I went over to the will-call line and picked up my ticket before heading to the back of the line outside. There were a bunch of people decked out in festive holiday sweaters. Some outfits, like mine, were clearly newly purchased, but I bet those outfits had been sitting in wrapped boxes earlier that day.

At seven-thirty, the theater opened its doors. Before long, I had passed security, had my ticket scanned, a *Playbill* and a cocktail in hand and was sitting in my seat in the eighth row of the Orchestra on the righthand side. Not where I normally preferred to sit, but last-minute purchases are up to the seller's discretion.

Before the lights dimmed, a guy in his early thirties was shown the seat next to me. I smiled and nodded my head as he sat down. It was nice to see I wasn't the only single guy at the theater that night.

"Good evening. Unless you want to be placed on the naughty list, please make sure you have turned off your cell phone. And while elves love candy, unwrap it now. Elves are also skittish, so do not take pictures or record this show. And like Santa says, 'He sees you when you're sleeping, he knows when you're awake and he knows if you're a good audience member.' Please sit back and enjoy tonight's special Christmas performance of The Naughty List.*"*

The lights dimmed, and the overture began. I sat back and tried to lose myself in the performance. Admittedly, the central romance in the show made me grouse a bit. Still, I did my best not to project my relationship dismay onto the poor fictional couple on stage.

During intermission, I learned my neighbor's name was Josh, and he was in from Texas for the week.

"I work for the Dallas Civic Light Opera," he told me. "I come to New York every Christmas and cram in as many shows as humanly possible."

"Sadly," I started, "I live here and rarely go to the theater. There are so many other things vying for my attention."

"What made you decide to see *The Naughty List* tonight?"

I accidentally rolled my eyes and said, "That's a long, loaded question." The poor guy raised his eyebrows, clearly realizing he'd opened a giant can of worms. "Let's just say I got out of a relationship and needed to keep myself busy."

"Ahh…" Josh said.

Thankfully, I was saved from delving into the entire story by the dimming of the lights and the entr'acte starting. The show finished sixty minutes later, and I jumped to my feet and applauded the cast. Once the bows happened, I said goodbye to Josh and made my way out of the theater.

Snow was lightly falling as I walked back to The Time. By the time I'd gotten to my room, I was ready to pass out. I brushed my teeth, washed my face, put on my pajamas and slipped into bed. I was asleep before my head hit the pillow.

* * * *

On Sunday morning, I went out for a much shorter run. The snow had picked up speed overnight, so the sidewalks were not that great. I made it a couple blocks before I realized I didn't have enough clear sidewalk to run on, so I headed back to the hotel.

"Too cold for you?" the doorman asked as I got back.

"I'm sure I could heat up if I could actually run, but none of the sidewalks are cleared yet."

"Can't say I'm surprised—between the holiday weekend and it being a Sunday and all. We have a small fitness room on the fourth floor. We also have a relationship with a fitness facility around the corner."

"Fourth floor, did you say?"

"Yep. Head up to the lobby, then catch the elevator to the fourth floor. You'll see signs up there pointing to it."

"Thanks," I said as I started climbing the stairs to the lobby. I crossed and nodded to the young guy who'd checked me in on Friday. I walked to the elevator and headed up to the fourth floor. Sure enough, the hotel fitness center had everything a guy could ask for – an elliptical rider, a treadmill, a stationary bike and an assortment of free weights. And best of all, I was the only one in the room.

I started by jumping on the elliptical rider. I did that for about thirty minutes while listening to Rachel Maddow's *Bag Man* podcast. I'd missed it a couple of years earlier when the book had come out. A friend at work had recommended it, so I'd downloaded it and had it sitting on my phone for a month. I figured as long as I was going to be running my legs in circles for a half-hour, I could put my brain to good use.

A cheerful song started the podcast with a nineteen-sixties ditty singing about "my kind of man... Ted Agnew is." I chuckled at how cheesy the political song was, but Rachel quickly talked about how Richard Nixon introduced Ted Agnew as his running mate in nineteen-sixty-eight. The podcast went from there. I watched myself in the mirror as I ran. I'm not one who likes to stare at myself in the mirror for long periods, but over the past few years, I'd grown to appreciate my body more and more. I would never be a centerfold model or a porn star, but I had to admit that all the work I'd done in the gym had paid off.

When Jeremy and I had first started dating, I was completely shy about my body. I didn't want to be naked anywhere outside a bedroom or bathroom. I even had problems changing into my workout clothes at the gym. I guess I had a lot of hang-ups dating back to when I'd been in high school. When I'd hit puberty, I had been the last kid in our class to notice the normal physical changes. I remember the day my first chest hair sprouted, and I'd been like, *finally*. Before long, my short, scrawny body took on the more normal appearance of a lanky teen, but I hadn't bulked up physically until I was in my thirties. I'd been your typical twink in my twenties. But once I'd hit thirty, I decided it was time to get more aggressive at the gym. I wasn't exactly a bodybuilder, but for a forty-one-year-old, I was more muscular than I'd been in my entire life.

The podcast episode ended. I had a few more minutes before my thirty-minute 'run' would be over. Another guy had come in and started on the treadmill. More than once, I caught him looking at me through the mirror. He was younger, probably in his late twenties. It was nice to know that someone that young could still take an interest in me.

Once I finished on the elliptical rider, I worked out all my major muscle groups. It's not like I had anything better planned for the day. Heck, I didn't have any plans until after the new year. I was supposed to be on vacation starting on Wednesday, but I planned on working remotely tomorrow and Tuesday. I needed to get my shit together, and sitting in face-to-face marketing meetings would not get me there. I should have been spending time with my fiancé. Heck, we were going to meet with our wedding planner this week. *I better make sure I call her and cancel the meeting*, I thought to myself as I lifted the weights over my shoulders.

"Come on," the young guy said, coming up in front of me. "You can lift something heavier than that."

I raised my eyebrows and chuckled. "Thanks. But I'd rather do more reps at a weight I'm comfortable with than hurt myself trying to show off."

"Then let me spot you. You can return the favor."

Now that I'd actually interacted with the young guy, he was giving off more of a 'bro' vibe than a 'bend me over and let's have fun' kind of vibe.

"Sure. Why not," I said. I picked up a heaver pair of dumbbells.

"Now that's more like it, dude." The guy looked almost gleeful at the idea of me lifting heavy things. *Wow, he is straight.*

"So, what has you in a hotel gym on a Sunday morning?" the guy asked.

"Caught my ex in a compromising situation on Christmas Eve and needed a place to stay for a few days."

"Dude…that fucking sucks. Did you know the guy she was fucking?"

I hadn't realized that I'd automatically used a gender-neutral pronoun for Jeremy. After being out for all these years, I'm still not one-hundred-percent comfortable with my sexual orientation, especially when dealing with strange straight guys.

"I did. Local guy. Gets around a lot," I said between pushing my shoulders skyward. Once I finished my set, we traded places. "What about you? Why are you here on a Sunday morning?"

"Have an interview at a marketing firm tomorrow. Drove down from the northern part of the state. I was told I would have to make a good impression on the gay guy who'd be my boss. So, want to look good, ya know?"

"Oh really?"

"Yeah," he said, struggling to keep lifting.

"Come on. You can do it," I encouraged. I put my hands under his elbows to catch them if his arms gave out. "So, what firm are you interviewing with?" I asked.

"You've probably never heard of it," he said, dropping the dumbbells to his side.

"Try me."

"It's a smaller agency called Tristate Marketing Technologies."

Oh, you've got to be fucking kidding me. "Oh really? What type of job?"

"I'd be working in the creative director's office."

"Good luck with that interview tomorrow."

"I was told by someone who used to work there as long as I'm young, hot and can give the dude an eye full of my ass, I'll get the job."

He went back to his routine, and I did my best not to smack the moron upside his head. *Should I tell him or not?* I debated. I had three interviews the following morning, and I guess this meathead was Richard Salzman. I deduced that because the other two applicants were female. This guy's portfolio was good, but his mouth could get him in trouble with human resources and our clients.

"Mr. Salzman," I said, right before leaving the gym.

"Huh?" he responded absently. It took him a second, but he finally caught up and asked, "How do you know my name?"

"Richard Salzman. Age thirty-one. Currently works for the Buffalo Institute for Design and Marketing. Your portfolio is good. I look forward to seeing you tomorrow for our interview."

"What the fuck?" Salzman uttered, the look of shock crossing his face.

"And tomorrow, we'll discuss your work and portfolio, not any other *assets* you may bring with you to TMT." With that, I left the gym with a smile on my face and a slightly lighter step. I'd still give the guy a fair interview, but hopefully, this would be a lesson he'd learn. Half the reason I chose this hotel was because I worked in an office practically across the street. I'd planned on going virtual tomorrow, but now I knew I had to show up for at least half the day.

I made my way back up to my hotel room and took a shower. Then, I got back into comfy clothes, ordered a pizza from room service and watched TV the rest of the day. The Giants were playing the Patriots, so I turned it on and kept my fingers crossed. The Patriots won. Sadly, my relationship status wasn't the only thing to disappoint me that weekend.

Chapter Three

I went to bed early, got up and hit the treadmill at six a.m., then headed into the office by eight. After dressing, I grabbed my briefcase and headed down to the lobby. While in the shower, I realized I did not know what I was doing after today because my reservation had ended. I crossed the lobby, and the front desk clerk looked up as I approached his computer terminal. He was dressed in a smart gray suit with a burgundy tie and matching pocket square. I glanced down and saw his name, 'Tommaso Gallo,' with the words 'Rome, Italy' written underneath.

"Good morning," Tommaso said, looking up from his computer in his Italian accent.

"Yes, I'm Roger Havemeyer in room eight-nineteen."

Tommaso clicked away on his keyboard for a second before asking, "Yes, Mr. Havemeyer, how can I be of service this morning?"

"I'm scheduled to checkout today, but I wanted to see if I could extend my stay by a few days."

There were more clicks on the keyboard. "That shouldn't be a problem, sir." He told me the rate, then asked me whether he could put the new reservation on the same card. I told him he could. "Your new checkout date will be for Thursday, December thirtieth."

"Perfect," I said. "Thanks, Tommaso."

"You're very welcome, Mr. Havemeyer."

I had half a mind to slip the young man my room key and tell him to drop by after his shift ended. *I wish I could be that forward*, I whined to myself. I walked out of the lobby and down the stairs. The doorman let me out with a nod.

"Not running today, sir?"

"I hit the fitness center again. Thanks for letting me know yesterday. I found it very equipped and *illuminating*."

I walked to the edge of the sidewalk and made sure there was no oncoming traffic before stepping out onto the street and crossing. The Brill Building, where my office was located, was right at the corner of Forty-Ninth and Broadway. At only eleven floors, the building wasn't the tallest in Midtown. Designed in the nineteen-thirties by Victor Bark, Jr., the building had been sold to the Brill Brothers, who owned the haberdashery that took up the bulk of the first floor. During the Great Depression, the owners had been forced to rent to—*God forbid*—musicians. The Brill Building became home to three music publishers—Southern Music, Mills Music and Famous-Music. Those three companies were quickly joined by other music publishers. By nineteen-sixty-two, the building housed one hundred and sixty-five different music businesses.

In fact, it has been argued that rock-n-roll was birthed in the Brill Building. The building was a one-stop shop for everything musical at its height. A young artist could find space to write a song, shop it to publishers, get an arrangement for the song, have lead sheets made, copies published, book a demo studio, hire musicians and singers and record the song all in one building. So many of the hits from the nineteen-forties through the nineteen-seventies all made their way through Brill. Composers like Burt Bacharach, Sonny Bono, Hal David, Neil Diamond, Marvin Hamlisch, Kander and Ebb, Carole King, Neil Sedaka, Dionne Warwick and Lizza — with a Z — had all called the building home at one point.

One thing I love about living in New York was how every building has such a fascinating history. Perhaps this building had a greater impact on pop culture in the middle part of the twentieth century than anyplace outside Hollywood. There are still a few music publishers in the building, but the tenants have become more varied. Sadly, a lot of the space had already been left unoccupied before the 2020 pandemic, and the building didn't refill as people came back to the city when it reopened. Thankfully, my agency liked the proximity to Midtown and the clients we had on Broadway, so it made an ideal spot for us up on the seventh floor. Our office space was formerly owned by Gerry Greenwich, a legendary music producer from the late sixties and seventies. Greenwich worked with the likes of New York Revival, Folk Service Supreme, Heart Puddle, Cerys Parker and the Funky Trolly, among a whole slate that had won awards around the globe.

I stared up at the ornate gold doorway that led to the building and wondered, *Whatever happened to Greenwich?* The face looking down at me wasn't Greenwich, but it was the polished bust of Abraham Alan Lefcourt, who stared down at me like he did every day. Alan was the original building owner's son, who died at eighteen-years-of-age. The ornate entrance with Alan's bust as the centerpiece made a lasting impression on anyone who crossed the building's threshold. *They don't make buildings like this anymore.* I opened the door and strode over to the elevator bank. The lobby was still empty at this hour, but I knew things would pick up once normal business hours started. I pushed the button for the elevator. I heard the click-clacking sound of heels across the marble flooring. I looked over to see my administrative assistant, Mitzi, making her way over.

"Morning, Mitzi," I said. "Good weekend?" The woman was maybe one or two years younger than me, and we'd both been with the firm for the same length of time. *Dear God, are we both going on twenty years now?*

"Went up and saw the family in Connecticut on Saturday. What about you and Jeremy?" I don't quite know how to explain the grumble that came out of my body, but it was enough to cause Mitzi's well-manicured eyebrow to arch as she widened her eyes.

"Let's just say I'm staying at The Time," I responded before she could ask.

"That's where we put up job candidates," she replied absently. I could tell she wanted to ask me what happened, but she was entirely too polite to do it.

"Yeah, I met one of those candidates in the gym. Let's say his 'interview' started with us doing reps in the fitness center and ended with him putting his foot in his mouth. Apparently, someone told him I was gay and was only concerned with hiring a hot guy with a nice ass."

"Wasn't me!" she said, then tilted her head sideways and added, "I always tell them you're looking for a gigantic dick."

"Mitzi!" I chastised with a grin. "I'm looking for a guy with a big...personality."

"Mm-hmm. And I'm looking for a man with a big...*bank account*."

"I wouldn't mind one of those, either."

She rolled her eyes. Several years ago, she'd helped me with our taxes. My dad had been an accountant, back when he was still with us. I was determined to do them myself but got utterly in over my head. I went from owing the city, state and IRS thousands of dollars to magically getting a refund after Mitzi worked her magic. So, she knew precisely what my assets looked like. I'd made some successful early investments that continued to pay off. I had enough now to play in the stock market—not enough to gamble it all away on any one stock, but enough to play. I won some, and I lost some.

We continued to chit-chat as we headed up in the elevator. We weren't even the first people to arrive in the office. My boss Colleen Dunham and her assistant were always there first. I rarely saw my boss, but her assistant, Stephen, was permanently stationed outside her office like a guard dog. I nodded my head as I passed him on the way to my office.

I spent the next few hours going over the new campaigns we were working on. A couple of different Broadway shows had hired us to get their marketing campaigns up and running before their shows opened in the spring. They'd already approved the artwork, so we were looking at marketing strategies. One of my younger associates had put together a report.

There was a knock on my door at ten-thirty, and Mitzi poked her head in. "The guy with the nice ass is here for his meeting," she whispered.

I rolled my eyes and wished I hadn't told her about Mr. Salzman. "Let him in."

I stood and greeted the guy with an extended handshake. "Mr. Salzman, I'm Roger Havemeyer, but I guess you've figured that out already."

"Mr. Havemeyer, I am so sorry about ye—"

"Take a seat." He unbuttoned his suit coat and sat down. I walked behind my desk and sat down in the overstuffed executive chair, which was just tall enough that I looked down at the cocky idiot. He refused to look me in the eyes. I was kind of sorry for him. He looked like a puppy who'd been scolded for chewing on a new slipper. I let out a breath and said, "Water under the bridge. You learned a valuable lesson yesterday. New York City is a small town. You never know who you're going to run into or what ears are listening." I picked up the folder with Salzman's name on it. "Tell me about yourself, your portfolio and why you think you're best for this job."

We spent the next hour discussing his work. Overall, despite the horrible first impression, he was intelligent, creative and appeared to have a good sense for marketing. From a sales standpoint, I couldn't deny his ridiculous good looks would help land a few accounts. Let's face it, sex sells. Before the interview had ended, I had already decided to extend him an offer. I was looking for two new associates. One interviewee had already informed me that morning that she wasn't interested and wouldn't be showing up. The other had been done via Zoom and seemed like a good fit as well. She'd be managing our digital assets and would be primarily working from her home in the Poconos. She'd come into the office as needed, which is what most of the employees did. Salzman would work with a lot of our clients face-to-face, so he'd need to be in the city full time. When I offered the young man the job, he stared at me, stupefied.

"I have to admit," he started, "I thought you were going through the motions after how I put my foot in my mouth yesterday."

"Bygones. Don't make that mistake again. If you ever say something inappropriate in front of a client, I'll let you go in a heartbeat. Our business is built on relationships, and if I'd been a client and you'd said that to me, we would have lost that account. Personally, I've been around the block a few times, so I don't get offended easily. Talk to Mitzi on the way out. She'll help you get in touch with HR if you decide to accept the position." And with that, the interview was over. As he left my office, I had to admit that he had a perfectly sculpted ass in those pants. I sighed as the door closed behind him. I can dream, but as someone told me a long time ago, "*Don't shit where you eat.*" I wasn't about to engage in an office fling. No ass is that good.

I waited a few minutes, then headed out into the office to see what was going on. I hadn't surfaced since I'd gotten there early in the morning. I headed over to the coffee station to make my late morning pick-me-up.

"Roger," a voice said as I finished brewing my beverage.

I looked up to see an old friend I hadn't seen in over a year. "Grayson Jackson, as I live and breathe, what are you doing here?" I asked, extending my hand and shaking Grayson's.

"My law firm hired you guys to handle our new marketing campaign. I was asked to come down and approve some things."

"Great. Who are you working with?"

"Just got out of a meeting with Estelle and Gerald."

"Solid people. They'll handle your campaign with the utmost professionalism." I leaned in closer. "And trust me, I would tell you if you should run. There are a couple of people around this place that I think just take up space."

"Good to know," Grayson said with a smile. "How are you and Jeremy? I heard through the grapevine you are finally getting married." For the second time that morning, I let out a sound that must have come from somewhere in the pits of hell. "Uh-oh, I don't like the sound of that."

I lowered my voice and said, "I caught Jeremy in bed with Avery Addington on Friday."

"What! You've got to be kidding me. Well, not about Avery. Everyone knows what kind of walking dumpster fire that asshole is. But Jeremy? I'm surprised."

"You and me both."

"Was this the first time he's stepped out on you?"

"Not from what I learned on Friday." I looked around and realized a couple of colleagues were staring, so I leaned in and said, "Gotta few minutes?"

"Sure."

I led Grayson back to my office, and I asked Mitzi to hold my calls. Grayson may have been a decade younger than me, but we'd hung out in a lot of the same circles because his best friend, Dale Devereux, had been a Wall Street player for many years. At one point, I had Dale managing all my stocks. When I'd found out he'd been let go from his firm the last year, I'd diversified my assets and now worked with a handful of brokers.

"So, spill," Grayson said as he took off his suit coat and hung it over the back of the chair.

I spent the next thirty minutes describing everything that had happened in great detail. For a straight guy, Grayson didn't freak out by any of the details.

"So, wait... You actually stood butt-ass naked in your living room having an argument? While Avery watched?"

"Yep. He might as well have popped some popcorn and enjoyed the show."

"Wow," he said, drawing out the word. "That kid. Thankfully, Dale finally cut him loose last year."

"Good for him. What did Avery do? Sleep with Dale's boyfriend?"

"Not exactly," Grayson said. He then told me the story about how Avery had inappropriately kept grabbing some kid who'd decked him.

"God, I wish I could have seen that. Sadly, it clearly didn't teach Avery any lessons."

"Nope. Dale had me drive Avery back to the city that night."

"I still can't believe Dale, of all people, is living on a farm in Woodstock."

"Oh, he's not living on the farm. You know Dale. He has a crazy large house and lives in luxury with his boyfriend, who just moved in with him."

"Maybe that's what I should do — leave the city and move to Woodstock."

"Maybe not move there, but getting out of the city could be a nice change of pace. I'm sure Dale and Talgat would love to have you visit."

"I couldn't impose on them."

Without asking, Grayson whipped out his cell phone and was texting before I even knew what had happened. Before I'd had a chance to breathe, I could tell Grayson was already getting texts back from Dale.

"Dale and Talgat say come on up any time. In fact, Dale suggested you come up for the New Year."

"What?" I spat out. "That was fast."

"What else are you going to do? Like you said, you need a change of scenery. Give it a thought. Do you still have Dale's cell?" Grayson asked me.

"I'm sure I do," I said, but clearly, I wasn't sure at all.

"Is your number still," and Grayson rattled off my cell number.

"That's it."

"Great." Grayson's fingers sped across his phone. "You have Dale's phone number as a text."

I picked up my phone and looked at my messages. Sure enough, there was a message from Grayson, and he was still listed in my contacts.

"Go on," Grayson said. "Text him. I'm not leaving until you do."

I started to say something, but Grayson shot me a look that seemed to say 'do it, mister,' so I did.

Hey, Dale, Roger Havemeyer here. Grayson is making me text you.

Almost immediately, I had a reply.

Sounds like Grayson.

That text was followed by, *I hear there is trouble in paradise, and you need to escape. My invitation to come up here this week is real. We're just hanging around the house. Would love the company. Let me know.*

"Wow, that was fast," I said to Grayson. "It's like Dale is hovering over his phone."

"He's been a bit bored lately. Once the fall ended on the farm, he's had a lot more downtime. Dale has *never* been good with downtime. Having company this week will be as good for him as it is for you. Besides, you'll get to meet Dale's new boyfriend, Talgat. I adore Talgat. He's the kind of guy I always hoped Dale would end up with—and the nice guy Dale never thought in a million years he would find."

"How so?"

"Talgat basically runs the Devereux Upstate farm with his siblings. I never thought Dale would get over himself long enough to enjoy a relationship with a farmer. I always worried he'd end up dating an Avery type and be miserable every second."

"Well, I guess I need to go upstate and meet this mystery man who has stolen Dale's heart." I took a deep breath and typed.

Why don't I come up on Thursday and stay through the new year? If it's not an inconvenience.

Dale texted back.

Awesome-sauce. We can hammer out the details later. I'm totally stoked you're going to come hang with us. You'll love Talgat.

That's what Grayson told me.

Grayson and I talked for a few more minutes before I saw him out of the office.

* * * *

The next few days flew by in a flurry of meetings and project approvals. On Wednesday, I took some time off to sneak home and pack up my belongings from the apartment. I had avoided dealing with

Jeremy. I had paid the rent on the apartment for January but would figure out what I should do after that in the future.

"I guess that's everything," I said, looking down at the large suitcases. *Dale's going to think I'm moving in when he sees all this.* I hadn't been packing for my trip north. I'd been packing all my essential belongings, period. I'd grabbed the important things – clothes, paperwork, toiletries and a few personal items I didn't want Jeremy doing anything to until I officially moved out. Basically, anything important fit into the suitcases I had.

On the way out, I left a note.

Jeremy,
I'm heading out of town for a bit. I came and packed up my belongings and am taking them and my car with me. I've already paid up the rent through January. You should probably start searching for a new roommate now.
Roger

I had wanted to say something nasty in the note but figured keeping it professional would be the best. Technically, my name was on the lease, so I would be on the hook if Jeremy didn't pay the rent, but I had figured I'd cross that road if, and when, we got to it.

I rolled the suitcases into the hallway and headed to the elevator. My building's garage was on the lower level. I'd made sure my car was there before heading up to the apartment. Technically, Jeremy didn't have a driver's license, but honestly, I didn't know what Jeremy would or would not do anymore. *Hey, I think I just hit acceptance*, referring to Elisabeth Kübler-Ross' stages of grief. As the saying went, "*God, grant me the serenity to accept what I can't fucking change,"* or something like that.

The doors opened to the underground carpark, and I wheeled the suitcases to where my Bentley Continental sat. I'd wanted something between a compact car and a huge gas-guzzling monstrosity, so the Bentley seemed to work perfectly. I pulled out my keys, pushed the button to open the trunk and lifted the suitcases into the back. It's kind of depressing when you realize how easy it is to pack your entire life into a couple of bags. Sure, I owned most of the furniture upstairs, but I didn't want to be bothered with it. It reeked of Jeremy, anyway. I wanted to cut him out of my life swiftly, clean and complete.

With the bags in the trunk, I got in the driver's seat, turned the car on and headed out into the mid-day traffic. Almost immediately, I regretted that decision. I'd forgotten how much I hated driving in the city. There's a reason the poor Bentley had a layer of dust. I navigated my way through Midtown and made it to the parking garage near the hotel. I planned to leave everything in the car overnight, so I didn't have to worry about taking anything into the hotel.

Once I was parked and had my ticket to get out the next day, I headed back to work and finished a few odds and ends. I'd informed everyone earlier in the week that I was heading to Woodstock for the new year. By that point, everyone had heard about the breakup. I wasn't sure how the gossip had gotten around the office so quickly, but it was easier than me having to stop my life and tell everyone.

After work, I went back to the hotel. My favorite desk guy, Tommaso, was on duty. I nodded my head, and he smiled back at me and said, "Mr. Havemeyer, I hope you've enjoyed your time with us. I see you're scheduled to check out tomorrow. Any chance you'll be extending your stay again?"

"Not this time. I'm heading upstate."

"Too bad. We've enjoyed having you here. If you need anything else to make your stay more enjoyable, let me know." And he winked. He actually winked.

Visions of me ripping off his clothes and taking his giant Italian cock down my throat rushed into my head. I probably blushed from the thought of it, and I could tell my southside partner was on board, because it started growing.

"Thanks," I somehow got out. "I'll let you know." I turned and hightailed it to my hotel room. I was thrilled that there was no one in the elevator, because my cock suddenly had a complete mind of its own. I shrugged out of my suit coat and folded it in half, so I could rest it in front of my all-too-obvious bulge.

"Good afternoon," a cleaning lady said as she entered the elevator with me. Even seeing the older woman hadn't stopped little Mr. Man from staying at full mast. Thankfully, my floor was next, so I hid my growing excitement as I exited the elevator. I hurried through the hallway and opened the room to my hotel room door.

My pants were off before I finished shutting the door. I ripped away my clothes and lay down on the bed. I spat on my hand and started stroking myself. Thoughts of all the things I'd like to do to Tommaso and what I'd let him do to me ran through my head. The first shot of cum hit me in the chin, and the second one hit the headboard behind me. I kept pumping myself until I had sticky white stuff all over me.

"Whoa," I said, looking down at the sheer amount of cum I had all over. "Guess I needed that." I let out a breath and let myself sink into the bed for a moment.

My dick was still standing, but the air was definitely being released slowly out of that tire.

* * * *

The buzzing sound of my cell phone woke me up. I was still completely nude, but the cum had dried. I looked over at the clock and realized I'd been out for over an hour. I reached over, grabbed my phone and saw it was Dale calling.

"Hey, Dale," I said as I answered.

"Hey, Roger. Checking in to see what time we should expect you tomorrow."

"Checkout time here is at eleven a.m., so I figure I'll be on the road by that time or shortly after. Then, however long it takes to get up to you."

"So, you'll probably be here around two. Great." I heard Dale yell, "Honey, he'll be here around two."

I let out a laugh. The joys of living with another person. A pang of hurt filled my heart, but I quickly wiped it away. *No. No regrets. Time to move on.*

"Talgat's siblings will be here tomorrow night for dinner. And as a heads up, we are not planning anything special for New Year's Eve."

"That's fine with me. I want to decompress and get away from life for a while."

"I've been there…" Dale said almost wistfully. "What? I'll ask him," Dale suddenly yelled. "Talgat wants to make sure you're not a vegetarian."

"Most definitely not a vegetarian," I said. "I don't have a problem eating vegetarian food, if you two are, though," I added as an afterthought.

"No worries. We are carnivores in this house. He just wanted to make sure."

We talked about a couple of things. I absently played with my dick while talking to Dale — not sexually, just playing with it. You know it's kind of sitting out there, so your hand goes down and starts messing with it. It's almost instinctual.

"We'll see you tomorrow," Dale said.

"Great. I'm looking forward to it." I hung up the phone and decided it was time to shower, throw on some clothes and head out into the cold to get something for dinner but figured I might as well shoot off another orgasm before I hit the shower.

* * * *

I woke up the following day around nine-thirty and packed my stuff from what had become my home for the last week. I'd had the hotel's laundry service clean all my recently purchased clothes, and I packed them into the duffel bag I'd grabbed the previous day from the apartment. I double-checked the room to make sure I'd left nothing, then grabbed my briefcase and duffel bag and was ready to leave.

"Well, it's been fun," I said to the room as I left.

I walked down the hall, grabbed the elevator and took it down to the lobby. My new best friend, Tommaso, wasn't working the front desk, so I walked up to the young woman there, gave her my name and checked out.

I walked downstairs, said goodbye to my favorite doorman and headed to the garage to pick up my car. Within minutes, I was in the Holland Tunnel leaving Manhattan for New Jersey. I hadn't left the city in a long time. It was nice to feel the tires spinning below me on the open road. The trip also gave me time to catch up on more of Maddow's podcast. Before I knew it, I was pulling off the Interstate in Kingston, NY, and catching the road west up to Woodstock. I quickly realized this part of the world had a hell of a lot more trees than people. It's not like I'm not used to seeing the skyline, but dear God, all I saw were trees in any direction. Twenty minutes later, I drove through the Main Street in Woodstock and expected to see something…different. I mean, I didn't quite know what I anticipated, but this place was very…normal looking. I didn't see a single hippie smoking weed on a street corner anywhere. I passed through town and followed my GPS device's directions to Dale's place. When my GPS told me to turn off the main road and onto a side road that had been recently paved, I figured I was on the right track.

What I saw up ahead was less a house and more a compound. It was a giant gray brick structure with a castle turret on one side with a wraparound porch. From the turret's size, I had to assume there was some kind of room that existed at the top. I wondered if it was the primary bedroom or a family room. I guess I would find out soon enough because I hadn't even gotten halfway down the driveway when Dale opened the door and leaned against it with a big goofy grin on his face.

I parked next to a big-ass SUV and got out. "Howdy, stranger," I yelled as I stretched and popped my neck."

Dale got off the porch looking like a cross between Grizzly Adams and the latest cover model for L.L. Bean. The look worked on him. He'd grown in a bit of a beard, but it looked more five o'clock shadow than full-on ZZ Top. He reached out and threw his arms around me.

"It's so good to see you," Dale said as he gave me a squeeze.

"Wow," I said, finally pulling away from him. "You're barely recognizable. And in that plaid shirt, you look like you stepped out of a gay episode of *Green Acres*."

"Yeah, I've changed since I moved up here full time."

"Did you get rid of your apartment at Twenty Exchange?"

"I may have become one with nature," Dale said, his smile quirking up at one corner, "but I haven't gone full native."

"Don't let him kid you," a voice called from the doorway. "He's way more native than he gives himself credit for. He even chopped wood in the fall to help us get ready for the winter."

I turned to look at him, a look of shock and a bit of awe on my face. "You chopped wood?"

"I did," Dale said with a bob of his head. "But don't let Talgat lie to you. If he hadn't been at my side, I probably would have taken a hand or leg off."

Dale's boyfriend walked over to us and extended his hand. "Talgat," he said. "It's nice to meet you. And from what Dale and Grayson have told me, you were one of the better people he knew down in the city."

"Thanks...I think," I said, scrunching my forehead in confusion.

"I told Talgat about your Avery problem..."

"Oh, dear God, you didn't!" I said with a bit more exasperation than I had intended.

"Don't worry," Talgat said. "I'm far from a fan of that little prick's. I'm sorry he fucked up your relationship."

"Well, Avery couldn't fuck up something that wasn't already on the way there." I let out a sigh. The sympathetic expressions on both Dale's and Talgat's faces suggested they understood. The last thing I needed was pity from these two. "So, where am I staying?"

The couple took the hint and put on big, fake smiles. They were kind of smiles the women on *Designing Women* always had right before they'd say, "*Well, bless his heart.*"

"Right this way," Talgat said. "Dale had me make up the guest bedroom on the opposite end of the house from ours, not that there's a room close to ours. We live up there," he said, pointing to the turret.

"Really? How big is this place?"

"It's not that large," Dale said. "It's only about six-thousand square feet."

"Oh, just five times larger than my apartment," I tossed out, looking at the structure in front of me.

I followed Dale and Talgat into the house, then they gave me the grand tour. Immediately in front of the door was a sitting area with comfortable-looking couches and an enormous fireplace. There was already a fire going. "Is that the wood you chopped?" I asked, pointing to the small stack next to the fireplace.

"Some of it," Dale let me know. "I have a stack of it away from the house."

"What he won't tell you is he found a Timber Rattler in the woodpile and wanted to burn the entire forest to the ground."

"It's a dangerous, venomous snake. I think killing it is a perfectly normal reaction," Dale said with a hint of the city-slicker kid I knew. "How was I supposed to know that killing the thing was illegal?"

"What did he do?" I asked.

"He went after it with a rake. The snake struck the rake. Dale dropped the rake and screamed like he was being attacked by the whole den. I came running from the other side of the house where I'd been doing some pruning in Dale's garden—"

"You have a garden?"

"Yes, he does."

"He has gone all country life on me." I stole another glance in Dale's direction.

Dale threw on an exaggerated pout before saying, "Hey, I'm right here, you two. You don't need to talk about me like I'm not in the room."

"Sorry, honey. That's right. I was telling a humiliating story about you." Dale sighed and rolled his eyes, but Talgat continued. "So, I came running around, and Dale was coming at me full tilt. I'm like, what's wrong? He screams, 'Rattlesnake!' From the way he was carrying on, I thought he'd been bitten. When I finally calmed him down, I went to investigate. And sure enough, there was a rattlesnake in the woodpile."

"Vermin sent from the pit of hell," Dale said, scrunching his face in disgust.

"All eleven inches of it. Now, don't get me wrong… Baby rattlers are still venomous."

"I thought they were more venomous than adult ones?" I asked.

"Nope. Old wives tale," Talgat said. "Now, getting a bite from one is still no joke, and you need to seek emergency attention and get anti-venom, but they're not more dangerous."

"What did you do?" I asked, turning my head to Dale.

"I stayed the hell away from the woodpile and haven't been back over there."

"Even after I transported the little guy to a place where he'd be safer and away from Dale."

"He," Dale said, gesturing toward Talgat, "was clearly more worried about the snake's safety than mine."

Talgat rolled his eyes. "Anyway," he drew out sarcastically, "I took the little guy and placed him in a different woodpile out in the forest behind us — and Dale hasn't seen his slithering friend ever since."

"He's small. He could hide anywhere."

"Dale called the exterminators the next day and had every inch of our property checked and snake-proofed. He was sure one was living in our walls and would drop and bite him in the middle of the night."

"I saw *Snakes on a Plane*," Dale said. "Those things can climb."

"Even I know," I said, cutting in, "that movie was beyond over the top and far from reality."

With the snake discussion behind us, I was glad to get the rest of the tour. Part of me was admittedly glad it was dead of winter, and I wouldn't have to worry about snakes or bears. *They have to have bears up here. Don't they?* I made a mental note to ask about bears at another time. The turret was more impressive inside than out. It had three levels. The bottom was a giant wardrobe area, complete with lots of hanging racks, spare bedding and rows of shoes. Dale's clothes took up the overwhelming majority of the wardrobe space from what I gathered. The second floor was a fancy bathroom with a nice, oversized bathtub. The top floor was the primary bedroom. Dale hit a button on the inside of the door frame and the blinds opened, revealing almost a three-hundred-and-sixty-degree view of the surrounding valley.

"Wow," I said. "I don't think I've ever seen this much snow sitting out in nature before."

"We had a new coating last night, so the animal tracks got filled in a bit," Talgat said. "I love sitting up here and watching the forest animals scavenging for food. They leave little footprints, so they're easy to track."

"That's kind of cool," I admitted.

"Don't encourage him," Dale said. "He already has a pair of binoculars up here and wants to get a telescope."

"Come on, Dale. Even you admitted it would be nice to take the telescope out on the porch up here in the summer. Imagine some of the awesome stargazing we could do."

I took a second to take the couple in. They couldn't be more opposite if they tried, but they somehow seemed to fit together. Dale was lanky and pasty white, but he clearly had put on some muscle since the last time I'd seen him. Talgat was shorter, stockier and Asian. Talgat looked like even his muscles had muscles. I took in the two men wearing their matching plaid shirts and looked at how Talgat's strained to keep his body covered because of his muscles. Dale had the figure fashion designers love because clothes hang on him naturally, like they were dangling on a clothing hanger.

"I just realized you two are wearing the same shirt. It's like a gay version of *Grizzly Adams*," I said as I widened my eyes exaggeratedly.

Dale narrowed his gaze at me, scrunched up his face and stuck out his tongue.

"Real mature, Dale," Talgat said with a smile. "Real mature."

I laughed, which caused Dale to chuckle. Before we knew it, all three of us were cackling all the way to the bottom of the turret. Dale showed me where I would stay on the other side of the house.

The guest room in Dale and Talgat's house was four times the size of the room I'd been staying in at The Time. It had a huge king-sized bed, an equally impressive bathroom, a small walk-in closet and a giant sixty-inch television.

"This room is almost as large as my apartment," I joked.

"I think this room is larger than my apartment," Dale responded.

"Whatever," Talgat said. "I've been in your apartment. It's not *that* small."

I'd never been inside Dale's place, but I had other friends who lived at Twenty Exchange, so I had a good idea of what his looked like. And knowing Dale, I seriously doubt he had an efficiency.

"So, how did you two meet?" Talgat asked.

"Great question," I said. "I think I met Dale and Grayson when Grayson was dating a woman in a play Off-Broadway. My marketing firm ran the advertising campaign for the show."

"Marigold," Dale said. "Gosh, I haven't thought about her in years."

"The show closed—"

"Because it sucked—"

"And when the dust settled, I kind of inherited Dale and Grayson."

"Basically, Grayson, Roger and I became drinking buddies. Grayson and Roger liked to watch football, and Roger and I liked to watch men, so we spent a lot of time at a gay sports bar," Dale told Talgat.

"You went to a sports bar?" Talgat questioned in mock shock.

"I've seen a sport or two in my lifetime," Dale said. "Hell, Grandad has tickets to the Yankees and that football team over in Jersey."

"He means the New York Giants," I filled Talgat in.

"See? I sort of know something about sports," Dale said, making a twirling motion with his right index finger, showing how much he cared about them.

"So yes, Dale and I would watch players' asses, and Grayson and I would watch the game."

"The best of both worlds," Dale said with a smile.

"But you're what...? A decade older than them?" Talgat asked.

"Yep. It was like big brothers for little orphaned gaybies," I joked. "In all seriousness, age never seemed an issue. Grayson was more mature than I was at the time—"

"Still is. That old fuddy-duddy," Dale joked.

"And Grayson and I took turns making sure this one," I said, hooking a thumb in Dale's direction, "did nothing that would get him hauled off to jail."

"That's *so* not fair. Name one time I almost went to jail?"

"The time you tried to pick up the undercover cop at the Yankee's game," I said without having to think.

"Oh yeah, I forgot about that one. He was hot. I still say he looked at me first."

"What happened there?" Talgat asked.

"Dale hit on an undercover cop. They thought drugs were being sold out of this one bathroom during games. The cop who was in there staking out the place looked like the twinks Dale used to play around with, so he hit on him. And apparently, Dale was a bit more forceful than intended and the cop missed the bust. The cop instead thought he could go after Dale on solicitation charges."

"The gall of that guy to think I was soliciting him for sex." He turned and looked at Talgat before saying, "Trust me, honey… I've *never* paid for sex."

"I don't have any doubt. I know men throw themselves at you, which is why I keep you locked up here in our little castle."

"Yep, you're my evil pet dragon who will bite off the heads of storming twinks," Dale said, trying to put on his most innocent angel face.

"Whatever… Anyway," Talgat started as he turned in my direction, "why don't you take some time to make yourself comfortable? We're going to have dinner around seven p.m."

"Want us to help you with your bags first?" Dale asked.

"Sure. Don't judge me by the amount of luggage I have. I kind of have my entire life in the Bentley."

"You moved out?" Dale asked. "I wasn't sure if your relationship with Jeremy was on pause or if it was over, over."

"It's over. It's done. It's a crispy critter at this point, and there's no resuscitating it back to life. It is what it is."

With that 'happy' thought, I led Dale and Talgat through their house and back outside to the Bentley. We grabbed my suitcases and hauled them inside. Before I knew it, my bags were on the bed, and I was unpacking what I planned on wearing over the next few days. The rest I kept in the suitcases and rolled them into the walk-in closet.

Once I was all set up, I lay on the bed.

* * * *

The sound of knocking stirred me out of my slumber. It took me a second for me to remember where I was.

"You awake in there?" Dale called from outside the closed door.

"I wasn't," I called back.

"You decent?"

"Never..." I joked back, "but I'm fully clothed." The door opened and Dale leaned against the door frame, looking down at me. "What time is it?"

"It's about six-thirty."

"Geez. What a great guest I am. I hadn't intended to take a nap."

"The body needs what the body needs, and clearly, yours needed time on the CloudBed."

"The *what*?"

"CloudBed? It's a brand," Dale explained, gesturing to the thing I was lying on. "Only the latest in ten-thousand-dollar sleep engineering. Remind me later, and I'll help you download the app for the bed. As you can already tell, the smart sensors do an amazing job of reading your body and adjusting while you sleep. But the app helps you have a bit more customization over the whole thing."

"You're not joking, are you?" I said, wiping the sleep from my eyes. I found a little eye bugger in the corner of my eye and did my best to flick it away daintily.

"Well, good news and bad news...," Dale said ominously.

I narrowed my eyes, saying, "Lay it on me."

"Talgat's siblings will not be joining us for dinner, so we ordered pizza."

"Which is the good news, and which is the bad news?"

"You can decide for yourself," Dale said with a wink. "Now, get up, lazyhead. The pizza will be here in twenty minutes."

"Yes, *Dad*," I called as Dale shut the door.

"And don't make me tell your mother," Dale yelled back, "or you'll be in big trouble, mister." He sounded like one of those comical fathers from nineteen-fifties television shows. I let out a little laugh. I couldn't help myself.

I forced myself off the bed, looking down at it as I stood. "Looks like a normal bed to me. But *no*, you're a smart bed. Who's a smart bed? You are," sounding like I was telling Fido he's a good boy before patting him on the head and giving him a biscuit. I walked into the bathroom and quickly relieved myself before washing my hands, face and brushing my teeth. I changed out of my traveling clothes, which were now a bit wrinkly after me having taken a nap in them.

Once I was presentable again, I made my way through my wing of the house. That's what it felt like. There were like four or five rooms over on this side, and I was the only one there. If these two ever had kids, there would be plenty of room for both them and an entire football team of little ones. I took one wrong turn and ended up at the door to the outside covered deck. In the moonlight's glow, the snow outside was beautiful.

The sound of knocking from somewhere behind me brought me out of my staring into the night aimlessly. I followed the sound of Dale and Talgat's voices and found them in the kitchen area with two pizza boxes.

"We have one meat lovers and one with half Canadian bacon and pineapple and half pepperoni."

"Canadian bacon and pepperoni? How…un-New Yorker are you people?" I joked.

"Don't blame me," Dale protested. "I will take zero responsibility for this man's"—he gestured with his head toward Talgat—"indefensible desire to eat both Canadian bacon and pineapple on a pizza."

"It tastes good," was all Talgat said. "Don't knock it till you've tried it."

"Never," Dale said with a slight shudder. "I think all my New York ancestors would disown me if either of those two things passed my lips."

"Whatever," Talgat said with an exaggerated eye roll. "The more for Roger and me—"

"I'm with Dale on this one. I barely get behind meat lovers. Too many meats can be added that are not quintessential New York pizza. Where do you think you are?" I let out a quick shudder before saying, "Chicago? Or, God forbid, California?"

Dale laughed at that one. "Isn't that where your brother is now?" Dale asked.

"Yep, and despite his defection to the opposite coast, I have not disowned him. I love my nieces and nephew too much to do that." I looked at them and asked, "Anything I can do to help?"

"Nope," Talgat said immediately. "I already set the table."

"And I cooked," Dale added quickly. "And by cooked, I mean I pulled out my wallet and forked over money—the way God intended."

"Tell me," Talgat cut in, carrying a bowl of salad over to the kitchen table. He gestured for me to take a seat, so I did. "Has he always been like this?"

"Like what? White, entitled, gay, crazy, eccentric…?"

"Well, that answers that question," Talgat said, barking out a laugh.

Dale came over with the two pizza boxes saying, "I resemble that remark. I am definitely the Whitest of the White. I'm *so* White that if I went streaking through the woods, I'd disappear into the snowy background."

"D'oh! Bad mental picture, Dale. I do not need to have images of you running naked anywhere," I chided him. "Lest you forget, I've already been there and seen that."

"Do tell," Talgat said, putting his elbows quickly on the table and resting his chin in his hands like an eager child waiting for a bedtime story.

"No," Dale said, narrowing his eyes in my direction. "We will not be sharing that story during dinner…if ever."

"Oh, now you *have* to tell me," Talgat said eagerly.

"Tell that story, and I'll tell the story about catching you in the alley at Pride," Dale warned.

"Ahh, yes. Mutually assured destruction." Then I put my hand up to my mouth, performing a bad stage-aside motion, before whispering loudly, "Ask me when he's not around."

Talgat turned his head and winked at me in an overly exaggerated motion that matched mine.

"I have a feeling I'm going to regret letting you come up and stay this weekend."

"Dig in," Talgat said, handing me the salad bowl.

I scooped some salad onto my plate, along with a slice of the meat lovers and a slice of pepperoni onto my plate. There was already a glass of red wine sitting at my place, as well as a glass of water. These two knew how to put on a simple dinner with a lot of style.

After a bite of salad, I tried the wine. "Tasty," I said, motioning to the wine.

"It's a 2015 bottle of Syrah from the Columbia Valley in Washington State," Dale explained. "It's supposed to be a great accompaniment to pizza. Of course, I should have pulled out a Vouvray or Riesling for Talgat... You know, since he's having a dessert pizza." Dale quirked his lip and shot Talgat a side-eye, who took a large bite out of his pizza while rolling his eyes.

"Grayson told me you bought this place. What's it like to be a homeowner?"

"Yeah," Dale said. Just like a good waiter, I'd asked him the question right after he'd gotten food in his mouth. He swallowed before continuing. "When I first moved up here, Granddad rented me this place while I learned the Devereux family business. After falling in love with Talgat, I reached out to the owners to see if they would sell. They were resistant at first, but I put in an offer they couldn't refuse."

"He enjoys living in the turret," Talgat said as he shot Dale a smile. "He wants to pretend that he's the king of his domain."

"Does that make you the queen?" Dale shot back.

"Only in your dreams, baby. Only in your dreams."

"What about you?" Dale asked. "Ever thought about buying a home?" My eyes flashed wide for a second, and I took in a quick breath. "You don't need to answer that question," Dale said quickly.

"No, no...it's okay. I...had been thinking about that already. I'd created a savings account and had cashed in some of my stocks. Thank you, by the way, for growing my nest egg. I wish you still worked down there. I haven't had nearly the same level of success since you left. You always had a good nose for that stuff. Anyway, I had been looking at properties to purchase as a wedding present."

"Oh," Dale said, drawing out the word as his eyebrows shot up his face.

"It's okay. I've reached the acceptance stage. All things considered, I reached the acceptance stage much faster than I would have expected. In retrospect, I think I knew the relationship was rocky. I just didn't want to see it."

"So, now what do you want to do?" Dale asked. He reached over and grabbed my hand, giving it a quick squeeze.

"I honestly don't know. I think I need a change. I don't know what that change needs to be."

"Are you considering a new job?" Dale asked. The look of shock on his face was obvious.

"No, no...nothing that drastic. I love my work. I need a change of scenery, I think. After the pandemic, more and more people left the city. I'm wondering if I should have been one of them."

"We know a few couples and two or three single guys who moved up here during COVID," Talgat said. "More and more companies realized their workers could be just as productive working remotely."

"I know Devereux Farms did. Even after reopening the corporate offices, we gave workers a choice to come back to the physical office or work remotely. We eventually downsized the space we were leasing. Even after we agreed to pay for workers' high-speed Internet, computers and other technology needs, we are still saving a lot of money."

"Look at you, finally taking an interest in the family business. I always wondered if Jameson would finally get his hooks into you."

"Yep. Granddad gave me an offer I couldn't refuse...literally."

Over the next fifteen minutes, Dale and Talgat told the story of how Dale had come to work at Devereux Upstate and how they had fallen in love.

"It was definitely not love at first sight," Talgat admitted. "Sure, I thought he was hot, but I put little stock in him as a person."

"And I thought Talgat was an unsophisticated farmer. Boy, was I wrong. I quickly learned Talgat's one of the smartest people I've ever met. Coming up here reshaped my view of the world."

"I can tell," I told Dale. "You've grown up so much since the last time we hung out. This is the first conversation I've had with you where you didn't tell me the price tag of your wardrobe and all the labels you were wearing."

"I really was that bad, wasn't I?"

"Yep. You were a label whore."

Dale groaned. "My new self and my old self could definitely not be friends. And in case you're wondering, country chic cost me all of sixty dollars from head to toe at Target."

My jaw almost dropped and hit the table at that revelation. "You've shopped at Target?" I must have sounded flummoxed because Dale nodded and shrugged.

"I even got him into a Walmart once," Talgat said. "I believe he said, *'It burns! It burns,'*" in an exaggerated vampiric voice, "as we stepped inside. The poor old man handing out carts wasn't sure what to make of us."

"In my defense, I grew up with the Walton grandkids. We went to the same summer camp in Maine, and I couldn't stand them. They were so backwoods Arkansas."

After clearing the table and loading the dishwasher, we enjoyed another glass of wine. We talked about life in the city and life in Woodstock. The more Dale and Talgat told me about life up there, the more I became intrigued. Around eleven, we finally said our good nights.

I headed off to my wing of the house and was ready to try my CloudBed again…now that I had the app downloaded.

Chapter Four

Wes

"Good afternoon," I said, looking up at the customer. "Welcome to Java Junkie Café & Roastery. What can I get started for you this afternoon?"

"Can I get an extra-large quad caramel macchiato, with skim, sugar-free with extra whipped cream?"

Four shots? Someone doesn't plan on sleeping anytime soon, I thought to myself as I put the order into the cash register. "Anything else?"

"No, that should do it," the young woman said.

"That will be six dollars and twenty-seven cents."

The young woman looked shocked by the price, but she kept her thoughts to herself. I guess she didn't realize all that customization cost extra money. She was clearly a woman from the city hanging out in Woodstock for the new year. The outsiders were always so easy to spot. First, no one who lived in Woodstock would ever order a drink that screams 'high maintenance'. Second, she didn't bother tipping and treated me like I was the help and not her barista.

I went about making her drink. For the fun of it, I totally made it with sugar. With all the caffeine that would run through her body, I figured a little shot of sugar would barely be noticed. When I finished the drink, I handed it to her. She didn't even bother saying thank you.

"Wow, she was a piece of work," my colleague and best friend Autumn said, coming up from behind me. "And I totally saw what you did."

"What?" I said as innocently as possible.

"Wesley Phelps! Don't you 'what' me?" Autumn said with a wink. "I would have used whole milk, too."

"What are you two gossiping about?" my manager Stefan Phillippe said in his crisp French accent as he walked up behind us.

"Another citidiot ordered a drink that made zero sense," Autumn said.

"Did you make sure you charged extra for the customization?" Stefan asked.

"Of course. And relished every button I got to push," I admitted.

"Well, get back to work. If we don't have any customers, start cleaning early. I would like to close by six."

"Sure thing, boss," Autumn said with a smile.

Stefan turned and headed back to his office in the rear part of the coffee shop. For New Year's Eve, the place had been steadier than I had imagined it would be. We had a couple pockets of people sitting at tables reading, working or quietly talking with friends. Autumn went about cleaning off tables and wiping everything down while I restocked. We would not be open on New Year's Day, but we'd be open bright and early Sunday morning for the church rush.

The twinkling sound of the wind chimes above the door sounded. The chimes were bought locally, and we even kept a selection of them in the story to sell to tourists. Sure, they could walk down the street and purchase them directly from Woodstock Chimes, but why do that when we carried them in stock?

I looked up and saw my other best friend, Dylan, sauntering into the store. "What's up?" I asked as he approached the counter.

"Not much," he said as he leaned his hip against it. He did a quick survey of the people in the store.

"Are you actually cruising in my coffee shop?" I asked.

"Hey, you never know when you'll meet someone, whether that be Mr. Right or Mr. Right Now."

I let out a low groan as I rolled my eyes. "Are you getting anything?"

"Sure. Give me a large coffee."

"That will be two-twenty-five," I said from memory.

He pulled out a five-dollar bill and said, "Keep the change."

"Thanks," I said, breaking the bill and adding the leftover to the tip jar. "So, what are you up to today?" I turned around and grabbed a large cup, a sleeve and a lid before filling it with our daily roast.

Stefan was a perfectionist when it came to his coffee. He was at the shop every morning roasting beans. Most of the day's roast filled our machines, but Stefan roasted enough to have two or three dozen half-pound bags ready to sell that day. Some regular customers checked in daily to purchase these small roast batches that were still for sale. The daily bags of coffee were generally snatched up before noon. We had larger batch roasts we sold, but the day-of ones disappeared by eleven a.m. most of the time.

"I've been working and doing a few odds and ends."

When Dylan used the word 'working', I was never sure what he meant. I knew he had a job, but he was always tight-lipped about what he did. He'd promised me it wasn't anything illegal, so I'd promised not to pry. I was still worried, but that's what best gay friends did. At one point, we'd tried dating. We had quickly realized that we were not romantically interested in each other. Sure, we had some pretty nice sexual chemistry, but we were just friends. Occasionally, when one of us was having a dry spell, we'd still get together and fool around. It was kind of nice to have an actual friend who came with real benefits every once in a while. One time, when we had been hanging out playing video games at his place, he had looked over at me and asked, *"Want a blow job?"* I had said, *"Sure."* I had pulled my dick out of my shorts and he blew me while I kept playing. No mess, no fuss.

"Hey, Dylan," Autumn said as she walked by to clean another table.

"Hey, gorgeous," Dylan responded. "You going to be at the boy's party tonight?"

"Wouldn't miss it," Autumn said, looking back at him. "It's not like there's anything better to do tonight in Woodstock." She shot me a giant fake smile, and I rolled my eyes.

"Without me, you two would be in your pajamas by nine, eating popcorn and falling asleep before the ball drops," I noted.

"I would be eating a pint of ice cream, not popcorn," Autumn countered. "And probably drinking a cup of coffee."

"When *aren't* you drinking a cup of coffee?" I questioned.

"When I'm sleeping, but I can't actually prove that. Who knows, I could totally be 'sleep caffeinating'."

To say that Autumn liked coffee was like saying Colonel Sanders liked fried chicken or Sara Lee liked dessert. Autumn lived for coffee. She was currently attending the Culinary Institute of America across the Hudson River. Her goal was to get her pastry degree, then become a 'Q Grader'. Yeah, I hadn't known what the heck that meant either until I'd started working at the coffee shop. A Q Grader was the coffee equivalent of a sommelier. Q Graders were certified expert tasters and cuppers of all that is coffee by the Coffee Quality Institute.

Turning to look at Autumn, Dylan questioned, "So, what is the coffee of the day?"

"I'm so glad you asked," Autumn said. "Today, we have a Guatemalan peaberry coffee. We have both a dark and medium roast. I believe we ran out of the medium earlier, so you're probably drinking the dark. The beans were sun-dried, and you should be able to tell hints of a strawberry undertone. The volcanic soil in the Antigua region makes for a wonderful growing situation for the beans."

She explained everything about the growing process, how Stefan worked to get the beans here into the store, then how Stefan roasted the beans to get the perfect balance to ensure all the notes in the coffee were still tasted, killing none of the actual flavor. I'd already heard the speech when I'd first arrived for my shift, so I tuned her out and went about wiping some things down to avoid a more intense cleanup later. "Oh, and if you don't know, Dylan, peaberries are only found in about five percent of any harvested crop, so finding peaberries within the coffee cherry is always unexpected."

"You don't say," Dylan said. I could tell he was being nice and placating her. He knew just as well as I did that once you got her talking about coffee, getting her to stop was almost impossible.

I looked up as the wind chimes went off again and another customer strolled in. I took the order, made the drink and handed it to the customer while Dylan kept getting a lecture on the amazing attributes of peaberries. I was glad I had something else to do than listen to another lecture on coffee from Autumn. I loved coffee and I loved Autumn, but the combination of the two was enough to cure an insomniac. I'd known Autumn most of my life, so I was ecstatic when she'd found her purpose in life. I never knew the extent to which her purpose would drag me into it.

Before long, we finished up the day's work. Stefan was glad to pitch in to make sure we got out of there earlier than expected since it was New Year's Eve. Clearly, he had some kind of date or party he had to get to that evening. After everything in the store was cleaned, shut down and locked up, we said our goodbyes and happy new years before heading off in opposite directions.

"I'll see you around ten?" I said to Autumn.

"Sounds like a plan." She waved goodbye.

At some point during the closing, Dylan had made his escape. I hadn't even realized he had gone until my cell phone vibrated and I had a text from him confirming the party plans.

I pulled up the collar on my navy-blue wool peacoat to brace my neck against the cold weather. Thankfully, we didn't have any snow scheduled for that evening. I rushed the four blocks to the apartment complex where I lived with my best friend, Pietro Lupi. Pietro was like my brother, best friend and guardian angel, all wrapped up in one gorgeous, straight package. He'd been born in Negrar, Italy, and moved with his family to the United States when he had been a teenager. Though he spoke both English and Italian flawlessly, he still kept the Italian accent when he spoke.

"How was work?" Pietro asked as I walked into our two-bedroom apartment.

"It was work. Surprisingly steady." I hung my coat on the overstuffed coat rack next to the entryway. I think we had something like twenty different coats between Pietro and me. We kept saying we needed to figure out which ones we hadn't worn in at least a year and donate those to a local charity.

"Are all your friends still coming tonight?" Pietro asked.

"Yep. I told them to be here around ten. Is Valeria going to make it back in time?" Valeria was Pietro's girlfriend. She'd gone into the city to see an exhibit at the Modern Museum of Art, so she wasn't sure when she'd make it back to Woodstock.

"Yes," Pietro told me. "I texted with her about thirty minutes ago. She was already in line at the Trailways station, getting ready to board the bus north."

"Great." I looked down at my watch and realized she would be here in plenty of time. "Well, it looks like we're good to go. I think I'm going to take a nap."

"You do that," Pietro said. "The last thing we need is you falling asleep before midnight at your own New Year's Eve party."

* * * *

I woke up from my nap around eight-thirty and immediately went to take a shower and get ready for the party. Thankfully, both bedrooms had their own bathrooms, but mine was right outside my room. Pietro's bathroom was connected to his bedroom. I had to shut the door from the kitchen into my part of the apartment when I showered or I'd give anyone a show who was cooking if I streaked from the bathroom to the bedroom. The only difference between Pietro's and my bathrooms was that mine had a small utility room connected, where the washer and dryer were hooked up.

After a quick shower, I put on the clothes I'd planned on wearing that night. Once I was presentable, I headed back into the apartment. Pietro and Valeria sat on the couch, snuggled up and taking in a movie.

"Whatchya watching?" I asked, heading to the refrigerator to grab a can of Coke.

"Some old movie called *It Happened on Fifth Avenue*. Ever heard of it?" Valeria asked.

"Can't say that I have," I admitted.

Valeria was a bit of a film buff. She loved all movies—classics, modern, independent, big budget, etc. She also volunteered year-round at the Woodstock Film Festival, so she was tied into the movie scene in the Hudson Valley. And because of these ties, she also had an extensive list of industry contacts in the city.

"It's convoluted," Pietro said. "There's a billionaire who is dating a girl whose father is pretending to be homeless."

"Okay, that definitely sounds different," I acknowledged.

Valeria swatted Pietro on the arm. "It's not nearly as convoluted as Pietro is making it out to be. It's actually straightforward. We're watching it because there's a New Year's subplot, and there are too many movies that explore the new year, so I thought this would be a fun movie to watch before our guests arrive."

I caught the use of the phrase 'our' guests, but decided against saying anything since Valeria was spending more and more time at Pietro's and my apartment. "Is everything ready in here?" I asked, gesturing to the kitchen.

"I need to get things in the oven. I figure I'll do that as soon as the guests get here," Pietro explained.

* * * *

By ten-thirty, all the guests had arrived. We'd put out the hors d'oeuvres. And by 'we', I mean Valeria and myself. Pietro served as host as people came in, directing them to lay their coats on his bed since our coatrack was too full. By eleven, we'd eaten and weren't sure what to do.

"Let's play spin the bottle," Valeria said out of nowhere.

"We don't exactly have an even number of guys and girls," I noted.

"And your point?" Valeria said. "Half the fun is not knowing who you're going to land on, guy or girl." Valeria looked around the small group before asking, "Who's game?"

"Sure, why not," Dylan said.

I was apparently the only one who didn't think this was a good idea, but I finally agreed. Thankfully, those in the group over twenty-one had been drinking, so we had an empty beer bottle to use as the spinner.

First up was Valeria, since it was her game. It wasn't a huge surprise when it landed on Pietro, so she leaned in and gave him a deep kiss.

"Get a room," Dylan joked as they finally came up for air.

Pietro then spun, and it hit Autumn. Autumn blushed, but she leaned in for a quick kiss. She spun the bottle, and it landed on Dylan. The two kissed. Then Dylan spun the bottle, and it landed on Pietro.

"Let's do this," Pietro said to Dylan as he leaned in. Dylan gripped both sides of Pietro's face and planted a huge kiss on him. Valeria laughed at the look on Pietro's face as they pulled away.

"I couldn't get upstaged by your girlfriend," Dylan said with a wink in Pietro's direction.

"Whatever," Pietro said. "You weren't the worst kisser I've been with." Pietro spun the bottle, and it landed squarely on me.

Great! Part number one fantasy and part number one fear. Pietro shot me a half-smile and leaned in for his kiss. I quickly pecked him on the cheek.

"Boo!" Valeria said. "That's *so* not how this works. Do it like you mean it."

Pietro grabbed the back of my head, pulled my lips toward his and gave me one of the hardest, deepest kisses I'd ever had. I was so lost in the moment that I'd almost forgotten I had been kissing my best friend. My nether regions stirred and I tried to squelch them, but that didn't stop me from getting aroused. Thankfully, my jeans kept everything in place, and no one seemed to notice. He jammed his tongue down my throat. I pulled away and let out a cough.

Pietro started laughing. "Dude, the look on your face is priceless."

"I... I wasn't... I..." I stammered, which led to a round of laughter.

"Your turn to spin the bottle," Valeria said, handing me the empty beer bottle.

I gave the bottle a big spin. Part of me hoped it would land on Pietro again, and part of me hoped it would land on anyone else. It landed on Dylan.

"Well, I don't know if I can measure up to Pietro," Dylan joked, "but I'm willing to try." Dylan grabbed both sides of my face and planted a huge, wet, sloppy kiss. The group laughed. I sat there in stunned silence, not sure what to do. I could only imagine how red my face was at that moment. I almost found it easier to kiss the girls than either Dylan or Pietro. At least with the girls, I knew I wasn't attracted to them. I thought I'd gotten over my crush on Pietro years ago. I figured it had been so long since I'd gotten laid, any physical interaction with another guy was going to cause me to get aroused. *Just look at how I responded to Pietro*, I rationalized.

The game ended shortly after that. We started watching the local coverage of the ball dropping in Times Square.

"Ten, nine, eight, seven, six, five, four, three, two, Happy New Year!" the group cried out in unison. Pietro threw handfuls of metallic confetti into the air as group members toasted in the New Year with glasses of champagne, except for me. I had sparkling grape juice. *Yippee!* The group immediately started singing *Auld Lang Syne* with the TV in loud, obnoxious voices that sort of resembled the actual key of the song. I also noticed that a few people in the room were making words up. I heard Dylan say, 'Old Lang's Eye', and I almost doubled over in laughter.

Being the only one under twenty-one, I couldn't drink, especially since I knew some of the group would need a designated driver to get home in one piece or they would get arrested for a DUI. I'd heard a couple of officers that afternoon in the coffee shop talking about the checkpoints they planned on putting up. Basically, every major way in and out of Woodstock would have one. The Woodstock Police Department was not taking any chances of accidents this year.

Once the midnight witching hour had passed, our guests trickled out. Dylan had only a small amount to drink, so he swore up and down he was sober and would pass any checkpoint.

"You better be," I said, narrowing my eyes flatly. "I won't be coming to get you in the middle of the night from county lock-up."

"I swear. I'm perfectly sober, not like these Bacchanalists up in here." I laughed since the only person in the living room at the moment was Autumn, who clearly could not drive, even if she wanted to.

"Okay, okay. I get your point. Drive safely…for my sanity."

"Will do, captain." With that, Dylan walked over and grabbed his coat from Pietro's bed. Pietro and Valeria were snuggled up on the couch. Dylan said goodbye and headed into the chilly night.

"You ready to get going?" I asked Autumn.

She nodded, and we grabbed our coats. Thankfully, there wasn't any snow that evening. Sure, things were nippy, but the heater in my car quickly heated us once it got going. I drove through the quiet back streets of

Woodstock until I was sitting in front of Autumn's house. She still lived with her parents.

Before leaving my car, she turned and asked me, "What did you wish for?"

"Huh?"

"At midnight. What did you wish for this year?"

"What I wish for every year, I guess."

"A boyfriend?"

"God, you know me too well. But yes, I wished for a boyfriend—a good, old-fashioned guy who is interested in me and wants to be with me for more than one night."

"God, that almost sounds romantic," Autumn joked. "You are entirely too young to be that cynical. What am I going to do with you?"

I shrugged and kept my hands on the wheel. Autumn leaned over and kissed me on the cheek before she exited. I sat in the car and watched as she stumbled her way to her front door. When she pulled out her keys and let herself into the house, she turned around and gave me one last wave before closing the door behind her. With Autumn safely in her home, I pointed the car back toward the apartment.

In minutes, I was back home. When I entered my apartment, the place was a ghost town. I could hear muffled sounds coming from Pietro's room, but I didn't want to dwell on what I figured was going on behind that closed door. I headed into my bedroom, stripped and threw on my pajamas. And by pajamas, I meant a tank top and a pair of shorts I liked to sleep in. I liked the silky texture of the shorts next to my junk, so I freeballed it under the shorts. I'd tried sleeping nude once but hadn't been able to get comfortable.

I ran through the bathroom quickly and headed to bed. I looked at my alarm clock and it read one-fifteen a.m. I thought about rubbing one out before going to sleep. You know? My first jerk of the new year. But I decided that sleep called instead. I turned off the lights, and I was dead to the world as soon as my head hit my pillow.

Chapter Five

Roger

The light broke through the cracks in the wooden blinds of the guestroom. I rolled over and looked at the clock. *Nine-thirty, already?* I had been enjoying the CloudBed a bit too much and was totally thinking I needed to purchase one of these magical bad boys for myself.

"Monday already," I told myself.

The weekend had passed in a blur. On New Year's Eve, I'd loved hanging out with Dale and Talgat and even Talgat's siblings, but I had been exhausted by ten. I never got to bed that early, but the guest room had called me — or maybe it had been all the wine I drank at dinner. Either way, I had spent the new year cuddling with a pillow on the bed and not in the arms of a hot guy for the first time in at least a decade...maybe longer. I had been a serial monogamist my entire adult life. I had gone from one long-term relationship to the next. I had thought Jeremy was my knight in shining armor. Now, he reminds me of Prince Charming's line of Stephen Sondheim and James Lapine's musical, *Into the Woods*, *"I was taught to be charming, not sincere."*

I'd finally spoken with Jeremy yesterday.

"Hey, Roger," Jeremy had said, picking up the phone.

"Hey, Jer." I'd always cut the last part of his name off when we were talking. He had never called me "Rog," though. *"So, what now?"* I'd asked.

"Well, we need to figure out how you're going to pay for my rent."

The conversation had deteriorated from there. Jeremy had some fantastical idea in his head that since we were engaged, he should get some kind of palimony.

"Sorry, Jeremy. In New York State, the courts have decisively rejected palimony. You are entitled to nothing." I'd already checked with Grayson, who had turned around and directed me to a friend of his who handled more traditional divorces. I knew he had zero legal footing. And since I had helped him file his taxes last year, I knew he had little in the world of legal assets, so he would not hire an expensive legal team and try to come after me. Besides, Jeremy had never known what I was worth. He knew I had some money, but we'd never talked about the subject, probably because he had nothing and I had paid most of the bills. In retrospect, I had been a complete idiot. *Talk about dodging a bullet.*

I pulled myself out of bed and walked into the bathroom. The guest bathroom was huge. It had a walk-in shower large enough for at least six people and a detached whirlpool bathtub with jets in all kinds of locations.

I let the rainfall showerhead pour water down on my body as jets from three walls sprayed me all at once.

Soap didn't stay on your body for long because streams of water were flying at you from every direction. I grabbed my shampoo and squeezed some into my hand. I lathered the soap goo into my hair, then rinsed it out. I grabbed my bar of soap. Yep, I like a bar of soap. Call me old-fashioned. No loofas for me.

I rubbed my nearly hairless body down. I'm not naturally hairless, but I'd done some manscaping before Christmas. I probably had another week before I'd start sprouting hair again in places I would prefer for hair to remain off. With soap in my hand, I pulled on my dick to make sure it was thoroughly clean. Then I looked down at my hairless testicles and thought they looked like some kind of bald hedgehog. I soaped them up and rinsed them. I repeated the same thing with my ass. Once all my two-thousand parts were cleansed. I stepped out of the shower and grabbed the oversized plush bath towel. I patted myself dry, shaved my facial stubble away and brushed my teeth. I slipped into a present Dale and Talgat had gotten me. They hadn't needed to get me anything, but they had bought me a nice full-length bathrobe and slippers in a lavender blue. The robe was made of the same material as the towel, and it was all warm and comfy next to my skin. I'd seen Dale and Talgat wearing matching ones my first morning here and commented about how much I liked theirs. The next thing I knew, Dale had ordered one online for me in a different color.

"*Got you a present,*" Dale had told me on New Year's Day. He'd handed me the box with the robe in it and said, "*I thought this might be your color. It matches your eyes.*"

Dale always had an eye for color and fashion, something I never understood.

"*How'd you get this here so fast?*" I'd asked after trying it on.

"*I have my ways,*" was all Dale would tell me.

I left the bedroom in my robe and slippers. I headed into the kitchen area to find Dale and Talgat wearing their robes, drinking coffee and staring at their iPads. The modern equivalent of a couple reading *The New York Times*.

"Good morning," I said. "What's on the agenda today?"

"Well, we thought we'd show you around the farm," Dale said between sips of coffee. "If you're still serious about talking to some realtor friends of ours, we thought we could hook you up with them today—"

"Not that we want to pressure you to move out here," Talgat added. "But now is a good time to look at real estate...." He let the words linger in the air.

The sleepy little town was already growing on me. And I quickly realized a lot of guys I knew when I was out clubbing in my twenties all lived up here in the Hudson Valley, at least part-time. Buying a house was a lot cheaper up here, so many guys kept their apartments or condos in the city and owned a house upstate. It was kind of like living the best of both worlds.

"I don't know," I said. "I'm still thinking about it."

"Well, you can still think about it and look at some houses that are on the market. Who knows? You may find one you fall in love with," Dale said with a wink.

"Or you'll realize that none of the houses on the market are right for you," Talgat said, shooting Dale a look. "And that's okay, too."

"Wow, it's almost like you two are playing good realtor, bad realtor."

Talgat gestured for me to sit down and turned over an empty coffee mug he had waiting for me on the kitchen table. He poured the coffee but let me add the cream. Not too much, just enough to take off the bite.

"Well, I'm not averse to looking," I said after my first sip.

"Great! Because we're meeting the realtor and her wife for lunch," Dale told me. Then he added a fun "Surprise!" for good measure.

I rolled my eyes and drank my coffee.

* * * *

After our coffees and protein shakes, we headed to the farm. Dale worked on something, and Talgat took me around the place in an old beat-up truck.

"Dale has been trying to pry this thing from my grip since we started dating," Talgat said, gesturing to the truck. "I've had it since I was a teenager. Why would I want to give it up now?"

"I guess… as long as it's still running—"

"That's exactly what I've been trying to get Dale to see!"

Talgat drove me up and down, in and out of various parts of the farm. I'd not spent any time on a farm before, so this was all new to me. I admittedly found the sheer size of the enterprise surprising. I guess the thought of how much room was needed to grow apples never crossed my mind before. I'd just eaten them.

After finishing the tour, we drove back to the administrative building and found Dale outside waiting for us. We switched out of Talgat's truck and into Dale's shinier SUV.

"I'm sorry you had to step foot in that monstrosity," Dale said as he glared in Talgat's direction. "I keep warning him that one day that old eyesore is going to have an *accident*."

"You lay one finger on my truck, Mr. Dale Devereaux, and I swear I'll —"

"What? Withhold sex? We both know you wouldn't last the week."

Talgat looked slightly offended before he said, "That may be true, but I can still do other things," Talgat said as he made a crude gesture with his fist. "Maybe I'll turn you into my human puppet! How would you like that?"

"He's probably done it already," I joked.

"I want the record to show that both of you are ganging up on me," Dale said as he threw the SUV into drive and headed away from the barn with us inside. "And also, for the record, I have not once been fisted… I tapped out after he got his fourth finger into me. Who knew? I'm not that stretchy."

"TMI," I said, leaning in between them from the back seat. "I could have gone my entire life without the visual image of Dale getting fisted running through my head."

"Oh, please," Dale said with an exaggerated sigh. "You're telling me you've never found yourself in a sling with your feet pointed to the sky and some leather daddy threatening to turn you into Ms. Piggy?" There was silence. "Maybe it was just me." There was another pause, then all three of us busted out laughing. We were still laughing when we pulled into a diner to meet the realtor and her wife.

Talgat still had the snickers as he exited the vehicle. "What are you laughing about?" A short, stocky Black woman said as she walked to the SUV. Behind her, a lanky blonde woman followed.

"Dale was telling us about the time he tried to be Ms. Piggy," Talgat said before all three of us busted out laughing again.

"Gays," the woman said. "I *so* don't get your species."

When I finally rubbed the tear from the corner of my eye after having laughed entirely too hard, I extended my hand and said, "Roger Havemeyer."

"I'm Ruby Nixon, and this gorgeous woman is my wife, Stephanie Blevins."

I shook Ruby's hand first. She had a good, firm grip. Stephanie's grip was firm, but I didn't feel like she was trying to win a handshaking contest when I gripped hers.

"Well," Ruby said, "let's get some food and we can talk about houses."

I followed Ruby and Stephanie into the diner. Dale and Talgat followed behind me. The waitress already had menus in her hand and was showing us to a table before we even said hello.

"Want me to get your usual, Ruby?" the waitress asked.

"Of course. I am a creature of habit."

"What about you, Stephanie?"

"I'll also have coffee. Thanks."

"And for you gentlemen?"

"Coke," "Coffee," "Water," we said in succession.

"I'll have these right out for you." And the waitress was gone.

"So, tell me about yourself, Roger," Ruby asked.

"Well, not much to tell, really —"

"Don't let him do that to you," Dale interjected. "He's a big-time marketing guru in New York City. He primarily works in the entertainment industry."

"Oh really? Any campaigns I may have seen?"

I leaned back and motioned for Dale to keep talking since he appeared to know as much about me as I did at the moment. Dale rattled off a few of the shows I'd worked on over the years. Ruby and Stephanie were sufficiently impressed. I was embarrassed.

"So, is he allowed to talk for himself?" Ruby asked.

I motioned for Dale to continue talking. "Yes. He can talk for himself," Dale admitted.

"But will I?" I asked. "Everything Dale said is true. But I'm also a forty-one-year-old gay guy who got out of a long-term relationship."

"Is that why you're looking at houses?" Ruby asked. "You realize houses don't make the greatest rebounds? You don't want to buy a house, then question your sanity two weeks later."

"I'm fully sane. I'd already been thinking about buying a house as a wedding present for my fiancé." As soon as the word left my mouth, I corrected, "My ex."

"Mm-hmm…" Ruby said. "I want to make sure that you're happy with what you buy. Don't want anyone ever to feel pressured into buying if they aren't in love with the house."

"Trust me," I said. "I will not buy a house unless I'm completely enthralled. I know it's an enormous investment. But I need a change, and this seems like the type of change I need to make."

"We get a lot of you former party boys up here looking to put down some roots," Ruby reassured me. "Look at how we tamed Dale."

Just then, the waitress approached our table with our drinks. She set them down in front of us, pulled out her pad, and said, "What's everyone having today?" Thankfully, Ruby immediately ordered. I hadn't looked at the menu, so I went with what I thought was a safe bet in a diner, a burger. When the waitress finished taking our orders, she collected our menus and was on her way.

I turned to Ruby and asked, "Where are you from, Ruby?"

"What? You don't think I sound like I'm from around these here parts?" she said with a thick Southern accent. "Do you expect me to scream 'the vapors, the vapors' while I fan myself, drinking lemonade on the plantation?"

"Wow," I said, drawing out the word. "You are not a shy one, are you?"

"Oh, heavens no. I left that when I left Louisiana."

"She was born and raised in New Orleans," Stephanie said. "She hadn't stepped foot on a farm until she moved to Woodstock and met Talgat."

"How did you two meet?" I asked.

"Yeah," Dale cut in, "how did you two meet?"

"Well, I was attending Tulane," Stephanie said. "I was born and raised over in Rhinebeck, across the Hudson River from here. When it came time for college, I wanted to get as far away from New York as possible, so I chose New Orleans. I'd always loved jazz."

"And yet, you somehow got stuck with the most nonmusical resident of New Orleans ever," Ruby said, her face lighting up as she laughed.

"Yeah? How did that happen?" Stephanie said, narrowing her eyes. "Let me remember... You ran into me on Bourbon Street and dumped your entire hurricane on my chest."

"She was wearing a white T-shirt. I screamed, 'Breasts!' at the top of my lungs, then proceeded to motorboat her."

"You didn't?" Dale said, clearly surprised.

"She did," Stephanie said, shaking her head. "I wasn't sure if I should feel assaulted or turned on. The next thing I knew, it was three years later, and we were moving to New York City to get away from the bigotry and racism of the South. That's not to say everyone in the South is bigoted and racist, mind you, but there were enough dirty looks and snide comments. Being from New York, I hadn't dealt with that level of open hostility before. I couldn't live there forever."

"So," Ruby said, picking up the conversation, "we moved to Manhattan for a while. Katherine went to law school at Columbia, and I got into real estate. After a while, we decided to find someplace slower, which was when we came to visit Woodstock."

"And yet, you stayed?" Dale questioned.

"You bet your ass we stayed," Ruby responded. "Sure, we realized Woodstock was one giant tourist trap, but when you peel back the hippy-schtick, you realize this is a nice, caring community. And Ulster County is fairly liberal, so it seemed like it made sense."

I turned to look at Dale and Talgat. "How liberal is it up here? I mean, I won't get run off some guy's property with a shotgun. Will I?"

"Never say never," Ruby but it. "I don't know what kind of kinky shit you gays get up to these days."

Dale looked at her and rolled his eyes. If this had been a play, even someone in the back row could have seen that eye roll. "No, I've never heard of anyone getting run off someone's property with a shotgun. Now, you go farther up in the Catskills than we are, and there are some less than hospitable places for us. Hell, go on the east side of the Hudson River and you'll find pockets of crazy conservatives. I mean, Donald Trump did own property up in Westchester. Need I say more?"

I knew the political landscape of New York to some extent. And that meant that there were a lot of conservative Republicans in New York State, once you got out of the city. Sure, there were pockets of progressives and even entire counties that were consistently progressive. Still, these were blue spots in a sea of red.

"Don't worry," Ruby said, grabbing my hand. "I won't let you buy a house next to any Republicans. I know the area pretty well, so I will make sure we get you some good neighbors who either don't give a shit or keep out of it altogether."

Just then, the waitress came back with our orders, and we all dug in. Now, at least, I was having coffee and a hamburger. I hadn't realized how unsatisfying coffee and a protein shake could be for breakfast.

"And so you know," Stephanie spoke between bites. "Everything at this diner is completely farm-to-table."

"Really?" I said, covering my mouth with my free hand since I was still chewing.

"It is. Many local restaurants work with local farmers to source their food. We're lucky we have several great farms in this area. We like to keep it in the community when we can."

"It's true," Dale said. "We supply a lot of restaurants with fruits and vegetables. We may be known for our apples, but we raise other crops on the farm."

"Interesting," I said, with a new appreciation for my meal.

"So, Mr. Havemeyer, how much are you looking to spend on a new home?" Ruby asked nonchalantly.

"Ruby!" Stephanie chastised. "Give the poor man a break."

"Well, I need to think about which properties to show him." Ruby turned her gaze back on me.

I swallowed and picked up my napkin to wipe my mouth — not because it was dirty, but because I needed to figure out exactly how I wanted to say this.

"I would say I'm very comfortable with something between one and two…" I drew it out.

"Hundred thousand?" Ruby asked.

"Million," I said flatly, doing my best not to look at Dale.

"Damn, boy," Ruby said, letting out a low whistle. "That opens up a lot of possibilities."

"Let's just say I had a great stockbroker for many years," I said, casually cocking my head in Dale's direction.

"Maybe we need to talk to you about our investments," Ruby said, eyeing Dale.

"I'm out of that world now," Dale said. "Sadly, I don't even know what's going on in it these days."

"That's not completely true," Talgat countered. "He still handles investments for his granddad and Deveraux Farms."

"True enough…" Dale said, pausing for a second to collect his thoughts. "I'm out of the individual wealth-building game these days. I used to love gambling with other people's money." He shot me a quick look and said, "It's what I did. I was good at it, but I was still gambling with your money."

"When I decided to invest my inheritance in the stock market, I looked at several firms. I went with you for a reason," I reassured him. "We sat down in your office, and you had a long conversation with me about whether this was something I wanted to do. You were bluntly honest with me. Thankfully, I saw how talented you were and went with you."

"Aw shucks," Dale said, putting on a cutesy smile. "He liked me. He really liked me."

"Whatever." Now it was my turn to roll my eyes.

Before long, we'd finished lunch, and I'd caught the bill. I'd intended to do so from the start, but Ruby made a joke of it. I was warming up to her.

"So, it's just going to be the two of us looking at houses," Ruby said. "Stephanie and the other boys have to go back to work."

We said our goodbyes, and I found myself in Ruby's large SUV going to look at potential properties. *Does everyone up here drive an SUV?*

We stopped at several places, and I wasn't too enthralled with any of them. The fourth house we drove up to was like something out of a dream. There was a stone driveway that had been laid, which included a small bridge that ran over a frozen creek. The whole thing looked old and rustic, but you could tell it was pretty new or had recently been remodeled.

"This house was built in 2002. You would be the second owner. The original owner passed last year, and the house fell to his estate, which is being managed by his eldest son, who lives outside Chicago," Ruby told me as she parked the car. "I can tell you they want to sell, but they are also in no hurry."

We got out, and I immediately heard my shoes crunch on the snow. Someone had been out in the past few days to plow, but there was still a good two inches of snow covering the ground. I looked off into the distance and saw a deer out near a tree quickly lift its head in our direction before running off.

I took a deep breath and noticed something. *Wow, nature doesn't smell like the city.* Even in Central Park, where you can lose yourself in nature and surround yourself with plants, it still smells like the city. There's this scent that exists everywhere. I took a deep breath in through my nose, the cold air tickling immediately at my nose hairs. The smell was...clean.

"So, the house itself is about five-thousand square feet, six bedrooms, six baths, eight-point-seven acres of land," Ruby said as I spun in a circle to look at everything in front of me. "The current asking price is two-point-two million."

"Okay," I said. She walked over to the door and quickly got into the lockbox before opening the house. Everything was wood. "As you can see, the foyer here is quite welcoming, and the glass windows are three stories high to allow the mountain sun to enter on this side. The backside is also completely glass, so you're able to catch the last rays of sun on that side."

"Did you say three stories?" I questioned.

"Yep. It's a big house."

"I'll say. It's like two and half times as much room as I could ever hope for at a fraction of the cost I'd pay for an apartment in the city."

"You must see the kitchen," she said, beckoning me to follow her. From the glint in her eye and the smile on her face, she knew she had already hooked me.

We spent the next hour going through the entire place. She even took me outside to a path leading to an outdoor, closed-in gazebo area with its own fireplace.

Right next to it was a hot tub. I could already imagine having friends over and hanging out in our swimsuits during a blizzard, then hopping into the hot tub to watch the snow fall.

I started working the numbers in my head as we walked back to the house. I easily had five million sitting in the bank. I didn't want to spend all of it on a home, but I was willing to spend about half. But I also needed to consider furnishing the place. That was going to cost me a ton of money, too. I'd have to factor in taxes and utilities, but my salary would cover that with no problems.

"How likely do you think they'll sell the house to me furnished?"

"I don't know the sellers myself, but we can always ask. Unless there is something in there that they are dying to get their hands on, I can't imagine them turning down an offer to buy it 'as is'. Chances are they'd be looking at an estate sale to get rid of a lot of this," Ruby said as she motioned to the living room furniture. Ruby motioned for me to take a seat on the couch, so I did. She sat in the chair opposite me. "What are you thinking? Again, no pressure."

"I think I love it. But I'm also thinking I at least have to try negotiating. What if we countered with one-point-eight million cash for the place furnished, as is?"

Ruby cocked an eyebrow at the word 'cash,' then asked, "How high would you be willing to go?"

"I can authorize you to go as high as two million before you'd need to check back in with me. At that point, I'll need to have my accountant look at a few things."

"Great! Let's get back to my office. I'll have a few papers for you to sign to get the ball rolling. I'll call in the offer as soon as we're there."

I took a breath in and held it as I looked around the grand living room area. This was more house than any one man ever could need. But it was only money, and I had no heirs besides Peter, so I might as well enjoy it. And this would give Peter and his family a reason to visit me and see the new digs.

As I walked out of the house and into Ruby's SUV, I couldn't help but smile. I was going to make a ridiculous offer on a ridiculous house—and I didn't need to ask anyone for permission.

* * * *

Wes

I walked from the storage room with a couple of boxes of to-go cups and lids. It was mid-afternoon, and the place was dead. All the tourists who had come to Woodstock for the new year had magically vanished from the town. Most had gone home Sunday afternoon, but a few stragglers Monday morning got their coffee on the way out of town as late as eleven a.m.

"What has you so bummed today?" Autumn said.

"Just life," I replied.

"It can't be that bad."

"It's not. I'm trying to figure out how I will pay all my bills in the next couple of weeks. You know how it is. December and into January, our tips skyrocket. They plummet as everything goes back to our regular customer base until the tourists come back in late spring and into the summer."

"I know what you mean," Autumn agreed. "The dead seasons are always harder financially."

"And you're still living with your parents," I said. Okay, I probably whined it more than said it.

"I know," Autumn said, laying a reassuring hand on my arm.

Living life without one's parents was hard. At a point where I could use their financial support, I could only depend on myself. Don't get me wrong. Pietro and his family had helped me so much after my parents had died. Just the fact that they let me live with their family during my senior year in high school was beyond anything I could have asked for, but there wasn't a day that went by that I didn't miss my folks. And I'm not just talking about missing their money. We weren't rich. We were your average family. Both my mom and dad had good, middle-class jobs. They had instilled in me my work ethic. They'd also pounded into my head the importance of getting one's education.

"Ugh," I said.

"What?" Autumn asked, looking a little more alarmed.

"Remembering that I need to budget for textbooks." I had a scholarship to Bard College on the other side of the Hudson River, but the scholarship didn't pay for books, so I had to manage them out of student loans. And I also used student loans to help pay for my half of Pietro's and my apartment. "I hate having to think about money. Why can't it grow on trees?"

"What are you doing to him?" a voice said. I turned to watch Dylan walking toward us.

"He was telling me all about his financial woes," Autumn said.

"How do you do it?" I asked, turning to Dylan. He was like me...in a way. As a teenager, he'd been kicked out by his parents, but he now had an apartment and stayed afloat. And he didn't have a job that I knew of. "I mean, it's not like you work."

"I work," Dylan reassured me.

"Where?" I asked.

"I work from home. I have quite a lucrative business at that."

"Please don't tell me you're a drug dealer," Autumn said. "I don't want to visit you in jail."

"I'm not doing anything illegal. In fact, everything I do is very legitimate and taxed by both the State of New York and the US federal government."

"Have you taken Mr. Holland's order?" Stefan said, coming out of his office. He always seemed to leave his office just in time to see Autumn or me talking to a customer or not working fast enough or hard enough for his liking.

"Yes," Autumn lied. "Mr. Holland is getting a large coffee, black." Thank God Autumn knew Dylan's order by heart. "That will be two dollars and twenty-five cents."

Stefan eyed us before turning around to look at something. He had a clipboard in his hands and appeared to be doing some kind of inventory. I put it out of my mind and poured Dylan's cup of coffee.

Dylan went and sat down at a small table in the corner, where he pulled out his cell and started reading something on it.

"Hey, Stefan," I said. "I'm going to go on break now. Is that okay?"

Stefan looked up from his clipboard and made a shooing motion. I wasn't sure if that meant 'sure' or 'leave me the fuck alone', but I took it as a sign that I could go. I grabbed my bottle of water and walked over to Dylan's table.

"What's up?" I asked.

"I was just doing my working schedule."

"What is this mysterious work you are talking about? I haven't seen you work a day in your life."

"Just because you don't see me work doesn't mean that I don't. I still have to earn money like everyone else."

I could tell there was something he wasn't telling me, so I finally said, "Out with it."

"Out with what?" he replied coyly. I leaned my head to the side and narrowed my focus. "Okay, okay. I started working as an online model about two years ago."

"Online model?"

"Yes, I… I do things online for people who want to watch."

It took me a minute to figure out what he was talking about. "You're a porn star?" I said a little louder than I intended, but thankfully no one around us turned to look. "You're a porn star?" I said in a more hushed voice.

"It's not technically porn. Well, it is, but it's not. I'm an independent contractor for an adult entertainment website called CammBate."

"So, you have sex with guys online," I said, less a question and more a statement of fact.

"Rarely," Dylan responded. "I will not say that I've never done that, but mostly, it's just me and my Internet camera."

I hated to admit it, but I was intrigued. "How does it work?"

"Basically, I put on a show. I talk to the viewers and pleasure myself. I get them to tip me, which is how I get paid—kind of like how strippers get dollar bills in a strip club."

"Like either of us has ever been to a strip club," I said.

"True, but we knew all the lines to *Striptease* in junior high."

God, I hadn't thought about that movie in ages. *Whatever happened to Demi Moore?*

"The more the guys tip," Dylan went, refocusing my attention on what he was saying, "the more I do. Basically, I have levels. I get one hundred tips, and I'll take off a shirt. When I get a thousand tips, I'll get naked. If I get three-thousand tips, I'll play with myself. If I get five-thousand tips, I'll have a cum show."

"And people are actually paying you for this?" I asked in disbelief.

"The Internet loves a good twink. And there are a lot of rich, older guys with a ton of money who are more than happy to tip me to watch me have sex with myself."

"How much money are you making?" I asked. I figured he was going to say a couple hundred dollars.

"I can easily make four grand a show if I play my cards right. I do four shows, and I'm making sixteen-thousand a week. I set about half of it aside for tax, but that still means I'm making eight thousand after taxes. But more often than not, I'm pulling in around ten thousand. And the more I'm willing to do on camera, the better my profits are."

"Wow," I said, letting out a low whistle. "I can't imagine doing that."

"Why not? You're hot. You're young. And God knows you have a gorgeous dick and a sweet little ass."

I looked down at my water bottle, hoping my face wasn't bursting into red flames as I blushed.

"You should totally come by tonight. I have a show at nine. I'll perform for maybe two to three hours."

"I will not fuck you on camera, Dylan," I said under my breath.

"I'm not asking you to be on camera. I'm just saying, come see what I do. If you decide it's something you're interested in, I can help set you up."

I looked at him warily. Then I thought about the cost of college textbooks, closed my eyes, shook my head and said, "I'll be there at eight."

When I opened them again, Dylan sat there drinking his coffee with a smug look on his face. *What did I just agree to?*

* * * *

As promised, I arrived at Dylan's apartment at eight o'clock. I'd been here before many times, but somehow the place looked different. Everything I looked at had been paid for by dirty old men watching Dylan masturbate on camera.

"What are you thinking?" Dylan asked, handing me a can of soda from the fridge.

"I'm... I can't—"

"It's going to be okay, Wes. This is a safe space. And I will not ask you to do anything you don't want to do. In fact, I will not ask you to do anything at all."

That seemed to let a little of the wind out of my sails. I leaned back on the couch and popped the can before taking a drink.

"Wanna help me shave my asshole?" Dylan suddenly asked. My mouth dropped open, and I tried to stammer out a response, but nothing came out. Dylan burst into fits of laughter. "I was joking... You should know my asshole is naturally smooth."

"*You're* such an ass," I said, then took in a deep, calming breath.

"Yep, and I have a great one—or so you've told me many times before."

"Oh geez," I said, taking another drink. "Keep this up and you're never seeing my cock again."

"Really?" Dylan said. He stuck his tongue out slightly as he licked over the top of his lip.

"Nope."

He inched closer. The muscles in my throat constricted as I tried to drink down my own saliva.

"Not even if I do this?" he said before he placed his hands on my knees.

"No," I heard a high-pitched sound escape my lips.

"What if I do this?" In one quick motion, he used his teeth to release the top button on my jeans and unzip my pants.

I looked down at my growing dick and said, "Traitor!"

Dylan flung himself back from me, leaning on the couch, and started laughing. "You should wear a belt," Dylan informed me. "It's much harder to get a guy's pants open when he has a belt on." Dylan's eyes looked toward my traitorous appendage, as it was now trying to poke out of my jeans. "Cute underwear, by the way..." he said, looking at my boxer briefs that were covered with pink flamingos. "They would look better on the floor of my bedroom." He reached out a hand and said, "How about a quickie?"

I looked at my watch. "Do you have time?"

"I always have time for you."

I accepted his hand as he pulled me off the couch and into his bedroom. He pushed me backward onto his bed, making quick work of the rest of my pants. He proceeded to perform a little oral *stress reduction*. I was so relaxed, feeling the soft tip of his tongue flitting about the head of my dick. I completely lost track of time and let him go to town. He could blow me for hours, and I would lay there and enjoy it without coming.

"Fuck!" he blurted. I opened my eyes and caught him looking at the clock on his wall. "I need to get set up."

He jumped off the bed. I threw on my underwear and followed him out of the bedroom, my hard-on guiding the way. We walked across the living room to the spare bedroom. He opened the door, and I was surprised by how simple the setup was. He had three cameras mounted on tripods that showed three angles of the bed. He had ring lights in the corners, and in the middle was a computer that apparently ran his whole operation. On the side table, he had lube and a bunch of sex toys. Many of them were ones we'd used with each other at one point or another.

"Whoa, this is some setup."

"That it is," Dylan said as he logged himself online. He pulled a folding chair from the closet and set it up for me. "You can sit here. You'll be out of camera that way."

"Okay." I sat where Dylan told me. "So, what's up with all the cameras and lights?"

"Just makes it easier for them to see me. I'm using a streaming software, so I can easily change between the cameras to give my audience the best vantage point. As for the lights, bad lighting makes someone look like an amateur. For me, I want to make sure my viewers get the best experience for their hard-earned money."

Within a few minutes, Dylan was up and running. At first, Dylan lay on the bed looking aloof. At one point, he pulled out a gaming console and made it look like he was playing a game. I could tell the gaming console wasn't connected to anything from my vantage point.

"What are you doing?" I whispered.

"You don't need to whisper. I haven't turned on the microphone yet."

"So, what are you doing?"

"There's this whole gamer fetish thing out there. Some guys are into it. If you look at the computer screen, you can see that some guys are already asking me what I'm playing."

I looked over. Sure enough, there was a chatbox on the screen, and people were already talking to Dylan. I looked at the screen name, pointed at the screen and said, "Really? SmoothBanger69?"

"I wanted something provocative. It worked." Dylan put the controller down and looked at the computer screen. He picked up the keyboard and started responding. I watched as he flirted, and guys tipped. "If you look down here," Dylan said, pointing to a number at the bottom of the screen. "This is my tip jar. See how it says what the viewers will get at the next tip level?"

It clearly said, *"One thousand, and SmoothBanger69 takes off his shirt."*

Within minutes, his virtual tip jar hit one thousand. Dylan turned to me and said, "My mic is about to go live." I nodded. Dylan turned to the center camera and said, "Thanks, cristoball1919," as he slowly removed his shirt. He felt up his chest for a minute and tweaked his nipples. From Dylan's face, you would think he was on the verge of having an orgasm. Having been someone who had caused a few of Dylan's orgasms, I knew that was not what his O-face looked like.

This kept going. Before long, Dylan reached his next goal, and he seductively removed his shorts. Even though he kept his underwear on, you could see his growing bulge inside. Dylan ran his hand over the length of his hard cock. "Come on, guys. He wants to come out and play. I need" — Dylan looked at the monitor — "seven-hundred-and-thirty-nine more tips for him to come out."

The dinging sound that came out of the computer monitor sounded like gamblers winning the slots jackpot in Las Vegas. I hadn't witnessed that sound personally, but I've seen enough movies involving Vegas to have a good idea what that sounds like.

I barked out a laugh. Dylan whipped his head in my direction. "Shit," I said under my breath.

Immediately, questions started popping up on Dylan's screen, asking who was there with him. Was I his boyfriend? His lover? His younger brother? *Eww!*

"He's a friend, guys. I'm showing him what I do. He's not a CammBoy. Sorry," Dylan said, making a pouty face on the screen.

A guy typed, *Will he fool around with you for a huge tip?*

"Sure, I'll play with him for ten-thousand tips," I joked, forgetting the microphone was live again.

His computer monitor practically exploded as the tips started pouring in. I stared at Dylan with a 'what the fuck?' look. I could tell from Dylan's expression he hadn't expected the tips to roll in that fast.

"Well, fuck," was all he said.

Chapter Six

Roger

I was hanging with Dale and Talgat when the phone call came in on my cell phone. I looked down and didn't recognize the 845 area code. I almost didn't answer, but realized before it went to voice mail that it was the Woodstock area code.

"Hello?" I answered.

"Hey… Is Mr. Roger Havemeyer available?"

"Yes?" I meant it as a statement, but I knew it came out as a hesitant question.

"Hey, Roger, it's Ruby."

I almost said 'who?' but I caught myself. I must have been half asleep or something. "Oh, hey, Ruby." Saying her name, I watched as Dale's and Talgat's heads whipped in my direction. I hadn't told them I'd put in an offer on the house. I'd just said the house hunting had gone well.

"I spoke to the other realtor… They accepted your offer at one-point-eight-five million."

"Holy shit," I mumbled.

"What?" Dale asked.

"My offer on a home was accepted." I wasn't entirely sure if that was a statement or a question as it left my mouth.

"Say *what*?" Dale asked, forcing me to focus on him.

"I'll tell you everything in a minute," I told Dale, then refocused my attention on Ruby. "So, when can we close?"

"Well, normally, it takes a couple of months...."

"Yeah, how soon can we close?"

"We need to get the house inspected. With the size of the place, it's probably going to take a team at least one full day. Then it's a matter of drawing up the paperwork, filing with the county and getting everyone in the same room together."

"That sounds ominous," I admitted.

"Thankfully, this time of the year is slow. And I know the realtor just returned from vacation, and the seller's lawyer is local. So really, it's going to be a matter of you and your lawyer. We can Zoom in the seller and your bank."

"I probably need to open a local bank account," I said, more to myself. "Will it be easier to do a bank check or a transfer of funds?" I asked Ruby.

"I'm sure we can manage either way. Oh, and the realtor told me that anything of value to the seller was already pulled from the house, so everything in there will be yours once you sign on the dotted line."

"How about Friday?" I asked.

"What about Friday?" she asked, then realized what I was asking. "Oh, you want to close the end of this week?" I could hear the disbelief in her tone. "That's a lot to figure out in a few short days."

"It's about shifting money and getting people in the same room once the inspection's done. Right?"

"Yeah," Ruby replied. "Let me make some phone calls first thing in the morning. I have someone I've worked with on these types of house inspections. As long as she has nothing else this week, I'm sure her team can do the inspection on Wednesday or Thursday. And barring any problems, I'll get everyone's schedules together for Friday." There was a brief pause. I could hear her scribbling on a legal pad for a second. "What about your lawyer? You need to have representation at the meeting."

Everyone has to have a lawyer? I'm sure some lawyer in the New York State Legislature came up with that rule. "I'll get one for Friday. I can have someone I know from the city run up or find one locally. I'll figure that out tomorrow."

"Well, I'll call you tomorrow afternoon, Roger, with any details once I hammer them out. Congratulations."

"Thanks," I said. We said our goodbyes, and I turned to look at Dale and Roger. "Well, that happened fast."

"What happened? We want the four-one-one," Dale said impatiently, looking at me.

"I kind of fell in love with this house. It's a little more remote out in the woods, but it's like my dream home. It's a tiny log cab."

"Uh-huh," Dale said dismissively. "I know better. Spill."

I spent a few minutes walking them through the house. I also pulled up the seller's website and showed them a video they'd produced, showing all the perks on the property.

"And I'm getting the house furnished, as is, by the end of the week if everything goes according to plan."

"Knowing you," Dale said, looking at me with slightly narrowed eyes, "I'm sure everything will go according to plan or you'll force it to happen."

"Wow," Talgat said. "I can't believe you're buying that place. I've been out there a few times for parties over the years. The guy who used to live there was a known philanthropist, and he often opened up his home for charity galas. The kitchen there is huge."

"Now I need to find someone who will cook in it for me," I joked.

"Maybe you should go cruising for a hot college student over at the Culinary Institute of America in Hyde Park," Dale joked.

"Where's that?"

"Across the river."

"There seems to be a lot of colleges across the river," I said.

"There are," Talgat added. "There's Bard, Vassar, Marist, the CIA and a handful of community colleges. On this side of the river, there are a few more community colleges and the State University of New York at New Paltz."

"Hmm... That's a lot of college students in one area."

"Yep," Talgat admitted. "You can't throw a rock around here without hitting one."

"I'm going to be a homeowner," I said absently, still a bit in shock.

"Do you have a lawyer?" Dale asked. "You know, to handle the purchase?"

"I figured I'd call Grayson and get a recommendation."

"No need. I know exactly who Grayson is going to recommend." Dale whipped out his phone, searched through the numbers and tapped the screen. "Talia? Dale Devereaux here. Sorry to be calling so late." There was a pause as Dale listened to the other end of the line. "Well, I have a new client for you. He had an offer on a house accepted and needs a lawyer. He's hoping to close on Friday if everything goes according to plan." He listened for a few more minutes. "Nope. He's like me. He's paying cash." More silence. "Perfect! I'll bring him by to meet you in the morning. Have a great night."

"Well?" I asked. I kind of already knew how the conversation went, but I wanted it confirmed.

"She said it's a slow week, and she has no meetings scheduled on Friday, so you're golden. She'll want at least twenty-four hours to read the contract. So as long as everything is standard, you won't have any problems there."

"Wow," I said. "This is all happening so fast."

"Yes," Dale said. "The transition to living up here may be fast, but once you're a resident, you'll love how slow things can be. I still miss the fast pace of the city. And I go down and hang out all the time, but I love coming home to peace, quiet and laid-back nature when I'm done."

"I guess Sondheim was right. 'I think there's a time to come to New York and a time to leave.'"

"What show is that?" Talgat asked.

"*Company*. I saw the revival with Raul Esparza and again when they gender flipped it with Katrina Lenk as the female lead. Bobbi with an 'I'."

"Wasn't that the one with Patti LuPone?" Dale asked.

"Yep. When she sang the line, 'The ladies who lunch,' I heard the sound of a thousand gay erections *rising* to attention."

"Yep," Dale agreed. "That's LuPone's superpower. She can make even the gayest man stand and salute the Almighty power of Patti."

"Well, it sounds like you had a busier day than you let on earlier," Talgat mused. "I'm glad you're going to be joining us up here...neighbor." He turned and looked at Dale. "I don't know about you, but I'm beat. I'm going to head up to bed."

"And with an offer like that," Dale joked, "how can I refuse? Good night, Roger." Dale stood from his seat on the couch, walked over and gave me a quick kiss on the forehead. "Welcome to the gayborhood."

"Night, Roger," Talgat said, already walking away. He extended his hand backward to catch Dale's. He hadn't even needed to look to know that Dale's hand was already stretching toward his.

"Good night, Talgat."

"Good night, John-Boy," Dale threw out.

"Wow, a Walton's throwback," I said. "I'm amazed you even know that one."

"I took a television history class when I was in college," Dale said casually as he disappeared from view. "Too bad I couldn't have seen the originals, like you." Even though I couldn't see the smirk on his face, I knew he'd just made an old man joke at my expense.

I got up and went over to my side of the house. In a few short days, I would have my own home. *What the actual fuck!* In the guest bedroom, I sat down at the makeshift desk and checked in with work to see if there was anything that I needed to deal with.

I shot Mitzi an email, letting her know the good news. She probably assumed I was having some kind of midlife crisis. I started scrolling through my inbox to see if there was anything important.

The first one that caught my attention was from my new hire, Richard Salzman.

Hey Boss.
Moved into an apartment in the city. Will be at the office bright and early tomorrow. I heard from your assistant that you're out. What should I be working on?
Richard

Welcome to the team. I'm sure you will bring a lot of energy and new ideas to the agency. As for tomorrow, plan on working with human resources most of the morning. After that, Mitzi will set you up for an orientation with one of the other people in our department. Let's catch up on Wednesday via Zoom. Again, welcome.
Roger

Nothing else was critical, so I started going through and deleting emails. *Spam, spam, spam,* I heard myself thinking as I deleted several. I went to hit the delete key on one and opened it by mistake.

CammBate… Get one hundred free tips on us.

The message was packed with a bunch of hot nude guys. "What the hell?" I clicked on the link and was immediately taken to a website. There were sections for women, men, couples and a few other categories. I clicked on men.

Suddenly, my screen was filled with images of men masturbating or engaging in a wide range of other sexual behaviors, either by themselves or with other men. My cock twitched. "Down, boy," I said.

I scrolled through the images. One had a guy sitting at a desk with another guy standing behind him butt-ass naked with his hands behind his back. The name read, 'MasterGregInTX'. Without thinking, I was unbuttoning my pants and whipping out my dick. I watched for a few moments until Master Greg applied some menthol cream to the poor boy's balls. I winced as I watched and closed that window.

I scrolled through a few more. Then I saw a profile for a brown-headed guy named 'SmoothBangr69'. The location on the profile said New York, so I clicked on the image.

"Sure, I'll play with him for ten-thousand tips," the guy off screen joked as the video loaded.

I stared at the screen as the number in the lower lefthand corner quickly climbed. *That must be the tip jar*, I thought to myself. Another number showed the number of people watching SmoothBangr69's show. In under a minute, there were over one thousand people watching and the 'tip jar' had reached over ten-thousand. A young man came into the frame. He was only wearing a pair of boxer briefs covered in pink flamingos.

The main guy, SmoothBangr69, said, "This is my friend...Erik. He's never done this before, so please be generous. The more generous you are with your tipping, the more I can convince him to do on camera."

I stared at the blond, blue-eyed man who looked nervous enough that he'd probably jump at his own shadow. There was something innocent about the young guy, almost angelic. I'm not into twinks at all, but this guy made my cock twitch in a way it hadn't in years.

I quickly learned that the 'host's' name was Jackson, and he started by reaching over to Erik and pulling him in for a kiss. At first, Erik was taken aback as Jackson and he pressed their lips together. I saw when Erik melted into the moment and began responding.

Jackson broke their kiss and circled Erik's nipples with his tongue. Jackson lightly bit Erik's nipple and pulled it in his teeth. Erik' tilted his head back, his mouth opened and he let out a soft moan. I instantly watched Erik's cock pressed against those pink flamingo boxer briefs.

I glanced down at my dick, which was standing at full attention, begging to be played with. I gathered some spit in my mouth and let it slide out onto the cockhead to help provide some lubrication as I started stroking myself, watching the men in action.

"Come on, guys," Jackson said, breaking away from Erik's body. "Show Erik some love. Let's get these off him," he said as he bent down and pulled at the waist of Erik's underwear with his teeth. Like clockwork, a stream of tips suddenly filled the tip jar. I was half tempted to create an account so I could tip the men myself.

Erik leaned back, and Jackson used his teeth to pull down Erik's boxer briefs, exposing the enormous cock that had been held back. Without a word, Jackson immediately went down on Erik, taking him all the way down to the base of his cock. I guessed Erik's cut dick was seven to eight inches but wasn't overly thick—not exactly a pencil dick, but more of a nice, average width. I stared at Erik's cock and wished I were Jackson, going down on him.

Jackson pulled away and looked at the camera, "You're right, GloryHole. His cock is delicious. Wish you were here to help taste it with me. And trust me, JackBater. It feels as good in my ass as it does in my mouth. And no, FlyGuy69, we're not boyfriends. We're long-term friends with lots of benefits."

Erik suddenly pulled Jackson on top of him and gave him a long kiss. Then, hesitantly, Erik flipped Jackson over, and he used his tongue to trail from Jackson's neck down to his — what had to be at least nine inches — cock. Erik used his tongue to lick around the head, teasing it. Then he engulfed the uncut cock, swallowing it to the base. Jackson gently grabbed the back of Erik's head and pumped the man's mouth. I heard a gagging sound, and when Erik came up for air, there were slight tears in his eyes. My dick became harder watching the young man gag.

Erik straddled Jackson and slowly lowered himself until all nine inches of Jackson were nestled in his ass. His back was to the camera, but Jackson clearly liked the warm ass that was now taking him to his balls. Jackson let out a moan of his own. Before long, Jackson was pumping Erik's ass, and I was keeping in rhythm pumping on my cock. I let down a bit more spit to keep myself lubricated.

"I'm gonna cum," Jackson said suddenly. He pulled Erik off him, then fisted his cock as he exploded his cum up Erik's back. The first shot hit the back of Erik's head. As Jackson continued to fist his cock rapidly, Erik's back was coated and coated in cum.

"My turn," Erik said seductively, getting off his knees and looking down at Jackson.

Jackson repositioned himself so the camera could see him and Erik sideways. Jackson grabbed some lube and rubbed it on Erik's cock. Jackson lay back against the bed, and in a heroic feat of flexibility, anchored his ankles behind his neck. I honestly didn't know that position was possible.

Erik placed the tip of his cock against Jackson's waiting hole. I pumped my cock harder as I watched Erik slowly push into the man. Before long, he'd built up a good rhythm. Jackson was already hard again, jerking himself in time with Erik's thrusts.

I notice a pool of pre-cum forming on the tip of my dick. I smeared it across the head, teasing myself but forcing myself to hold back. I didn't want to come yet.

"Fuck, I'm gonna co —" Erik's sentence was cut short as he threw his head back and his whole body spasmed.

Immediately, my orgasm hit me in waves as stream after stream of cum coated my stomach.

I wasn't the only one having an orgasm. Jackson's second one coated his chest. Erik slowly pulled out. From this angle, I could see a trail of cum seeping out of Jackson. *I wished it had been my hole.*

"Wow," Jackson said. "I hope you enjoyed that as much as we did." He looked at Erik, who had flopped over onto his back, clearly exhausted. "Let's give a hand to my friend Erik for his first time on CammBate. I have a sneaking suspicion you'll be seeing more of him."

Jackson scooched to the edge of the bed, then the camera went dark and a message appeared on the screen, *This performer is currently off-line. Check out our other CammBaters now for a pumping good time.*

I let out a breath as a sense of exhaustion roll over me. I stared down at the sticky mess I'd created. *Guess I need to run through the shower.*

Chapter Seven

Tuesday had involved meeting my real estate lawyer and hiring a home inspector. Thankfully, everything with the county had been fine, so there was no need to have a survey done of the property, which could have caused delays. Wednesday and half of Thursday had been taken up by virtual meetings at work. I had talked to the partners, and everyone was cool about me working virtually for the time being. We had called it a 'test run'. I had promised that I could make it down to the city in a little over two hours, if necessary, which had seemed to ease any of the concerns they'd had.

By noon on Thursday, the home inspector had called to let me know that her team had found nothing that would prevent the sale of the house. She had several recommended fixes and upgrades, but they had been primarily cosmetic. By Thursday evening, the home inspector had dropped by a notebook outlining all her findings. She had also brought by her bill, and I asked if I could Venmo her. Thankfully, she hadn't looked at me like I had grown a third head. She had provided me with her information, and I switched money into her account.

By ten-thirty a.m. on Friday, I was ready for all this to be over. We had decided to meet at Ruby's office, because she had a nice, big conference room. I walked in and found my lawyer, Talia, already there.

"Anything amiss with the contract?" I asked Talia after Ruby showed me into the conference room.

"Not at all," she informed me. "It's one of the most straightforward contracts I've seen. As for payment, once everyone is here, we can sign and have you call your bank to initiate the transfer of funds. Are they ready on your end?"

"I spoke with them this morning. They received the bank account information for the seller yesterday afternoon. They started a small test transfer of funds, and it had worked."

"Perfect!"

Ruby's assistant brought us in a cup of coffee. I didn't recognize the brew, so I asked Ruby when she finally joined us in the conference room. "Where did this coffee come from?"

"It's a local coffee shop. They roast their own coffee beans. The guy who owns the place is from France and takes his coffee seriously. They only make small batches, so the day-of coffee often sells out before noon. I go in at least once or twice a week before coming to work to pick some up."

"We do that, too," Talia said. "Ever since Stefan opened that place, it's become the roast of choice in my office."

"Guess I'll have to check the place out now that I'm going to be living here."

"Hello, hello," an older white man with frizzy hair said as he entered the office.

"Roger, this is Peter Sinclair. He's the seller's real estate agent." Sinclair nodded his head and took a seat at the table. "Everything good on your end?"

The ominous nature of the question had my stomach drop. In that instant, I knew something had gone wrong. Had the seller backed out?

"Oh, no, nothing's wrong. I was showing a couple a house this morning. They were late and took forever to walk through it. I was like, the place is only twelve-hundred square feet. How much time do you need to see it?"

Ruby nodded her head knowingly.

Sinclair asked, "Who are we waiting for?"

"Well, we need to set up the Zoom connection with your client, and we're still waiting on your client's lawyer?"

"I'm here," a loud voice said. "Sorry I'm late. I got held up in court. It should have been a simple probate hearing, but things went awry when an unknown child appeared in court and threw everything in a tizzy." The Latina sat her things down and threw her coat over the back of the chair. "You must be Mr. Havemeyer," she said, reaching her hand across the table. "I'm Alejandrina Sagardia." I stood and greeted the woman.

"Okay," Ruby said, drawing everyone's attention. She looked at Peter and said, "Let's get your client on the phone and get this signing started."

In minutes, we had the estate's executor and his lawyer on the videoconference monitor.

"Gerry, Gerry, can you hear us?" Alejandrina said, looking into the screen. "Honey, I think you're still on mute."

"Can you hear me now?" a man's voice said through the computer monitor.

"We can now, Gerry," Alejandrina said. "I see you have someone with you there."

"Hello all, I'm Marc Woodward. I'm representing Mr. Greenwich and his late father's estate up here in Chicago. It's nice to meet you finally, Ms. Sagardia."

"Likewise, Mr. Woodward. Thanks for helping Gerry navigate through this process."

The lawyers talked over Zoom for a couple of minutes. Before long, I felt like I was signing my life away. It was all "sign this," "initial that," "sign this over here" and "we need you to initial every page of this multi-page document...and go." During all this, I called my bank and started the transfer of funds. Once the seller had them in his account, they initiated another sequence of transactions to pay his lawyer, his realtor and Ruby. I still had to pay my lawyer out of pocket, but she wasn't charging me that much at all.

"Well, it looks like everything is good on our end, Mr. Havemeyer," Mr. Woodward said.

"Great!"

"Take care of my dad's place. He loved that house," Mr. Greenwich.

"I promise I will, Mr. Greenwich." As the words came out of my mouth, it was like a lightbulb flashed on. They were about to stop the Zoom call when I blurted out, "I have to ask a quick question. Gerry Greenwich, your father wasn't *the* Gerry Greenwich, was he?"

The other people in the room looked at me like I'd grown a second head or something. Thankfully, Gerry knew what I was asking. "Yep. I'm Gerry Junior. Did you know my father?"

"In a way. My firm took over his former office space in the Brill Building a few years ago."

"Holy shit," Gerry Junior said. "I haven't thought about that place in years. I loved hanging out there as a kid. Dad would sometimes take me in on Saturdays when he had work to do. My babysitters were a who's who of musicians and movie stars. I didn't know who anyone was back then, but the people who paraded in and out of my father's office..." His voice trailed off as he got lost in a memory.

"I can't believe I hadn't put it together," I said, looking into the screen. Now that I was staring at Gerry Junior in the face, I could totally see the image of his father in his face. "First, I start working in your father's office space, and now I'm buying his old house. What are the chances?"

"Well, Mr. Havemeyer—"

"Roger. Please, call me Roger."

"Well, Roger, my dad loved three things in life—his family, his music and his house. Welcome to the legacy."

"It's an honor. I wish I could have met him."

"You have. You met him in the music, and now you've met him in the dream home he built. Hell, I still think there's a Grammy award in that house somewhere."

"If I find it, I'll make sure I send it to you."

"Don't worry about it," Gerry cut in. "The Grammy goes with the house. The statue bought the place—or at least that's what Dad said. He used the money he earned from Cerys Parker and the Funky Trolly's second or third album to build the place when he retired. Dad said he hid it somewhere when it was being built. Of course, he may have told his ex-wife that so she wouldn't try to steal the thing." The other man laughed at the memory. I couldn't be entirely sure, but I swear I saw a tear in his eye before our Zoom call disconnected.

I leaned back and let out a sigh. I couldn't believe I'd bought Gerry Greenwich's dream home. Now, it was my dream home.

"Congratulations, and welcome to the neighborhood," Ruby said, after I'd had my moment of nostalgia. She handed me my keys.

"Just like that, I'm a homeowner," I said, leaning back in the chair.

"Child, I know. It's a lot to take in."

I looked at her. "Child?" I said as I lowered my brows and smirked.

"Oh, you know what I mean," she said, playfully swiping me on my arm.

"You all saw that, right? Ruby just assaulted me," I joked.

"I know Talia won't take the case, but I'd be happy to represent you in court," Alejandrina said, grinning widely at Ruby.

"You go and try that. Let's see when you get invited next to lesbian poker night."

"Lesbian poker night?" I asked.

"Yep, all the professional lesbians get together every couple of months for a potluck and poker. We only play with like pennies, nickels and dimes, so it's not about the money."

"Ain't that the truth," Alejandrina said. "If it was, I would wipe out all your bank accounts."

"You wish," Ruby said. "Yeah, she beats us almost every time. Most of us don't have good poker faces. Alejandrina is always calm, cool and collected."

"It's years of experience in a court. Anyway," she said, "I really have to be getting out of here. I have another appointment at one, so I wanted to grab a quick bite." She turned to me and said, "Congratulations. And make her invite you over for lesbian poker night sometime. We occasionally let one of the gay guys in town join us. We don't want too many at once."

"I will keep that in mind." I stood and shook her hand. Quickly, everyone was standing and getting into their coats. Before I knew it, Ruby, her assistant and I were the only ones left.

"I'm going to lunch," Ruby's assistant said. "Be back in an hour. Text me if you need me."

"And then there were two," I said. "I should probably let you get back to your life."

"I wish I could sit and shoot the shit with you all afternoon, but I have another client I'm showing houses to at two. Not spending nearly as much as you did, but they're still looking to spend eight-hundred thousand, so I need to see what's available. Around here, medium-priced houses go pretty quickly."

I stood, put on my coat and offered Ruby my hand. "Thanks for everything this week. You've been a godsend. I don't think I could have gotten this house inspected in a month if I'd been trying to do all this on my own."

"That's why I make the big bucks," Ruby said with a grin. I wanted to ask her what her commission was but knew that would be inappropriate. All I knew for sure was that my home purchase just put a sizable chunk of change in her bank account, while taking it out of mine. "I left you a home-warming present. Since you don't have neighbors exactly near your house, I didn't think anyone would drop by with a plate of cookies to welcome you to the neighborhood."

"Probably not. One thing I liked about the house was how large and remote the place was."

"Oh, don't forget to have someone come out and look at your generator. You may need to upgrade at some point, so you might as well put that on your to-do list going forward."

"I have a sneaking suspicion my 'to-do' list is going to keep growing."

"Welcome to the joys of homeownership."

I shook her hand one more time and saw my way out. I sent a group text saying I was officially a homeowner. Dale and Grayson were both part of the group, so I wasn't surprised when they responded quickly.

Dale texted back almost immediately.

Congrats! We were hoping everything was going smoothly. Can't wait to come out and see the place now.

Missing you guys already. My house is going to be a lot quieter with only me in it.

I'd packed up my stuff that morning and was ready to move my stuff in.

Not missing you at all. I can finally fuck Talgat in the kitchen again.

Grayson chimed in.

I didn't need to know that. How can I ever have breakfast in your house again if all I can see is you and Talgat screwing where we eat?

Then, as if almost an afterthought, he added another message.

Congrats, Dale. Can't wait to see the new place.

Earlier in the week, I'd gone out to the home, my home, with Ruby to check out the furniture and what was there. They'd left me everything. I had dishes, silverware, a coffee pot, chairs, linens, cleaning supplies, etc. You name it, and they already had it stocked in the house. For a starter home, I couldn't ask for more. One thing I knew I didn't want was to keep the current bed in the primary bedroom. The other furniture and the giant television in there could stay. I felt weird about sleeping in the same bed as Gerry Greenwich had before he'd passed. Thankfully, I now had a new bed that I was in love with, thanks to Dale, so I had ordered a CloudBed for myself, along with pillows, sheets, comforters and everything else I would need.

I pulled up the UPS app to see when my delivery would be made. The app was saying everything should be there between three and five p.m. I looked at the current time on my phone and realized I still had a good two and a half hours before I had to be home.

"Might as well get lunch," I said to myself.

Thankfully, Ruby's office was right off Main Street, so I walked down to the main drive and started looking for someplace to eat. A few places were opened, but nothing called to me. Then there was a gorgeous wooden sign hanging over the sidewalk on the other side of the street that read, "Java Junkie Café & Roastery." *That's the place Ruby gets her coffee.* I crossed the street and walked inside. Immediately, I was bowled over by the delectable smell of roasted beans. I know some people like the smell of apple pie or vanilla. To me, nothing beats the smell of excellent coffee.

I took in the small café. The place was pretty cool. There was an octagon-shaped area that faced the corner of the street. I could immediately tell that the tall glass panes could be opened to make the place an open-air café in the summer. Several two- and four-top tables were scattered around the open space. Off to the right, as I entered, was a glassed-in roastery area. After taking in the ambiance, I walked up to the counter and looked up at the overhead board to see their food options.

"Good afternoon, welcome to Java Junkie. What can I get started for you today?" the young cashier said. I looked up to see a pleasant-looking woman in her early twenties with a broad, beaming smile.

"Any chance you have any of your fresh roasted coffee left? I was told I had to get some."

She took on a pitying look. "I'm sorry. Today's roast was gone before eleven. We make it in such small batches that we rarely have any past noon. We have some of our regular roasted coffee. Admittedly, it's not as amazing as our fresh roast, but it's still delectable."

"Sounds perfect. I'll take a pound of whatever is your boldest blend."

She grabbed two bags from underneath the shelf and put them on the counter. "Would you like for me to grind these for you?"

"Nah, I can do that at— On second thought, I probably should have you do that. I don't remember if my new home has a coffee grinder. I should probably figure that out when I get home."

"Probably," she said with a smile. "Can I get you anything else?"

"How about a large flat white and your ham-and-cheese panini?"

"Yummy," she said. "You'll appreciate both." She rang me up and told me that my drink and sandwich would be at the end of the bar in a couple of minutes. I turned to walk away, and I heard her say, "Wes, I need a flat white."

"On it," a guy's voice responded.

I glanced over and saw a guy at the espresso machine with his back to me. I leaned against the counter with my back to the barista and took in the group of people eating and drinking. At this time of the afternoon, a few business types were taking a late lunch and a handful of younger people were reading or studying. There was even a group of older men and women in one corner knitting.

"Flat white," a voice said behind me. I turned to take the drink from the barista, and I looked into a pair of amazingly blue eyes. I'd had dreams about those eyes all week. I reached for the saucer, and I clumsily couldn't grasp the drink as I stared in absolute shock.

"Fuck," the guy said as I dropped the cup and saucer and it tumbled to the ground, shattering on impact.

"I am *so* sorry," I said once I got my wits about me. "That was totally my fault."

"I'm sorry, sir," a French voice said. "Wes, don't be so clumsy. Get this cleaned up."

"It wasn't his fault," I said, but the French guy waved me off.

"What did you have to drink?" the Frenchman asked. "I'll make a new one immediately."

"A flat white," I said, looking as the barista of my fantasies went to grab a broom and a mop. I watched him walk away. His ass may have been covered by a pair of jeans, but I couldn't help but stare. I knew what those jeans held. Blood rushed southward as images flooded my memory. I pulled my coat around my midsection to prevent my erection from causing a disturbance in the café.

That's the problem with suit fabric. If you get an erection, there's nothing to hold that bad boy down. With jeans, the fabric can hold it in place to ensure the world doesn't see what's going on.

" — panini," I heard a voice say to my left.

I pulled my eyes away from the guy barista and saw the woman barista handing me my ham-and-cheese panini. "Thanks," I said.

She smiled at me, knowing that she'd caught me staring at her coworker. I turned my attention back to the manager, who was finishing up my new flat white.

"Here's your flat white, sir. And again, I'm so sorry my barista was clumsy with your drink."

"It was completely my fault. I lost my grip on the edge of the saucer."

"It's nice that you're apologizing for him," the manager said, "but he knows better. Come again." The manager shot me a winning smile.

I took my drink and sandwich to a table in the corner. I took off my coat, hung it over the back of one chair and slipped into a chair on the opposite side. Thankfully, my boner had already deflated, so I didn't have a third appendage pointing across the room. I pulled out my phone. I zoomed in on the barista and snapped a picture of him. The picture wasn't great, but it would help me later that night as I got lost in my fantasies.

I drank my flat white and ate my sandwich. I did my best not to stare at the young man, but I couldn't keep my eyes off him. And the female barista caught me looking in their direction a couple of times. She would smile knowingly and say something to the other barista. I would glance down at my phone, but I could feel his amazing eyes peeking in my direction.

* * * *

Wes

At first, I was pissed that Stefan blamed me for dropping the flat white. I didn't drop the cup. I don't know what happened. All I know is I handed the guy in the suit the cup, and the next thing I knew, it was out of his hand and crashing at my feet. I'd had to jump back to keep my sneakers from getting soaked with hot coffee.

"That was totally not your fault," Autumn said as she approached me later. "Honestly, I think Stefan was flirting with the guy."

"Really?" I asked. I hadn't even paid attention to the man. I couldn't pick him out of a police lineup if I had to.

"Yep, you should have seen the way Stefan practically threw himself at the guy. Too bad for Stefan that Mr. Hotty over there clearly only has eyes for you."

I cocked my head to the side, furrowed my brow and said, "Not funny."

"I'm not joking. He keeps staring at you. And trust me, I know he's not looking in this direction to check out my charming personality."

I tried to look in the direction Autumn nodded her head inconspicuously. As soon as I looked over, the guy's head went down to his cell phone. Was he looking at me, or was I imagining things now that Autumn planted the idea in my head?

"I have to admit, he's kind of hot…for an older guy," I said with a shrug.

"Get over yourself," Autumn said. "If I had a hottie like that looking at me with lustful eyes like those, my panties would be wet and I'd be fucking him in the bathroom already."

"Autumn!" I said, shocked.

"Just saying. Hot is hot. I don't care how old hot is. You gays are so weird about age. It's just a number. Ugly is ugly at any age, and hot is hot at any."

"Well, it doesn't matter. I don't fool around with out-of-towners. I've done that before. It's good for them, but then I'm the one still here once they leave."

"Well, you're in luck. Your new boyfriend mentioned he just bought a house in the area."

I ignored the 'boyfriend' comment. In fact, I'd gotten so caught up in our conversation that I'd lost track of my new friend. When I looked up, he was standing in front of me. He had a chiseled square jaw and piercing blue eyes. I thought my eyes were blue, but his were an Alice-blue shade. I honestly didn't know that shade was possible in nature.

"Sorry about earlier," the man said.

I looked at him. I might as well have been drooling. I finally said, "It's all good."

The man handed me his empty saucer, cup and plate his panini had been on and said, "See ya around."

"Not if I see you first," I said, then immediately wished those words hadn't escaped my mouth.

The guy threw a bill in the tip jar. He turned one last time and looked at me before heading out.

"*Not if I see you first?*" Autumn repeated.

"I know!" I leaned forward and hit my head against the counter. "He probably thinks I'm on work release from a mental hospital," I groused.

"Who knows? Maybe you'll get to see him again once Stefan gets his claws into the guy." Autumn motioned with her head, and I caught Stefan staring after the man as he left the building. I let out a sigh and got back to work.

Chapter Eight

Roger

I was basically hard the entire trip home to my house. All I wanted to do was get inside and spank one out, but I noticed the UPS van was already there as I pulled up the driveway. I let out a quick, "Fuck," as I parked beside the van.

"Good afternoon," I said, pulling myself out of the Bentley. I slipped into my suit coat, then my wool overcoat.

"You must be Mr. Roger Havemeyer," the man in brown said.

"That would be me."

"I have a package for you. Quite a big one, from the looks of it."

I bit back a laugh as I tried not to hear the double entendre coming out of the guy's mouth.

"That package of yours is definitely a two-man job," the UPS guy said as he walked around and opened the back of the truck. "I don't know how they thought I was going to manage this thing on my own. I can call in another guy, but who knows how long that will take?"

"Shall we see if the two of us can handle my...package?" I bit my lower lip to keep from giggling. I hadn't seen much of UPS Guy so far, but when he turned and looked at me, I totally went a little weak in the knees. The dude could have been a model.

"Do you know where the bed is going?" he asked.

"It's going to the second-floor primary bedroom" — I looked at his name tag and read—"Chad." *Of course, he's a Chad.* He had every 'Chad' attribute down. He was young, tall, white, gorgeous, cocky and virile. He looked like he could fuck all the cheerleaders and half the football team without breaking a sweat.

He jumped up into the back of the van and started pushing the bed out. We'd have to make two different trips. One for the bed and the other for the box spring.

"Oh shit," I said. "Let me go unlock the place."

I made sure Chad had a firm grip on the bed, and I ran toward the house and quickly opened the front door. Here it was the first time I was crossing the threshold of my house, and I was doing it in haste so I could help 'Chad' carry my new bed upstairs to the primary bedroom. Something about that made me laugh.

"What's so funny?" Chad asked from behind me. He got a grip on the mattress and had followed me up the stairs.

"All this, to be perfectly honest. I signed the paperwork today for the house. I'm still getting used to the idea that this is now mine." I held the door open, and Chad walked inside.

"Want me to take this up to the primary bedroom?" he asked.

"If you don't mind."

"Not a problem. I love to be of service to my customers in any way I can."

Oh, you can service me, all right.

Chad started walking up the stairs and knew which way to turn at the top. "I take it you've been in here before?" I asked as I followed him into the hallway.

"Yeah, the previous owner occasionally needed help, so I'd do the neighborly thing and help a fella out whenever it fit into my schedule."

I was beginning to think Chad preferred the *full-service* delivery. I lingered on Chad's impressive arms for longer than I should have, because little Roger was starting to have a mind of its own again. I tried to shove the fucker down and caught Chad looking at it. Chad let one corner of his lip smile as he laid the bed down in the room.

"Let's go get that box spring now," I said, trying to sound chipper.

"Then I can help you get it put together. I know these CloudBeds are complicated, and you'll need a helping hand."

I spun around and started heading away, but I swear I saw Chad lick his upper lip right before I turned. *You are so reading into things that are not there. He's just the UPS guy. Not everyone in Woodstock wants to fuck you!*

Outside, we lifted the base, and it was a lot heavier than I had expected it to be. Thankfully, Chad bore most of the weight. I wasn't out of shape, and I had some decently toned arms, but Chad seemed to be a giant moving muscle. He had a thin sheen of sweat across his brow by the time we got it into the primary bedroom and onto the steel frame.

He helped me put the mattress on it and showed me how to hook the whole thing up. For someone who was just the delivery guy, he sure was handy to have around. Before long, I had the bed all put together. I didn't have any of the sheets and pillows yet.

"I'm guessing you had nothing else for me today?" I realized how the question sounded before continuing. "I have another package with the sheets, comforter, pillows, pillowcasing and such getting here today."

"Order it on Amazon?" Chad asked.

"Yep."

"Their driver is probably delivering it. I pass them all the time. They should be here in another hour or so. They're always later than UPS in their deliveries up here."

"Good to know. And thanks for all your help."

"My pleasure. Remember, if you need any special deliveries, don't hesitate to ask."

This time when I glanced down at his body, I noticed he was running his thumb over his semi-erect cock. "Oh," I managed to say. "Can I get you a bottle of water?" I asked. I wasn't even sure if I had bottled water in the house. I headed off in the direction of the kitchen.

"Nah," he said. I turned back to look at him. "I prefer to get it straight from the spigot."

I was about to ask what he was talking about, but he took two steps in my direction, grabbed the back of my head and pulled me into a kiss. I don't think I'd ever had a guy be so forward with me before. He had my wool coat off and flung over the back of the chair and my suit coat followed. He then grabbed my necktie and used it as a leash as he dragged me into the living room in front of the fireplace.

"Too bad you don't have a fire going," he said. "Guess I'll have to warm you up myself." In seconds, my tie was off, my shirt was off and my pants landed somewhere in a pile. Before I registered what was going on, I was standing completely naked, only wearing my black socks. He eyed me and rubbed his hands over my chest. "Nice." He leaned in so I could feel his breath on my ear. "I want to fuck you so bad." He grabbed my hand, forcing it to feel the growing Chad in his pants.

"Yeah, I'm pretty much a top," I said. Without waiting for a response, I took the hat off his head and put it on mine. Then I put my hands on his shoulders and pushed him to his knees. I may have been the naked one, but I wanted to make Chad understand that I wasn't the one who was going to be giving up control. He thought he was an alpha. He was about to lose that game.

When he was on his knees, I took out my cock and slapped him in the face a couple of times. I already had some pre-cum coming out, and I watched as it lightly splattered across his cheek. I was going to do it again, but I didn't get a chance because he inhaled my shaft. His chin hit my balls. That's when I learned Chad had no gag reflex. He came up for air and went down again. I grabbed the back of his head and pumped his face rapidly. He didn't even choke a little. He also had incredible breath control. When my dick was nice and wet, I sat on the edge of the couch. I pointed at my third arm and said, "Sit on it."

He scrambled to get his pants off, and I was halfway inside him before I thought about protection. *Fuck!* He was already balls deep in my lap when I leaned and whispered, "I'm on PrEP."

"Me, too," he said as he raised his ass up from my lap and slid down again.

I leaned back, locking my hands behind my head, watching as he used his thigh muscles to go up and down on me repeatedly.

"Oh fuck," I whispered as my load coated Chad's insides.

"What?" he asked as he kept going up and down.

Did he not feel the orgasm?

"Nothing," I said. "Keep going."

"Oh, yeah. Right there," he cried out as he started lifting himself faster and faster. I was still rock hard, watching my shaft slide in and out of him, now aided by one round of cum as a natural lubricant. He slid off me and turned around so he could watch my face as he rode.

I was beginning to feel a little like a pogo stick. My cock was sensitive, to begin with, but being ridden this hard after coming once was driving my senses to the edge.

"I'm going to come," he whispered. I hadn't realized he'd been jerking off the whole time. When his first spurt of jizz caught me in the chin and his ass muscles clenched tighter around my dick, my second orgasm escaped.

"Fuck, I'm coming," I spurted out hoarsely between breaths.

His ass muscles did something to my rod I'd never dreamed before as he tried to milk every last drop of cum from me. When he finally slid off my dick. I looked down and saw how red it was. From the looks of it, my cock wouldn't want to be touched for days after this workout.

"Gotta towel I can use?" Chad asked.

"Fuck, I don't know. I know I have some new towels being delivered today…by Amazon."

He leaned down and gave me a kiss. "You're cute when you're flustered." I wanted to say something in response, but my brain had stopped working at some point. "What about paper towels? Any in the kitchen?"

"There should be. Well, I mean…there were paper towels in there the other day when I was here."

"Perfect." I watched as Chad's perfectly sculpted ass containing two of my loads walked away. He apparently had some amazing ass muscles, because I didn't see any cum dripping out. Well, either that, or I shot so far up into his bowels that his stomach was processing my cum for nutrients.

A minute later, Chad came back with a roll of paper towels. He wiped the cum from my chest. "Thanks. You didn't need to do that."

"I like to take care of my customers. I believe in being a full-service delivery man."

"I can tell," I said, still a little breathless. He'd done all the heavy lifting, and he barely looked like he'd broken a sweat. He found his discarded clothes as I still sat on the couch, catching my breath.

When he was dressed and looked like nothing had happened, he came over and plucked his hat from my head. I'd forgotten that I'd put it on me until he took it back. Before putting the cap back on, he leaned down and gave me another kiss.

"Until the next time I deliver a package here." He turned around and walked toward the front door.

Only then did I realize how dark the house had gotten. I looked out of the giant windows, thankful that I didn't have any close neighbors, because they all would have gotten the show of their lifetime if they had stumbled up to this side of the house. I heard the front door open.

"Oh hey, it looks like Amazon got here. I'll put your boxes just inside the door."

I paled... *oh fuck*. The poor Amazon guy...or gal. I hoped we hadn't given them a show. I hoped they didn't see us in here with the lights off. I heard the rumbling of the UPS truck down my driveway, and I forced myself to stand. In the dark, I tried to remember where my underwear had ended up. I finally found them and put them on. I felt sticky. *I hate sticky*. I would shower just as soon as I opened boxes. I preferred the idea of washing my new towels, sheets and comforter first, but I needed one of those towels so I could take a shower. I walked to the front entryway and grabbed the Amazon boxes. I carried them into the kitchen, where I pulled out a knife and sliced through the tape on each box. I made quick work of the packages and started a giant load of laundry that included everything but one towel. Once the washer load was going, I climbed the stairs to my new bedroom and drew a nice, warm bath.

Chapter Nine

Wes

The rest of the week had been pretty dull. I don't quite know how one tops getting fucked for the world to see for the first time. I won't lie. It had been a huge fucking turn-on. In all honesty, once my cock had been in Dylan's mouth, I had completely lost track of what was going on. I kind of went with it. Dylan had controlled the show and guided me through where I had needed to be to ensure our Internet audience had the best view.

Dylan had gotten in trouble with CammBate, because they didn't have evidence on file to prove I was actually over eighteen-years-of-age. Before they had been willing to deposit the money in Dylan's account, I had to create an account and upload my driver's license. Dylan had walked me through how to do this on Wednesday.

On Friday, Dylan had come by the coffee shop and handed me a giant wad of cash. All-in-all, our little experiment had landed me enough money to cover my rent and my college textbooks. Dylan had also informed me that he'd purchased me a set of ring lights and a digital camera and had them sent to my apartment so I could perform on my own when he wasn't available. I had made Dylan a promise that I would still appear on his channel occasionally.

I shocked myself. I had expected to have huge regrets about the show, but it had been a giant turn-on. Something about controlling my sexuality that way made me feel empowered. *I am a sex worker.* The thought of that caused my cock to twitch. I couldn't wait to try it out on my own. I had ordered a few sex toys and a couple of different types of lube.

After work on Saturday, I raced home to get my purchases off the front doorstep of our apartment and into my bedroom before Pietro asked. The last thing I wanted was for my straight roommate to come home and start asking me a lot of questions.

I parked the car and made my way to the apartment. Sure enough, a stack of boxes was sitting on my doorstep waiting to be unwrapped. My member did a happy dance in my pants. The idea of setting it all up and broadcasting it to the world made me smile.

I opened the door to the apartment and nudged the boxes inside with my foot. "Pietro?" I yelled, to see if he was home. Silence. Good, he was supposed to be gone until late tonight, but you never knew if his plans would change. I took the packages into my bedroom. Using a key, I sliced through the tape and unwrapped everything, laying it out on my bed. I had two ring lights, a high-definition webcam, a couple of dildos, a vibrator, nipple clamps, three masturbator toys and two different types of lube. Oh, and most importantly, a new anal douche contraption. This one was reusable. I didn't want any accidents while I was trying to be all sexy.

I set up the ring lights and the new webcam right in front of my bed. I laid out all the toys, so I'd have easy access to them. Once I was happy with the setup, I went into the bathroom and started the douching process. I was running clear water in a matter of minutes, so I hopped in the shower to make sure everything was clean. I toweled off and did my hair. I was pretty sure it would get messy while I was on camera, but I wanted to put my best foot forward.

I threw on a jockstrap, a pair of shorts and a tank top. Dylan had suggested I always start by wearing clothes, then let the viewers tip me to the point where I was nude. I had to admit, Dylan had a lot more business sense than I would have ever given him credit for. He saw his camming as a business, and he saw everything he did as part of marketing.

"If your viewers want you to climax, make them pay for it. It's no different from when the waitress at the diner comes by after dinner and asks if you want dessert. Remember, the climax is dessert. Once you've climaxed, the guys will lose interest in you, so you need to get as much out of them before you come as possible," Dylan had told me matter-of-factly.

I turned on my computer and waited for my new camera to start. I pulled up my web browser and logged in to CammBate. *"Welcome TwinkErik69,"* the splash screen read. I'd kept the name 'Erik' that Dylan had given me on the spot. It seemed to make sense. Some people already knew me as 'Erik', so I might as well stick with it.

I tried to remember my crash course in camm work from Dylan the previous afternoon. I clicked on the button that said 'Broadcast Now', and immediately, I saw myself on the screen. What had Dylan told me to do?

"When you first open your room, it will take a few moments for people to trickle in. While you're waiting, do something," Dylan had told me.

"Like what?"

"You saw how I fake played video games?"

"Oh yeah, I forgot about that part."

"That was me hanging out being a normal twenty-something. Guys, especially older ones, like that. They love being able to see you in your normal habitat doing something."

"Any suggestions?"

"Play video games, watch TV, read a book...pretty much anything that draws people into your world. Hell, you're an artist from what I remember, so draw."

I pulled out my sketch pad and pencil set. I sat cross-legged on my bedspread and started to sketch. I wasn't sure what I wanted to draw, so I let the pencils guide me. Before I knew what I was doing, I had roughly sketched out the hot older guy who had been in the coffee shop earlier that week. I still remembered his eyes, lips, nose, high cheekbones and cute, turned-up nose. I smiled as I drew.

Ding! The sound of a tip coming into my virtual tip jar drew me out of my flow. "Hey, thanks, RiversGuy. That was very generous of you." I went back to drawing. Every time I heard the tip jar, I raised my head and thanked whoever had contributed.

At one point, after saying thank you, I changed the tip goal to 'taking my tank top off'. In a matter of minutes, that goal had been met and beat. I put my pencils down and slipped out of my tank top. I took a moment to caress my hairless torso before I got back to drawing.

For the next hour, I drew and stripped, drew and stripped. Before long, I was completely naked on my bedspread, still drawing.

What are you drawing? AveryHeadGiver asked.

"Hey, Avery," I replied. "I'm drawing a guy I saw the other day. Not my usual type, but I haven't been able to get him out of my mind."

What makes him 'not your usual type?' AveryHead-Giver typed.

"Most of my boyfriends and sex partners have been close to my age and build, but this guy was older. I would bet he was in his forties, and he was fucking gorgeous. I wanted him to wrap his arms around me and have his way with me." As I talked about my mysterious fantasy man, my cock grew. I looked down and said, "See what I mean? Just talking about him causes me to get rock hard."

Can we see the pic? GirlBot asked.

"Uhh… I probably shouldn't. Ya know. I don't want to expose him on here. He's a random guy I met. Who knows? It could be your best friend or uncle. That would be awkward," I said with a little laugh.

I had absently started stroking myself. I leaned over, flashing my ass to the screen as I grabbed my new bottle of lube. I dropped my art supplies on the floor beside my bed. I held the lube up for the camera and squeezed out a glob onto my cock and let it dribble down the head.

The tip jar exploded. I stared into the camera. "What do you think? You all like my nice cock? I wish you were all here showing me how to use it." Okay, so I kind of sucked at dirty talk. But it seemed to work, because the tips kept pouring in.

Any chance you can show us that ass of yours again? 40sCammGent asked in the chat window.

I rolled over onto my knees and pressed my head sideways into the mattress. With my hands free, I spread my cheeks so the world could see my pink hole. I had to admit that I have a picture-perfect asshole. I stroked myself with one hand while my other hand, still lubed up from jacking off, started exploring it. I could barely contain myself. I wanted something inside me, so I let a finger slide in. I played with my hole this way for a couple of minutes.

I flipped back over and stared into the camera. I grabbed the towel I had nearby and wiped my hands off to scroll through the messages I was receiving. They were all amazingly complimentary. I'd always thought I was kind of cute, but these guys were making me feel like I was some kind of sex god.

Any chance you have a nice dildo you can use on that pretty hole of yours? 40sCammGent asked.

"Hey, CammGent. As a matter of fact, I got a new dildo that I'm dying to take for a spin." I leaned over and grabbed the new toy and held it up for the camera. "Think I can manage it all? Let's find out." I set the new room goal to 'dildo in my ass'.

I went back to stroking myself as the tips rolled in. Once the goal was reached, I lubed up the dildo. I faced the camera, putting my legs behind my arms, so my hole faced the camera, and the viewers could watch my facial expressions.

"Maintain eye contact," Dylan had told me. *"Eye contact with the camera makes people feel they're in the room with you."*

I lubed up the dildo and eased it inside. Instead of this massive monstrosity, I probably should have gone with a starter dildo. I grimaced as I got the head inside. I let out a breath and gently pressed the rest in. Slowly, inch by inch, I inserted all ten inches of the dildo into my ass. Once it was all the way in, I let it sit for a moment before I gently pulled it out before pushing it back inside. I kept this up, slowly at first. Before long, I was pumping my hole fast and furious with my new toy.

I leaned my head back and moaned. Normally, I'm not a colossal moaner, but Dylan had coached me that being verbal and showing the audience what I was feeling was crucial to making a good connection.

"Hey, Wes," Pietro said as he threw open the door to my bedroom. "Holy fuck!"

"Out!" I screamed. I can only imagine the look of shock and terror that crossed my face. In seconds, the dildo was out of my ass, and I shut off the computer.

* * * *

Roger

I hadn't intended to jump on CammBate and search for my new friend, but the giant house felt lonely this evening. I'd spent the day setting up my office in one of the rooms on the house's second floor. This time, I went all in and created an account.

The screen looked at me, asking for a username. I tried a couple of generic ones and was quickly informed that the username was already taken. I finally went with 40sCammGent. Once I had my username created, I started searching through the profiles.

There he was, TwinkErik69. My cock twitched as soon as I saw him. He was wearing a jockstrap. He was furiously drawing something. I wish I could be a fly on his bedroom wall to see what he was drawing.

I stared at the screen. I don't know when my pants had opened and my dick had sprung free. I was so lost in watching him.

I looked at the computer and typed, *Any chance you can show us that ass of yours again?*

Erik flipped over onto his knees and spread his cheeks without saying a word. He played with his meat with one hand and felt around his hole with his other. When he slipped his finger into his ass, I almost shot my load. I removed my hand from my shaft because I was not ready to have an orgasm.

A few minutes later, I asked, *Any chance you have a nice dildo you can use on that pretty hole of yours?*

I waited for Erik to read my message. Finally, he saw it and said, "Hey, CammGent. As a matter of fact, I bought a new dildo that I'm dying to take for a spin." He leaned forward and changed the tip goal of the room to 'dildo in my ass'.

I hadn't planned on tipping, but I pulled out my credit card and bought tip points so I could hurry things along. Working with your credit card while your cock is dying for attention is an interesting experience. Once I had purchased tips, I saw he was only fifty tip points from meeting the dildo goal, so I sent him over the goal with a click of my computer's mouse.

I had figured he'd roll over onto his knees and take the dildo that way, but he opted to lie on his back with his legs locked under his arms. Watching his face as he took the dildo inch by inch was almost too much to take. I wanted my cock to be that dildo sliding into him. I pumped myself harder and faster. Soon I was pumping in rhythm with the dildo. I was trying to hold off coming.

"Hey, Wes… Holy fuck!" a voice off-screen suddenly said.

"Out!" Erik said, looking mortified. I don't think I'd ever seen a dildo shoot out of a guy's ass so fast as he moved to turn off his computer equipment.

I came right as the screen went dark.

* * * *

Wes

I cleaned myself up and threw on some clothes. I could practically feel Pietro's presence in the living room as I got my shit together. When I was finally in a calm place, I opened the door and left my bedroom.

"Dude, I am so sorry about that," Pietro said. "I don't think I'll ever get that image out of my head." He put his head in his hands as if closing his eyes would make what he'd just witnessed go away. "What were you doing?"

"Which part? The dildo or the camming?"

Pietro's eyes grew as his eyebrows shot up. "Camming?"

I rubbed my eyes, pinched the bridge of my nose and let out a sigh. I guess I should tell him everything, so I did.

"Whoa," Pietro said as I finished the story. "You made how much money?"

I tilted my head to the side. "That's what you took away? Not that I'm gay or now a sex worker?" I probably sound incredulous.

"Dude, I've known you were gay for years. Hell, my whole family knows you're gay."

"What? Why didn't anyone say anything?"

"I don't think anyone thought it was a secret."

"Wow, just wow. I've never talked about that part of my life for fear that you'd freak out and stop being my best friend."

Pietro's face suddenly flooded with emotion. The primary one was hurt. "I can't believe you would think I was so shallow that a little thing like who you're fucking or who's fucking you would make me stop being your best friend."

"I'm sorry. You're the only family I have. I couldn't bear to lose you."

"You could never lose me... Well, maybe if I saw what I just saw again." He shook his head as if he could somehow shake the memory of a dildo up my ass from his head. "Maybe, next time, tie a sock to the door handle or something."

"I promise. The last thing I want to do is scar you for life," I said as I rolled my eyes. "You know, you could make a mint online yourself."

"You think?"

"Pietro, look at you. You're basically an Italian Stallion. Men and women would throw money at you."

"Tempting," he said, clearly pondering the idea for a second before dismissing it. "Nah. All this only gets seen by Valeria. If she found out I was showing the goods to other people, she'd have my balls in a vise."

"Very good point."

"Well, I'm going to go watch a ton of straight porn in an effort to forget this evening."

"Have fun," I said as Pietro stood and headed toward his room. "Don't do anything I wouldn't do."

Chapter Ten

Two weeks went by, and my older hunk hadn't come by the coffee shop again. Maybe my dropping the cup of hot coffee had scared the poor guy off. I had kept camming and was growing a nice following. I had played around with Dylan about once a week, which always brought in a lot more money than either of us had gotten on our own. One evening, Pietro had stuck his head in, despite my having put a sock on the door handle to warn him off.

"Pietro! I'm live. Didn't you see the sock?"

"Yeah, but I thought I'd poke my head in and say hi."

"What if I had another dildo up my ass?" I asked. I had been wearing my usual shorts and a tank top. Without warning, he had come over and sat on the corner of the bed.

"Hey," he said with a wave to the camera, "I'm his roommate."

Almost immediately, the requests for what they wanted Pietro and I to do to each other had streamed in the chatroom. Pietro had looked at the conversation and his eyes kind of bugged out. I don't think I had ever seen Pietro blush in my entire life, but his face grew red as one of the local apples in September.

"Well, then. Umm... I will...let you get to it then." He stood and left, shutting the door behind him.

"Well, you just scared off the straight boy," I said with a laugh. Instantly a barrage of comments filled the screen.

How straight is he?

Even the straightest arrow can bend.

I got something straight for him.

"Nope. I promise you. He is perfectly happy being one-hundred-percent straight. He's as straight as I am gay."

Don't you fantasize about him? I would totally jack off to him every night, PartyBoy1999 had written.

"Eww," I said. "That would be like masturbating thinking about a family member. He's basically my brother. If I ever caught him having sex with his girlfriend, I would be traumatized for life. Let me tell you a story," I said. Then I had dived into the story of my first solo camm show when Pietro had walked in on me with a dildo up my ass. As I had told the story, my tank top tip had been achieved, and I had slipped out of it without missing a beat.

* * * *

"What are you smiling at?" Autumn asked.

"Oh, nothing. I was remembering a conversation I had with Pietro."

"Are him and what's-her-name still together?"

"Yep, I think this is officially the longest dating relationship he's had. I think Valeria has whipped him into shape."

Before he'd met Valeria, Pietro had a line of ex-lovers a thousand miles long. He had never entered a dating relationship planning on dropping the woman, but he had a short attention span. Valeria not only kept his attention, but she also demanded it. Honestly, I didn't think I'd ever see the day when a woman had this much control over Pietro.

"What time do you have class today?" Autumn asked.

"Not until two. You?"

"One." Autumn looked down at her watch. "Wow, I can't believe it's already noon. Need to be out of here by one." Woodstock to Hyde Park was thirty to forty minutes, depending on how fast one drove and whether you got stuck behind a slow-moving vehicle. My school was closer than Autumn's, but not by much.

"How's Stefan going to run this place in the afternoons without us?" I asked.

"I'll do fine," Stefan said, coming out of nowhere. "Autumn, I already have your schedule. Wes, I still need your completed class schedule for the spring."

"I need to see about dropping and adding a class today. Once it's finalized, I'll bring it in to you."

"It's hard to put together the work schedule when I don't know your availability."

With that, Stefan had gone across the shop, stopping by a table to talk to some out-of-towners I'd never seen before. I had busied myself cleaning things up and making coffee whenever people came. Before I had known it, Autumn had left for the day. I had wiped down everything one last time before telling Stefan that I'd see him first thing in the morning before I headed off to campus for my first day of classes.

I had grabbed myself an extra-large coffee with a couple of shots of espresso before I took off. That's one thing Stefan ignored. He didn't mind if we took coffee with us. If we had anything to eat, we had to ring it up. If we had a bottle of water or a can of soda, we had to ring those up. But coffee, he let us have for free. Between my late nights camming, early mornings slinging coffee and afternoons in college lecture halls, I knew I was going to be running on caffeine. I might as well get an IV bag on rollers with a caffeine drip and drag it behind me.

By the time I had gotten back to the apartment that night after class, I was drained. I walked in and found Pietro and Valeria hanging out in the kitchen.

"Just in time, little guy," a nickname Valeria had started calling me. "I was cooking *pastelon* for Pietro. Have you ever tried it?"

"I don't even know what it is," I admitted.

"It's basically Puerto Rican lasagna. It's made with sliced plantains instead of noodles."

"Sounds different…" was all I could think of saying.

Valeria barked out a laugh before saying, "Sit your white ass down and get ready for an amazing dinner."

"Sure, let me put my stuff in my bedroom."

"Make sure you wash your hands when you come out of there. I hear what goes on in there. You be *nasty*!" I must have paled because she added, "I don't judge. I have a ton of friends who are sex workers. You ain't doing nothing I haven't heard of before. But I wish I could have been there when Pietro caught you with the dildo up your ass."

"You..." I started to say, but the words didn't form in my mouth. I shot Pietro an 'I'm going to kill you in your sleep' look and headed into my bedroom. I didn't slam the door. I wanted to, but I needed to cool off. I had to have known that Pietro would tell his girlfriend what he'd witnessed. Hell, she had probably talked him off the ledge. I sat down on the corner of my bed and put my face in my hands. *Does everyone know? What the fuck am I doing?* I had to know that people would find out. Whether Pietro told them or some guy at school jerked off to me one night before going to bed, I couldn't keep this a secret forever.

There was a double knock at my door. "Come in," I said.

"Hey, buddy. You, okay?" Pietro said, a concerned look on his face.

"Yeah... I hadn't realized you'd told Valeria is all."

"I promise, she's the only person I've told. And I swore her to secrecy, so your activities are safe with me."

I took a deep breath and let it out in a quick huff. "I decided to do this," I said, gesturing to the O-lights standing in front of my bed. "I knew it wouldn't stay quiet forever. Woodstock is a tiny town. All it takes is one person watching me and everyone will know."

"And if that happens, we'll face it...together."

"Yeah, but what will your family say?" Once the words left my mouth, I realized I was more worried about his family finding out than anyone else.

"They'd be cool with it. If not, I'll read them the riot act and stop talking to them. Valeria may be my girlfriend, but you're my best friend. If you had tits, I'd call you my soulmate."

"I could get those implanted," I said, glancing to the side to see his reaction. His eyes grew wide. "I'm joking. I'm not transsexual. I'm a one-hundred-percent cis-gender gay man. I was just fucking with you."

"Good, because I don't know how I would explain that to Valeria. She'd come walking in and find me playing with your tits. It would be awkward."

It was my turn to be speechless.

"Boys!" Valeria called. "Now that you two have spanked each other off. Wash your hands. Dinner is served."

I did as she'd requested. Once my hands were clean, I walked into the living room and looked at Valeria and said, "If you want to see what goes on in my bedroom, you can pay like anyone else."

"You're assuming I haven't," she shot back.

* * * *

Roger

I had spent the next couple of weeks sitting in Zoom meetings with clients. Thankfully, Richard had been a godsend once he figured out how to get his foot out of his mouth. He was great with clients, and I was already letting him handle sales pitches to new ones. He was also a 'Chad', but he knew how to use those attributes to close a deal, and he had the creative prowess to back up his 'Chadness'.

I had hated to admit it, but my house was huge. I'd actually gotten myself turned around several times. I had dinner alone in the dining room one night—just me and a good book. I had looked up and realized how long the table was. If I had a guest at the other end, it would have reminded me of that scene with Michael Keaton and Kim Bassinger in *Batman* when the two are having dinner in Wayne Manner.

"I think I need a dog," I had whined. *"A big dog. To keep me warm at night and guard me in case someone plays* The Purge *and makes me their first target."* I had taken to talking to myself out loud a lot. I hadn't realized I was going stir-crazy until I looked down at my calendar and saw that it was already the twenty-sixth of January. It was mid-morning, and I needed to do something…anything. I called Mitzi.

"Hello?" she answered on the second ring.

"Hey, Mitzi. I need to get out of my house for a while. Is there anything that I have to get done today?"

"Let me see." I could almost see her pulling up my virtual planner to see if I had any meetings. For years, she'd been keeping me on the straight and narrow with time management. Even now, we checked in at the beginning of almost every workday to make sure I didn't miss anything important. "Nope. You have a three-p.m. appointment, but I'm like ninety percent sure they're going to cancel on you, anyway."

"Perfect… Cancel on them first for me."

"Should I make up an excuse?"

"Car troubles," I said without skipping a beat.

"Oka-ay," she said, drawing out the word.

"I am having car troubles. I have a car, and it's not big enough. I need a new one, so I'm going to go buy one." I had been tossing around the idea in my head for a couple of weeks, anyway. We'd only had one major snow so far in January. A whole eight inches, but my little car had not been designed to drive in snow, let alone snow that actually went past my ankle.

"I'll get that meeting canceled. And happy car shopping."

I hung up on Mitzi and called Talgat.

"Talgat," he said, answering the phone.

"Talgat, it's Roger. Any chance you have some free time today to help me pick out a new, more substantial vehicle?"

"Getting rid of the matchbox car finally?" Talgat joked.

"It's not that small," I fussed.

"Sure, keep telling yourself that, Roger. It's a big, *manly* sports car."

"Whatever," I said. I almost threw up the 'w' sign with my fingers but stopped myself because I realized that would show my age. Oh, how that would show my age. And though no one else in the house would see, I would have known that I had done it. "So, you free?"

"Doing a little paperwork. Nothing that can't wait until tomorrow. When's good for you?"

"Now? I figured we could drive down to Kingston. I remember there were a couple of dealerships right when we cross the interstate."

"Yep, there's a Nissan and Ford place right next to each other," Talgat told me. "See you in thirty minutes?"

"Perfect. I'll head on out now."

We hung up the phone, and I grabbed my coat. I almost left my house when I remembered I'd need the paperwork for my current car to sell it to the dealer. Not that I'd get much for it, but it was still good to have a trade-in.

I was out of the door and picked Talgat up in twenty-five minutes. Dale wanted to go because he thought it would be funny to watch me buy a car, but Talgat informed him he wasn't invited. I watched Dale pout as we drove away.

"You know you're going to be in trouble later," I said. "Dale can be a whiny little toddler when he wants to be."

"Tell me about it," Talgat said, watching the wintery landscape pass by as we drove down the mountain. "But you know what? Sometimes, just like a toddler, Dale needs to be told 'no'." Talgat turned in his seat and looked at me. "And if you tell him I said that, I will lie through my teeth."

We got down the mountain and pulled into the Nissan dealership. Talgat said he had a friend who worked as a mechanic there, so he went to say hello while I started looking at vehicles.

"Good afternoon, sir. Can I help you find something?" A young woman came over in a professional-looking pantsuit.

"Yeah, I need to get a car that's better suited for driving in the snow. My Bentley is fun to drive, but it's not exactly designed for the wintry mess we get up here."

"How old is your Bentley?" she asked.

"About three years," I told her before adding, "but it has low mileage. Most of that time it sat in a garage down in the city."

"Great. We should be able to get you a nice trade-in on the car if you decide to purchase. What are you wanting?"

"Something that will drive in the snow. I live up past Woodstock, and I don't want to be stranded. Right now, if it snows, I'm not going anywhere. If there was an emergency, it'd be faster for me to whittle a pair of skis than wait for the plow people to come dig me out."

"I think I know what you should look at," she said. She turned to walk away, and I followed her. She showed me the latest Pathfinder in the showroom. She explained the size of the vehicle, its weight, the tire height and other features that would make it a magnificent vehicle to get around snow in. "Now, I wouldn't go plowing through six-foot drifts or anything, but it should be handy, unless it gets terrible out there."

"Hey, Jolene," a voice called. The saleswoman looked over at a short woman wearing a mechanic's outfit standing next to Talgat. "You taking care of that guy all right?" the mechanic asked as she walked up to us.

"Of course, I am," Jolene said. "He a friend of yours?"

"Not yet," she said. She wiped her hand on the front of her pants and extended it to me. "Carly Chisholm," she said, grasping my hand when I offered it. "Any friend of Talgat's is a friend of mine. Unless you're a friend of Dale's... then that just makes you a bit suspect," she said with a grin.

"He's not that bad, Carly."

"You," she said, turning to look at Talgat, "are not the greatest judge of character when it comes to rich, pretty boys from the city."

"Oh yes, because I've known so many of them."

"You used to be so normal. Then you met Dale and went all 'high society' on us."

"Uh-huh," Talgat said, wrinkling his forehead. "And how many posh farmers do you know?"

"Besides Dale?" she joked.

"Have you seen Dale plant anything?" Talgat said. "He wouldn't know a ripe apple on a tree from a pineapple tree."

"Wait," I said. "I thought pineapples grew out of the ground on a plant?" I asked.

"Exactly," Talgat said. "You already passed the first test. Dale failed when I tried to explain how fruit was grown."

"He didn't really think pineapples grew on trees?"

"Oh, he did," Carly said. "Talgat had him believing it, too—well, long enough to make sure he talked about wanting to grow pineapple trees with the Kudaibergen siblings and me."

"I knew no one would believe me if they didn't hear it for themselves," Talgat said. "I know it was mean, but I couldn't help myself."

I had to laugh. I love Dale, but he'd lived a ridiculously sheltered life. "I'm amazed Dale realized pineapples didn't come from a can called Dole. Give him credit where credit is due," I joked.

A voice cleared its throat, and all three of our heads turned to Jolene, who was standing there. "So, about buying a car…"

"She was thinking a Pathfinder would be good for me."

Carly looked at Talgat, who shrugged, so she said, "Knowing where you live now, a Pathfinder is probably your best bet. I would have recommended a truck if you were going to plow your own roads." She looked at me, then asked, "You're not going to plow your own roads, are you?"

Something about how she said it clarified that the correct answer was, "Nope. I already have a contract in place to have them done for me."

"Good," Carly said, nodding her head. "A Pathfinder is an impressive vehicle in the snow. It handles well with the auto four-by-four, but I still wouldn't recommend driving in anything deeper than three to five inches."

"Really? I figured a Pathfinder would plow through the snow," I admitted.

"Only if you want to get stuck in a snowbank or slide off the road and into a ditch. Unless you have a plow hooked up to the front of your vehicle, driving in any amount of snow can be dangerous," Carly explained.

"See? I'm learning new things every day I live up here."

"So, what color do you want?" Jolene asked. "We have black, silver, gunmetal gray, deep ocean blue pearl—"

"Really, that's a color? I'm surprised they didn't call it gay-ass blue," I asked.

Jolene looked across the lot and pointed out one to me. It was a delicate shade of deep blue. "I want that one."

"Let's go inside and see what kind of deal we can get you."

"You're planning on paying cash, aren't you?" Talgat asked.

"Probably... Does that matter?"

"Ahh...the joys of rich people," Carly said, rolling her eyes. "Not as bad as Dale, but still in the same league. If we get too many more of them up here, I'm going to move to Sullivan County and live in a cabin with a couple of wolfhounds for protection."

I had a slightly puzzled and confused look on my face. Talgat stared Carly down. "Don't scare the new people. That's not nice."

"Yes, *Mother*," she said. "It was nice to meet you, Roger. I probably better get back to work. I work better with engines than I do with gays from the city."

With that, she spun around and walked away. "What was that?" I asked when she walked away.

"That was the lesbian equivalent of a runaway train," Talgat said, shaking his head. "Take nothing she says personally. With cars? Listen to her. With anything else? Pay her no mind."

"So, that was a 'yes' to paying in cash?" Jolene said, clearly just as lost as I was.

* * * *

Forty-five minutes later, I drove a brand-new gay-ass blue Pathfinder off the lot.

"It handles nicely," Talgat said. "Dale's been trying to get me into one of these. I didn't want to tell you this, but Dale also has a Pathfinder — just last year's model."

"I knew it looked familiar. Wow, I really am the crazy city-dweller who has moved to the country?"

"Nah, you're not nearly as crazy as Dale was when he moved here. Sometime, ask him about the time he thought he could walk to the farm from the house. Darn right near killed himself. So far, I have seen no reason to worry about your safety."

"There's clearly a story there," I said. "I will definitely put that on my list of questions to ask Dale when I see him."

I drove by the farm, dropped Talgat off and showed Dale my new Pathfinder. When he asked me what the color was called, Talgat and I both said, "Gay-ass blue," then started laughing.

I drove into Woodstock. I was going to run to the grocery store, but when I saw the awning for Java Junkie Café & Roastery, I realized I hadn't been in there in weeks. I felt like I was in a weird relationship with Erik at this point. I saw him a few times a week... He didn't see me.

I parked and walked inside. The glorious scent of coffee bowled me over. I looked to see if Erik was working, and sure enough, he was standing behind the cash register. I started walking toward the counter. Erik looked up, and we made eye contact. A grin flashed across his face before he took on a professional countenance. *Is he glad to see me?*

"Hey there," I said, trying to act all cool.

"Good afternoon," he said, looking up at me with those blue eyes. "What can I get you today?"

Besides you, I wanted to say. Instead, I said, "Flat white."

I paid, then wanted to hit myself in the forehead repeatedly for acting so obtuse. I looked over to see who was making the drink. The manager was standing there. I could tell he was checking me out the whole time. He wasn't good at hiding it. Worst of all, Erik knew his manager was checking me out. *Fuck.*

"Your order will be ready at the end of the bar," Erik said.

I turned and looked at him and those amazing blue eyes and grumbled, "Yeah, I'd rather not, Erik." My eyes flashed wide, and I said, "Oh shit, I shouldn't have said that." I looked pleadingly at Erik, and his face lit up like the ball in Times Square on New Year's Eve. I broke eye contact and felt like a teenager. I shot Erik a quick sideways glance. Only then did I see the kid's nametag, 'Wesley.'

Fuck, fuckity, fuck, fuck fuck! Wesley continued to smile. I hoped he hadn't heard me call him by his stage name. *Do Internet porn stars have stage names?*

I leaned against the bar and did my best not to look at Wesley in a way that would be creepy—as if him knowing that I watch him have sex online wasn't creepy enough.

"Here's your flat white," Wesley said.

"Roger, I'm Roger," I said, turning to look at him.

"Well, Mr. Roger," Wesley started as he handed me my drink, "I hope you enjoy your drink. And you'll come see me—I mean us—again soon." This time, it wasn't my face that looked mortified.

I pretended like I heard nothing. I smiled, dropped a fifty in the tip jar and practically ran out of the place.

Once I got inside my Pathfinder, I hit my head against the steering wheel. "Dumb, dumb, dumb. Why am I so dumb?" I said, practically screaming the word. I looked out of the window and saw a woman staring at me with a perplexed look on her face. I smiled, waved and got the hell out of there.

* * * *

Wes

Did he call me Erik? No. I must have misunderstood him…but maybe I didn't. I had a million thoughts running through my head. Then I basically asked him to come back and see me again soon. *Oh geez.* "Smooth, Wes, real smooth," I said under my breath as Roger left the store.

"Why didn't you send him to the end of the bar to pick up his drink?" Stefan asked suddenly. "You're supposed to send them to the end of the bar to keep the line moving."

"I told him to, but I don't think he heard me," I lied. "He seemed distracted." *Yeah, that sounds believable.*

"Make sure you follow the process in the future. If they don't move, politely tell them their drink will be at the end of the bar. If we had been busy, he could have held up the line."

"Sure thing, Stefan. Sorry about that. I will make sure they pick up their drink at the end of the bar." The part I didn't say out loud was, "when they're clearly avoiding *you*." But was Roger avoiding Stefan or wanting to be near me? I didn't know. Why are men so complicated? Why can't they come out and say, "Hey, I think you're hot. Wanna hang out?" But then, he may also have been shocked if he recognized me. I mean, how often does one meet a guy they've spanked off to in person while they're trying to get coffee?

"Hello?" a voice said. I looked up to see Dylan.

"Oh, hey."

"Oh hey?" he questioned inquisitively. "I called your name like three times. You were clearly off in la-la land."

"Actually, this is perfect timing. I need your advice. Give me a minute," I said, and I turned around.

"Can I get my coffee first?" Dylan said pleadingly. "I need my coffee. I can't fix your problems without caffeine."

"Fine," I said. I grabbed a to-go cup, slipped a sleeve on it and filled it with the daily bold. I handed it to Dylan without ringing him up, which I did every once in a while when Stefan wasn't hovering.

I looked around to see where Stefan had gone. *Must be in his office.* I headed to the door and knocked on it.

"Come in," Stefan said.

"Hey, boss. I still haven't had my break yet. Since we're a little slow..." I let the question hang out there.

"Sure, give me a couple minutes and I'll relieve you."

"Thanks."

I went back to the cash register and waited for Stefan to come out. Of course, a couple of minutes turned to fifteen. Dylan complained about me taking too long, so I gave him a refill. When Stefan finally came out, he motioned for me to take my break. He didn't bother apologizing for taking so long. He never apologized for anything. Part of me wanted to quit just so I wouldn't have to deal with Stefan anymore. Sure, he was a genius with coffee, but he was a crappy person. Okay, maybe not a crappy person, but he was completely aloof and lived in his own little world, where he didn't pay attention to anyone or anything else.

"Sorry that took so long," I told Dylan when I finally got away.

"What was so important that you gave me not one but two free coffees?"

"I told you about the hot older guy who came in here a while back?"

"The one you lusted after for a week?" Dylan asked. I shook my head. "Yeah, I remember you talking about him a few dozen times."

I rolled my eyes. I hadn't talked about Roger that much. At least, I didn't think I had. "Well, he was here today...."

"That's it?" Dylan looked at me expectantly.

"I think he might have called me Erik."

"You *think* he called you Erik, or you *know* he called you Erik?"

"I don't know," I admitted. "I was slightly distracted, staring into his eyes and not looking at his chest."

"Oh, brother," Dylan said. "Did you do anything to embarrass yourself?"

"Maybe," I said in a way that clarified that I had.

"What did you do?"

I let out a slight huff and told him.

"Big whoop," Dylan groaned. "It's not like you dropped your coffee on him. Oh wait, you did that the first time you two met."

"Hey! I didn't get any coffee on him the first time. It was all over the floor."

Dylan laughed. "You are too easy to mess with." He took a drink. I was regretting my decision to give him free coffee. "You wouldn't be the first CammBoy who has met a fan off-line. Hell, you wouldn't be the first CammBoy who slept with a fan off-line. There's a Reddit forum where a group of us performers on CammBate talk about our off-line sexual conquests."

"Wait! You've slept with someone you met on CammBate?"

Dylan looked at me. His mouth dropped open as he realized he'd let that little tidbit of information out of the bag. He almost looked smitten. "Maybe," he replied. I knew him well enough to know he wasn't even attempting to lie to me.

"You have! I can't believe it."

"Hey, don't throw stones in glass houses. Besides, it's not like I have time to date."

"Doing what?" I countered.

"I work...and I do other things. And this isn't a conversation about my sex life. This is a conversation about getting you a sex life."

"Fuck you," I snapped.

"Is that really a sex life when you're doing it to earn money?" Dylan asked. "I mean, sure, we both have sex all the time, but it's not the same. When we fuck on camera," he said, lowering his voice, "we don't have the feelings that go along with fucking someone you're romantically interested in."

"True," I agreed. "I mean... You know I love you, Dylan, and would do anything for you. But we are *so* not compatible as boyfriends."

"Tell me about it. But we have great chemistry on the screen. Everyone tells us that. In fact, a lot of my followers swear up and down that we're secretly dating and don't want our fans to know."

"What would be the point of that?"

"I think some believe we're afraid that they won't tip as much if we're seen as a couple. I mean, half the fun of watching us fuck on screen is wishing they were one or both of us. It's the fantasy. If we were in an exclusive relationship, I guess that would kill the dream."

"But there are several guys on CammBate who work their boyfriends or husbands."

"I know that and you know that, but people are weird. Anyway, we have gotten way off-topic here. So, what are you going to do the next time you see your future husband?"

I tilted my head to the side and narrowed my eyes. Dylan threw up his arms in surrender. "I don't know what I'm going to do," I admitted. "What if he's only into me because I'm some kind of pervy porn conquest fantasy he has?"

"Pervy porn conquest fantasy? Well, that should be the title of your autobiography," Dylan joked. "Don't overthink it. Let it happen. It sounds like he's into you. If he is, don't throw up those defenses of yours. You can't keep all potential boyfriends at arm's length."

"I don't—"

"You forget who you're talking to. I know you better than you know yourself, Wes. I want you to be happy. Because a happy Wes...is a profitable Wes."

I groaned. "It always comes back to you, doesn't it?" I joked.

"But of course, it does. I'm the most important person in your life. Now, go get me another coffee. And get one for yourself. You're looking a little tired. We have a show tonight. I need to make sure my friend Erik is as perky as ever and ready to play."

Chapter Eleven

Roger

I drove home in my new car and kicked myself the entire way for acting like an idiot schoolboy with a crush. What's worse, Wesley saw right through my 'cool' pretense and realized I was a dirty old man watching him online.

As I pulled up my long driveway, I noticed another set of tracks leading up to my place, so I knew either Amazon or UPS had made a delivery. *Hmm… What did I order?* I felt like going on my social media and updating everything to 'In a complicated relationship with Amazon Prime'. It was simply too easy and convenient to order from them. Running low on toothpaste, *"Alexa, add toothpaste to my cart."* Running low on laundry detergent, *"Alexa, add to cart."* Need more protein shakes, *"Alexa…"* Honestly, if Jeremy had been as easygoing as Alexa was in my relationship, we'd probably still be together.

*Ahh…*Jeremy. We still hadn't agreed about the whole rent situation. He had his lawyer send me a letter asking for palimony. He had found some kind of two-bit hustler who would file a lawsuit. I swear, getting rid of Jeremy was worse than a game of Whack-A-Mole. Every time I thought I had him out of my life, he'd pop back up, wanting something else. Thankfully, my lawyer had filed a brief with the court asking the judge to *"involuntarily dismiss the case with prejudice."* As a non-lawyer, I had smiled and signed checks to my lawyer. Apparently, mine was trying to get the judge to dismiss the case against the wishes of the plaintiff in a manner to prevent Jeremy from ever bringing it up again. I was told to expect a ruling on that any day. If it happened, I could finalize any legal entanglement I still had with Jeremy. I mean, technically, he owns nothing. Mostly everything in our apartment was stuff I purchased. Hell, even the apartment was in my name. So, the fact that I was letting him stay there was only out of my generosity. My lawyer warned Jeremy's lawyer that if this judgment came our way, Jeremy should be ready to vacate the premises immediately. Technically, Jeremy was a squatter with no legal rights to the apartment. I had hoped we could be adults about all this, but Jeremy didn't seem to know how to let that happen.

On my doorstep was a set of documents from my lawyer. He'd emailed me the motion, but this was a copy of the official one filed with the court. Stuck to the package was a sticky note.

We should play again soon. Here's my number.
Chad, the UPS guy.

My cock twitched, remembering how nicely Chad had ridden me the first time we'd met. If I didn't figure out what I wanted from young Wesley, I would probably have a couple more rounds with Chad soon.

I had mistakenly told Dale and Talgat about my hook-up with Chad when we had been having dinner one night. I had invited the guys over and made spaghetti—one of the few meals I knew how to pull off without fear of needing the Woodstock Fire Department on standby.

During the middle of dinner, Dale had asked me, *"Have you met any of the local guys yet?"*

"Yeah, I've met a couple. There's one guy I'm kind of interested in. He's younger than me, so not sure if that will go anywhere."

"Really?" Talgat had asked. *"How'd you meet?"*

"Coffee shop," which was technically true. *"I also met some guy named Chad."*

"Chad Powell? The UPS guy?" Dale had asked.

"You know him?"

"Honey," Dale had said flatly, *"everyone has met Chad. He's like a one-may gay welcoming party. He's fucked more guys than Avery has."* Hearing Avery's name had made me visibly cringe, so Dale had appended, *"Too soon?"*

"Yes," I had admitted. *"Too soon. As for Chad, I take it you fucked him when you first got here."*

"A few times. So has Talgat."

"Hey, keep me out of this. I was young and naïve. I thought I was in love."

"That's not the story your sister tells. I can get Ayala on the phone and ask her." For added emphasis, Dale had whipped out his cell phone and held it up, a menacing thumb hovering over the screen.

"Don't you dare, Mr. Devereaux," Talgat had warned. *"You do that, and I'll start my own* Lysistrata *campaign – no sex for you."*

"So, basically what you're telling me," I had said, doing my best to steer the conversation back to me, *"is that I've slept with the town slut."*

"Well, yes. But then, Chad wouldn't be the town slut if everyone hadn't slept with him. It's like a Gay Woodstock Merit Badge, right up there with going to Hannaford's and buying a house."

One would think I would have shied away from Chad after finding out that information, but nah. I hadn't seen him since our first encounter, but I wasn't actively trying to avoid him. I had been busy and hadn't answered the door when he had delivered things.

I opened the pack of legal documents and scanned them. They were identical to the ones I'd been emailed, so I took them upstairs and filed them. Once that was taken care of, I went into the living room, turned on my Apple TV, opened my TV app and turned on live streaming of the nightly news. I only half paid attention to what was going on. I had my entire house synced, so streaming in the living room could also be seen in the kitchen, which was where I headed to make an early dinner halfway through the news. After leaving the coffee shop, I realized that I still hadn't had lunch. I had planned on getting it there. Still, I had forgotten about that completely when I'd had my awkward encounter with Wesley.

'Wesley'… The name suited him more than 'Erik'.' My cock twitched as I let him run through my mind. I looked down at my watch and saw it was after six p.m. I knew if he was going live today, he wouldn't do it until after nine, so I had plenty of time to eat and take a quick nap before watching. I hated to admit it, but he'd quickly become my favorite thing on the Internet to watch.

I threw together a salad and heated a frozen dinner I'd picked up at the grocery store for those rare evenings when I didn't eat out or order in. I focused on the television. A fresh scandal came out of Congress down in DC, and another came out of the Albany Governor's mansion. I swear, politicians could never get their shit together. They were either the most corrupt group of people who have ever walked the planet or the dumbest criminals. I mean, who accepts an envelope filled with cash from a constituent and thinks that's legit?

Ding! The sound of the microwave reverberated off the walls. I had assumed wood would absorb sound, but I had assumed wrong. Wood, especially when treated and varnished, could bounce noise as much as marble could. I sat down at the kitchen island and ate my dinner on a stool there while I finished watching the news.

As soon as dinner was over, I cleaned my dishes and put them in the dishwasher to dry. I know that sounds weird, but I don't go through dishes that quickly. After the first time I found something growing on a plate in the dishwasher, I'd decided I needed to clean the dishes by hand and use the dishwasher as a drying rack most of the time.

After dinner, I headed up to my room and laid down on the bed. I don't know if it was the amazing CloudBed, sleeping alone or not stressing out over Jeremy all the time, but I was getting the best sleep of my adult life. I was practically in la-la land within a few seconds of my body hitting the bed.

I woke a couple hours later, and my room was pitch black. "Alexa, turn on bedroom light," I said into the darkness. There was a short beeping sound as my lights turned on. "Thank you," I said into the void. I swung my legs over the edge of the bed, stood and headed into the bathroom for some relief. I looked down at my watch and realized it was only eight-thirty, so I still had a bit of time before my evening show with Erik…Wesley.

I walked down the hall to my office, sat down and got to work. True to her word, Mitzi had cleared my calendar and ensured I hadn't been interrupted that entire day. I shot her an email letting her know I'd bought a Pathfinder and described the color. I refrained from calling it 'gay-ass blue', but I had typed the words and deleted them.

I read through a few other work emails. I had a couple of projects to approve for a client. I looked at the designs, made some suggestions and sent them back to the graphic arts department. Before I knew it, it was nine-fifteen. I opened the CammBate website and clicked on the 'male' tab and searched out TwinkErik69, but he wasn't on. I did a quick search and found SmoothBangr69. Wesley and whoever his friend was were sitting on the bed talking to the livestream. They were already shirtless.

"Look at that," Jackson said, staring at the screen. "We just hit the 'lose our shorts' goal. Erik, want to do the honors?"

Jackson refocused the camera on Wesley, who stood and did a bit of a striptease as he slid his shorts down. He turned around for the camera to reveal his perfectly round — and completely fuckable — ass, outlined by the green straps of the jock he was wearing. My cock was a full raging hard-on. Wesley had done a quick bend over and grabbed his ass cheeks, exposing his hole for a moment.

"Well, that was a bit more than they paid for," Jackson joked. "My turn." Not to be out done, Jackson performed his own little striptease and flashed his cock for a second to the camera. He said, "Whoops," then covered his mouth, quickly faking innocence. "I'm going to change the room to the next tip level, which is when we'll lose our jocks. If you want to see both of us in all our glory, keep those tips rolling in."

I knew what I wanted to see. I still had a balance on my tip account, so I sent it all to Jackson and Wesley, hoping to see the tip jar fill quickly. Thankfully, I didn't have long to wait. Before I knew it, Wesley was wiggling out of his jockstrap. His dick sprang free and laid flat against his stomach.

"Yes, ChatterGuy, Erik can suck himself off," Jackson said, looking at the screen. "In fact, we'll make that the next tip level. Self-sucks for both of us."

Wesley nodded his head and did a quick demonstration where he put the tip of his tongue right on top of his cockhead. *Wow!* I pulled out the bottle of lube I kept in my desk drawer and started jacking myself off. The tip jar filled quickly.

Wesley locked his arms around his legs and pulled his head down to his dick, and he started bobbing up and down. He couldn't get all the way down to his balls, but he got about halfway there. I'd seen self-sucking in porn before, but watching Wesley do it made me incredibly horny. With little fanfare or warning, I shot my load.

"Ugh," I whined. I grabbed a couple of wet wipes I kept on hand for these types of sticky situations, and I cleaned myself off. Then noticed a shot of cum had gotten on my computer keyboard, so I did my best to blot it up before sanitizing the keyboard itself. Thankfully, the cum landed on the wrist bar and not on any keys. Even though I had already climaxed, I leaned back and watched the entire show. It wasn't long before I was fully hard again and ready to go for round two. I wasn't sure if I would be able to come again, but I knew I would give it the good old college try.

The next tip was sixty-nine-ing, so I watched as both CammBoys sucked each other off. I enjoyed watching the skilled way Wesley's lips circled Jackson's cock and took it to the balls. I imagined what it would feel like to have those lips wrapped around my rod.

By the time we moved on to the fuck goal, I was already spanking my meat. This time, Wesley started by fucking Jackson. They lay sideways across the bed, so it was easier to see both men as Wesley repeatedly plowed into Jackson's ass. I pumped my fist in time with Wesley's strokes and wished it was my ass he was plowing—and I'm not usually a bottom. Wesley was relentless. He pinned Jackson beneath him.

"Where do you want my load?" he suddenly asked Jackson.

"In me," Jackson said. "Breed me like the stud you are."

Okay, that line was cheesy, but when Wesley threw back his head and let out a guttural growl, I shot my second load of the night in time with him. Once he was done pumping Jackson full of cum, he grabbed the camera and held it down to Jackson's hole so we could all see Wesley's cum leaking out.

Jackson smiled at Wesley and said, "My turn."

* * * *

I had slept like a baby last night. I had dreams of everything I wanted to do to Wesley and have him do to me. I had bit the bullet that afternoon and made my way into Woodstock and to the café. Unfortunately, when I had opened the door, I saw only the manager and the female barista. No Wesley around.

I strolled up to the cash register and ordered my usual flat white, then waited for Stefan to make it himself. Autumn stared at me a couple of times. At first, I was afraid I had something hanging out of my nose or something. Thankfully, I didn't. I got my coffee and headed over to a corner table. I pulled out my phone and started reading and responding to emails.

There was a sudden sound of a chair being pulled back from the table, and I looked up to see the female barista sitting with me.

"Hi, I'm Autumn," she said, extending her hand.

I twisted my head slightly as I furrowed my brow and shook her hand. "I'm Roger."

"You see my friend over there?" She pointed to a spot on the other side of the room. There he was. Wesley stood looking mortified in my direction.

"Yes, I see him." In that moment, I almost expected the worst.

"So, he has a thing for you. And from what I can tell, you have a thing for him, so I'm here to play matchmaker. Wes is entirely too shy for his own good." *He goes by Wes. Good to know.* "So, are you interested in him?"

I choked back a gasp. I wasn't used to people being this abrupt in their approach. "Yes, I'm interested in him," I choked out. "I think he's gorgeous, and I have since the moment I laid eyes on him."

"Perfect," she said. "That's what I figured, but he's too shy to take the first step."

"I can't blame him for that. I know I am always horrible at taking the first step when I'm into a guy."

She motioned for Wes to join us. As he approached the table, he pulled out a chair and added it to my two-top, making it a three-top.

"I am so sorry for this," Wes said as he sat down. "I don't know what she said—"

"Don't worry about it," I responded. "I'm Roger Havemeyer," I said, extending my hand.

Wes grabbed my hand tentatively but firmly. "I'm Wes Phelps. It's nice to put a name with a face."

He's thought about me. I watched as the realization of when he told me he'd been thinking about me crossed his face. "Don't worry. I've admittedly been thinking about you too. Anyway, tell me about yourself."

Autumn practically rolled her eyes at that question. Instead of making a clever comeback, she said, "You two be good and play nice. If you need anything, holler."

"Sorry about that," Wes said when Autumn had gone. "She means well—"

"I'm glad she helped us break the ice. I've wanted to talk to you for quite some time now."

"You have?" Wes asked.

"Ever since I met you. I find you ridiculously attractive—"

"I'm average," Wes said. "I mean…thank you for the compliment. I'm trying to get out of the habit of self-deprecating humor."

"How's that working out for you?"

"Well, as you just saw…I'm far from perfect."

We sat around in the café for another ten minutes before I finally worked up the nerve to ask him on a date. "So, I don't want to be pushy or anything, but would you like to go on a date with me?"

"Yes," Wes said, not even attempting to play it cool. "I haven't been on an actual 'date, date' in forever."

"Me neither."

"Really?" Wes asked, his eyebrows knitted together in confusion.

"Here's the gist. I was in a long-term, committed relationship. Well, I thought it was committed, until I walked in on him and some guy having sex in our apartment in the city."

"Ouch… I take it that means you two weren't in an open relationship?"

"Not at all. Honestly, we'd never had the conversation."

"What are your thoughts on open relationships?"

"Wow, talk about getting to one of the tough questions quickly," I said.

"You don't have to answer that."

"No, it's okay. Honestly, I haven't thought about it before. I know a lot of gay guys in open relationships, and it can work. But I think there need to be ground rules, and both parties must be on board for it to be successful. And I mean, both parties must agree, not *one* party agrees, and the other party goes along with it. I knew a couple who was like that, and the one who wasn't enjoying the *open* part of the relationship just grew resentful until everything fell apart."

We talked like this for the next hour. I noticed the manager staring at us a couple of times. "What's his deal?" I asked.

"Who?" I pointed my finger discreetly in the manager's direction. "Oh, Stefan. He's a decent boss. He may be jealous. I think he had the hots for you."

"Even if he did, I was only coming in to see you."

"Aw… That's almost romantic-sounding, if not a slightly bit stalkerish," Wes said, beaming.

"I'm an introvert by nature," I admitted. "A friend called me an extroverted introvert. Basically, I can put it on when I'm at work and dealing with a client, but then I need downtime and alone time to rebuild my energy reserves."

"I'm the same way. When I'm here, I can plaster on the friendly smile — or when I'm at my second job — but then I need sleep to recover from all the smiling."

"I remember growing up and hearing 'it takes fewer muscles to smile than to frown.' I took biology in college and found out that it takes ten muscles to smile and six or less to frown. By my math, it takes zero muscles to have resting bitch face."

Wes let out a loud laugh. Then he started laughing because he was laughing. His laughter was contagious. His alabaster skin took on a reddish hue as he grew slightly flustered.

When he finally stopped laughing, I asked, "How does Saturday work for you?" A confused look crossed the other man's face, so I clarified, "For our date?"

"I work until five, so I should be ready no later than seven."

"Perfect, I'll see you on Saturday."

We talked for a little longer. When we finally stood to go, Wes threw his arms around me in a big hug. He was a little shorter than me. I took in the fruit scent of his shampoo as I rested my cheek on top of his head for a moment.

"Break it up, you two, or I'll have to get the fire extinguisher," Wes' friend Autumn said, walking by to wipe off our table.

Chapter Twelve

Wes

Between slinging coffee and doing homework, I hadn't had too much time to get crazy nervous about my upcoming date with Roger. When Saturday afternoon finally rolled around, I realized I was beyond excited. I hadn't been on a proper date with a guy in a couple of years. Sure, I'd had the 'let's meet for coffee then screw in the car' or 'hey, let's go for a hike and fuck in the woods,' but a date that involved getting dressed up and going to dinner at a nice restaurant was not something I was used to.

I narrowed my outfit options down to three, but I wasn't sure which I should wear. "Pietro!" I yelled from my room. "I need you."

He walked into the room a few seconds later. "How can I be of assistance, Master Phelps?" he asked, putting on his best butler-sounding voice. He glanced over at the bed and saw the three outfits I'd laid out.

"I can't decide what to wear."

"They all look nice. I think you can pull all three of them off. But then, you have that kind of body designers like. You're built like a hanger."

"I think that's a compliment, but you are zero help." I turned away from him and yelled, "Vale—"

"I'm here," she said, sauntering into the room. "When I realized it was about clothing, I knew this one"—she nodded in Pietro's direction—"would be of little use. Show me what you've got."

I held up three options against my body. "Yeah, that outfit is a definite no. You're going to a restaurant, not a gay bar."

"You're right. The leather pants are a bit much, but they make my ass look great."

"This is a first date," Valeria reminded me. "You're not auditioning for a role in twink monthly. Next."

I held up a pair of jeans and a red button-down shirt. "Definitely better. But that reads more 'going to Applebee's' than fine dining."

I had to agree with her on that one.

"Hope you like this." I held up a pair of pressed chinos and a maroon cashmere sweater. The sweater hugged me in all the right places without being completely tight. And it ended right at my waist, so my best *ass*ets were still on display.

"Yeah, why you bothered showing me the other two options is beyond me. This one makes the most sense…by far."

"Thanks. You're a godsend, especially since he was no help."

"It's not my fault that all clothes look amazing on me," Pietro said. "Besides, most people don't look at my clothes… They're imagining what I look like without them."

"Can this boy's ego get any larger?" Valeria said.

"Someone had to come along and tame it," I joked. "I'm glad it was you."

"Come on, stud muffin," she said, grabbing Pietro by the arm and tugging him out of my room. "This boy has to get ready for the ball."

"Does that make you my fairy godmother?" Pietro asked.

"He's the fairy," Valeria said, nodding at me, before adding, "but you can call me *mami* in bed."

"Eww…" I let out reflexively.

Pietro grabbed the corner of my bedroom's door on his way out. "I may not see you until tomorrow. Have fun on your date." He flashed his eyebrows at me and stuck out his tongue before grinning mischievously.

I so didn't need to know the mating habits of straights.

I put the clothing choices I wasn't going to wear away. I was about to head into the shower when my phone went off. I looked and saw it was Dylan calling.

"What's up?" I said, after hitting the green button on the splash screen.

"Not much, checking in on how your date preparations were going."

"I got the seal of approval from Valeria for my outfit."

"Valeria is fierce. She won't steer you wrong."

"Are you all psyched up to go on your date with your new sugar daddy?"

I let out a quick huff before saying, "He's not my sugar daddy. He's just a fucking hot guy who is into me, who happens to be older."

"Yeah, but how old. Autumn said he's like old, old."

"Dylan, you think thirty is old, so I don't know if you and Autumn are expert judges of age."

"Maybe, but that didn't answer my question. How old is the sugar daddy?"

"I don't know. I'm guessing he's in his late thirties or early forties, but I suck at guessing people's ages."

"Well, if he's forty, that would mean he was your age when you were born. So, technically, he could be your father's age, making him your *daddy*." He said the word with as much sex as he could over the phone. "I mean, we both know girls who got knocked up in high school. And they had their children when they were younger than us. So, he could be older than your dad."

"Guess I'm lucky my parents didn't have me until their early thirties then."

"I'm messing with you. You make it too easy."

"Yeah, well, tonight is not a good night to mess with me. I'm already a bundle of nerves."

"He likes you. You like him. You've already gotten over the hardest hump in all this. At least you two know you're interested in each other. It could be one of those awkward first dates where you don't even know if there's mutual attraction until you're both ripping off each other's clothes."

"We're having dinner. I don't imagine there being any clothes ripping in the steak house."

"Come on. Give those old Woodstock ladies a show. Teach them a thing or two about pleasuring their husbands."

"Anywa-a-a-y," I said, drawing the word out as long as possible. "What are you up to tonight?"

"I'm heading out of town."

"Where are you going?"

"Down to the city to hang out with a friend of mine. He's been doing drag for about a year and has been trying to get me to come for a show."

"That sounds like it could be fun."

"It should be. Afterward, I'm staying at his place. I'll drive back first thing in the morning."

I looked over at the clock on my nightstand and said, "Shit! I've got to go. I need a shower. I'm running late."

"And by running late, you probably mean you're still running forty-five minutes early."

"You know me too well."

"Have fun. And don't do anything tonight that I wouldn't do with…your sugar daddy."

Dylan hung up the phone before I responded.

I tossed the phone on my bed, stripped out of my work clothes and headed into the bathroom to shower.

* * * *

Roger

I'd recommend we meet up at Silvia's because Dale had told me it was one of the nicer establishments in Woodstock. I felt like a kid getting ready for his high school prom. Maybe it was because it had been so long since I'd actually gone on a date, but I was nervous. First, what was I thinking? Taking out a guy who is half my age? I mean, I could literally be his father. I'd never considered myself to be the kind of man who was commonly referred to as a 'chick hawk' in gay circles. Those are the scary old dudes who hang out in bars and flirt overtly with every young guy who walks by them. And here I was, forty-one and going on a date with someone half my age. Sure, we were both adults, but the age difference still worried me. We were at two very different points in our lives. I'm on the cusp of middle age, and Wes is becoming an adult.

I pulled up in my Pathfinder about ten minutes early. Thankfully, there was plenty of parking, so I didn't have to drive around trying to parallel park the SUV. As much as I was enjoying the power of the Pathfinder, I still wasn't the most adept driver when it came to navigating it smoothly. As I pulled into the lot, the snow started to fall. I knew we were supposed to get some, but I didn't think it would amount to much.

I leaned against the car, not wanting to go inside just yet. I took in a deep breath of the icy mountain air. I could smell the fragrance of the food wafting through the front door as someone exited. I checked myself out in the side mirror to ensure my hair was combed. I was ready. I'd gone business casual with my outfit. I'd thrown on a pair of black chinos and a maroon sweater. Any reds and blues always looked good on me because they made my eyes shine even brighter than they usually did.

Wes slipped in behind me and wrapped his arms around me in hello. I knew it was him because I recognized the floral scent of his freshly washed hair. "Well, hello to you, too," I said, spinning around in his grip.

I looked down and realized we were basically wearing the same outfit. I let out a laugh. Wes looked at me. "What?"

"Our outfits, we're practically twins." My blond hair was a bit lighter than his dirty blond. And my eyes were a lighter shade of blue compared to his dark ones, but we had similar haircuts. I was more filled out and had a few inches on Wes, but we looked like a couple that had purposefully dressed the same.

"I guess great minds think alike," Wes joked. "I went through a lot of clothing options before picking this one."

"What were the other ones?" I asked.

"One was deemed more Applebee's than Silvia's, and the other was a bit too risqué for this place. I didn't think black leather pants were that bad, but...."

I pictured him wearing nothing but those leather pants and wanted to steal him away from the restaurant and head straight to dessert. I finally tore my eyes off him and asked, "Shall we go inside?"

"I thought you'd never ask." Wes casually grabbed my hand, and we walked from the parking lot to the front door. When I had been his age, the idea of casually holding a guy's hand wasn't even something I'd dreamed of. Public displays of affection were a surefire way to get oneself hurt back then.

I broke off the handgrip for a second to open the door. Someone was pushing, and they stumbled outward.

"I'm so sorry. Are you okay?" I looked down to see the woman who had stumbled and looked into a face I recognized. "Hey, Ruby."

"Roger. Good to see you. That door has always been a problem. You can't see if someone is on the other side."

She looked up and saw Wes, then looked back at me, cocking her head slightly.

"Is Stephanie here?" I asked.

"She's finishing up with the check. I needed to get some fresh air." She looked over at Wes and said, "I see you're making new friends."

"Wes is an old family friend," I said. I don't know why I lied. I just did. I caught the look shared between Wes and Ruby, but neither contradicted me.

A second later, Stephanie came through the door putting her coat on. "Hello, Roger," she said when she saw me. The look of surprise flashed across her face before she said, "Wesley Phelps. It's been a few years since I saw you last. How are you doing?"

"I'm doing well, Mrs. Blevins. Working at Java Junkie and going to school across the river."

"Great. I wish your parents were here to see this." Stephanie shook her head. Something passed between Wes and Stephanie – a mournful look that went unsaid. "Well, I hope you two guys have a nice dinner. Try the pork chop. It's amazing tonight."

"Good to meet you, Wes," Ruby said. "I'm sure I'll be seeing you around town, Roger. I still need to invite you up to the house when the girls get together for poker." What she didn't say was 'to grill you about your intentions toward Wes,' but I definitely felt the subtext in her stare.

"Sounds like a plan."

"Maybe you can bring Wes with you," Ruby said.

"Why would he invite Wes?" Stephanie said in puzzlement. Like a Mack truck hitting a tree, realization splattered across Stephanie's face, and she said, "Oh."

I held the door for Wes and motioned for him to go inside as Ruby dragged a slack-jawed Stephanie away from the entrance.

"Well, that wasn't awkward at all," I said, following Wes inside.

"Do you have a reservation?" the hostess asked.

"Yes," I said. "Party of two for Havemeyer."

She looked down her list and said, "Perfect. If you'll follow me."

The place was modern and cozy. There was a giant open kitchen that took center stage. Along one wall was a plush velvet green bench. Spaced evenly along the bench were marble tables and a chair on the other side. We were placed at one of these.

"Do you want the bench or the chair?" I asked Wes as we neared the table.

"I'll take the chair. If I'm on the bench, I'll see everything going on behind you. I'm like the dog in *Up* some days. I can get so easily distracted by things moving in the background. Squirrel!" he said, flipping his head to the side. I think he was referring to a movie or a television show. I didn't know which one, so I smiled.

"Yeah, you have no idea what I'm talking about."

I shrugged. "Sorry. I'm not always the most up-to-date on movies and television. When I lived in the city, my job had me going to plays and musicals almost every night. I never had time to see things."

"Here you two go," the hostess said. I took off my overcoat, and Wes gestured for me to put it on the bench next to him, which is where he'd already put his own coat.

"Wow, we really are wearing the same outfit," Wes said, taking me in as he sat down and accepted the menu from the hostess.

"Yep, we are two peas in a pod."

Wes looked over his menu at me and lowered it slightly before whispering, "A fucking sexy pod."

The corner of my lip twitched up instinctively. My smile made Wes smile, which I barely glimpsed before he disappeared behind his menu again.

"Have you been here before?" I asked.

"A couple times with my family…" His voice trailed off.

I wanted to reach out and caress his hand, but I didn't think we were there yet, so I just said, "You all right?"

"Yeah, sorry. My memories of my parents just hit me out of nowhere some days."

"Like coming to a restaurant you haven't visited since they died?" I asked, remembering what that felt like all too well after both of my parents had passed.

"You sound like you know what I'm talking about."

"My mother died from breast cancer when I was in college. My father was not the same after that. He died of a massive heart attack later that same year. I was devastated, but my younger brother, Peter, was still in high school, so I had to keep my shit together for him."

"Where are you from?" Wes asked, setting his menu down.

"I grew up down in Westchester. Went to school at NYU but had to take a year and a half off to raise my younger brother. His world had already been upended. I didn't want him to go to a new high school. I had to petition the state to be his legal guardian, and Peter was legally emancipated the next year."

"Where's he now?"

"He lives out in California with his wife and three kids. What about you? Any siblings?"

"Not any blood siblings, but my roommate is as close to a brother as I'll ever have."

"How so?"

Wes took a deep breath in.

"Welcome to Silvia's. Have you looked at the menu yet?" a young man in black pants, a white shirt and a bowtie asked.

"Not yet," I admitted. "Can you give us a few more minutes?"

"Certainly. Can I get either of you something to drink?"

"What's the best Bordeaux blend you have?"

"That would be our twenty-sixteen La Gaffeliere, sir."

"Sounds great."

"Bottle or glass?"

I looked over at Wes, who said, "None for me. I'll have a Coke."

"I'll have a glass of wine and a glass of water. "

"Great. I'll be back with those in a few minutes," the waiter replied as he turned to go get our drinks.

"Not much of a wine person?" I asked.

"I'm not legal yet." My eyes must have flashed in surprise because Wes quickly added, "Let me rephrase that. I'm not twenty-one yet. I will be in June. When it comes to alcohol, not legal yet. For everything else, I'm very much legal... Wow, that was awkward."

I smiled. "So, you were telling me about your parents?"

"I had hoped you'd forgotten about that already."

"You don't need to tell me if you don't want to."

"No, it's not that, I... I still have a hard time with it. It's been almost three years, but it's still rough. My parents were coming home from a party at some friend's house on the Fourth of July. They were sideswiped by a truck that lost its brakes. Pietro, my roommate, his family took me in during my last year in high school. We'd always been best friends, and I didn't have anywhere else to go. My parents hadn't been rich, but we'd been decently well off. I was their only child, so everything was left to me, but I don't have access to most of it until I turn twenty-one."

"Have you tried petitioning the court?" I asked without thinking.

"I had that conversation with my lawyer. She thought it was best for me to wait. But she also told me if things ever got bad, I could call her, and we'd push it through."

"She sounds like an excellent lawyer."

"And I've been fine. I'm not going to say life is easy, but working at Java Junkie helps pay my rent, and I'm on a full ride at Bard, so I'm covered there."

"So, Pietro is still your roommate?"

"Yep. Though these days he's wrapped around his new girlfriend's little finger. Her name's Valeria, and I completely approve of their relationship."

"What about you? How did you end up in Woodstock?"

"I thought I told you about my ex the other day?"

"That's right. The guy you found fucking someone else in your bed?"

There was a clearing of a throat next to us, and the waiter sat down my glass of wine. I did the obligatory smell and swirl test before taking a swig. "Very nice," and nodded appreciatively as the waiter put down the Coke in front of Wes.

"Are you two ready to order?"

Fuck, I still hadn't looked at the menu. I motioned for Wes to order while I scanned it quickly. "I'll have the pork chop," I said, remembering that Ruby — *or was it Stephanie?* — one of them had recommended it.

"That will be two of the pork chop specials." The waiter reached out, and I gave him my menu.

"Sorry about that," Wes said when the waiter left.

"For what?" I asked.

"Blurting out your business in front of the waiter."

"No worries. It's not like it's him I want to fuck." The words were out of my mouth before I had a chance to blush.

Wes took a sip of Coke before narrowing his eyes at me. He got a mischievous smile on his face while he sucked on the straw. He set the drink down and asked, "So, who is it you want to fuck?" As he said the word, he moved his foot so it rode slightly up my leg. Part of me wanted to scream, 'check', race from the restaurant and have my way with Wes in the Pathfinder.

"You are a tease, aren't you?" I said once I'd gotten my hormones under control.

"I'm young, hung and full of cum," he whispered.

I smiled, and without thinking, said, "Trust me, I know." *Fuck.*

Wes tilted his head, and his mouth twitched up at the corner. "Care to expound on that?"

"Do I have to?" I whined.

"Yes."

I took a deep breath, leveled my eyes and said, "I guess you'd find out eventually. And if this causes you never to want to see me again, I'll understand."

"I seriously doubt that," Wes said. "If it's what I think it is, I kind of already guessed." I wasn't sure if he'd guessed or if he was fishing, but I decided honesty was the best policy.

"Before I met you at the coffee shop, I saw you online—"

"On Grindr?" Wes said with a smirk. In that moment, I knew he was fucking with me.

"On CammBate. I had just moved up here to Woodstock, and I had gotten an email from that website. I hadn't even heard of it before that night. I had logged on to see what it was, and I saw when your friend Jackson had roped you into your first scene. Then a few days later, I saw you at the coffee shop."

As if a lightbulb blinked on, "That's why you looked like you saw a ghost and dropped the cup and saucer."

"Guilty as charged," I said sheepishly. "I won't be mad if you don't want to see me again. I feel like I've dragged you here under false pretenses."

"I'm not going to let you off the hook that easily," Wes said. "Trust me. I thought about you several times during those first few weeks while I was…performing. I've earned quite a lot of money thinking about you."

That was not the answer I had expected. "You're not freaked out then?"

"Not anymore. I had an epiphany when I realized eventually someone would recognize me. I figured when they did, at least I wouldn't have to explain my job."

We kept chatting all the way through dinner. Before long, the waitstaff was looking at us funny, since we were one of the last tables still seated.

"I guess we should get out of here," I said. "I think they want to clean up."

I motioned for the waiter, who was hovering closer than I would have liked, and asked for the bill. I didn't bother looking at it. I handed him my credit card. We were out of the restaurant and in the parking lot in a few minutes. The snow had really started to come down.

"Well, fuck," I said when I looked at the streets.

"What?" Wes asked.

"I was going to ask you back to my place, but I'm a bit out of town. Unless you have a four-by-four, it's probably not safe to drive out there."

"That sucks," Wes grumbled. He shivered slightly against the snowy night. Without thinking, I reached out and wrapped my arms around him.

He laid his face against my chest. "I can hear your heartbeat," he said. "And I can feel...oh my," he let out as he positioned his thigh pressing into my hard bulge. "Someone isn't bothered by the cold."

He reached his hands up, grabbing the back of my head and pulling my face down toward his lips. Their smooth texture against mine caused my whole body to shudder. There was more intimacy, more vulnerability in that one kiss than I had felt from years of being with Jeremy. I kissed Wes back. I quickly realized I wasn't the only one getting excited standing there in the dark snowy weather. A set of car lights lit us for a second, which caused us to break apart and catch our breaths. I glanced down and saw both of our pants were tenting.

"Can we go back to your place?" I asked.

"No, dammit. Pietro and his girlfriend are there tonight. But...I have keys to Dylan's. He told me I could use his place anytime."

"Who?"

"Sorry. You know him as 'Jackson'."

"Ahh. And he won't mind you bringing a guy home to his place?"

"He's out of town. And would he mind? No. If anything, he'd encourage it and ask if he could join in."

"Well, that would be a hard pass from me if he did. I have my eyes set on you." I knew it sounded cheesy once it left my mouth, but Wes wrapped his arms around my neck and kissed me harder.

"Follow me?" Wes asked.

"Sure. Drive slow. As much as I want to be with you, I don't want to get into a car accident on the way."

"Don't worry. I already drive like a little old lady going to Kentucky Fried Chicken on Sunday after church," Wes said.

"Wow, that was oddly specific."

He reached out and kissed me again. "Follow me." He broke away from my grip and headed over to his car as I got up into the Pathfinder. I looked through the window and saw him waiting for his heat to come on. I kind of felt bad because my heater was already on and at full blast. I almost rolled down my window and told him to come hang with me while his car heated, but he looked at me and gave me a thumbs-up as he pulled away from his parking spot. I threw my car into drive and followed Wes' taillights as they left the parking lot.

Chapter Thirteen

Wes

The snow was coming down much harder than I'd expected it to. I checked my rear-view mirror every few seconds to ensure that Roger was still behind me. Thankfully, he did a good job of following without being too close. I wanted Roger to rear-end me, but not with his car. The heat in my car finally kicked on. The heat was constantly either freezing or sauna, with very little in between. By the time we approached Dylan's apartment building, I was sweating bullets — and not because I was excited.

I parked in an empty parking space a little way from Dylan's front door so Roger could pull in beside me. I jumped out of the car. I wanted the cold, snowy air to drop my body temperature and hopefully take a little sheen of the sweat away before Roger got out. I wiped my brow with my coat. Thankfully, I didn't think he'd be able to see my sweat in the dark. I took a few steps up to the sidewalk and waited for a second before Roger stepped out and joined me.

"What's the name of this place?" Roger asked.

"Woodstock Estates Apartments," I told him before quickly wiping my sweaty palm discreetly on my chinos, then I grabbed Roger's hand. I lightly tugged, and he fell into step beside me. We walked over to Dylan's place, huddled together on the sidewalk. I think my body was radiating enough heat for both of us. When we got to the door, I pulled out my key chain, found the key and opened the door.

"You have a key to his apartment?"

"Yep. I've had a key to his place for as long as he's had one. If I've ever needed some alone time, I've come over here and just chilled. Dylan's been a great friend that way. He always knows when I need cheering up, a shoulder to cry on or some peace and quiet."

"Those are definitely the best friends."

I flipped on the light switch and motioned Roger to join me inside. "You can hang your coat on the coat hook," I said, gesturing to a set of hooks lining the entry hall. Roger slid out of his and hung it before turning to help me with my jacket. *Such a gentleman.* "Let me give you the five-cent tour."

I started by showing Roger the living room and the kitchen. I can say Dylan has damn good taste. His home looked like a cross between Pier 1 and an Ikea display floor, but without the need to edit. The only thing garish in the living room was a set of black-and-white nudes of himself. When he had first shown me the new images, I had been like, *"Why in the world would you want nude photos of you on the wall?"*

In his typical fashion, Dylan had said, *"I wanted something pretty to look at. And you can't get much prettier than this,"* motioning to himself.

I showed Roger the primary bedroom and saw it was a bit of an unkempt mess. I led him into the living room, and we sat down on the couch. I sat on one side, and Roger sat on the other.

"Nice place," Roger said, sitting down.

"It has a nice balance between looking like a photoshoot and being homey. Obviously, Dylan's bedroom was not meant to be seen tonight."

"I think we all have those days where we don't pick up after ourselves immediately."

"Yep," I said, not knowing what else to say. We'd had such great conversations all night, but suddenly we both were at a loss for words, which felt strange. A slight chill overcame me, and I shuddered. Dylan must have turned down the heat when he left. Roger saw the shiver and scooted across the couch to put his arm around me. I leaned into him, laying my head on his chest. I could hear his heartbeat again. It was still racing, but not as much as it had been in the parking lot a little earlier. Guess I needed to do something about that.

I looked up at him. He was staring down at me. I reached my right hand up and caressed his face with my thumb. Up close, I could see tiny laugh lines developing around Roger's eyes. I ran my hand down his face, then traced around his ear and jawline with my index finger. I got to the tiny cleft in his chin and used my thumb to trace around his lips. When I got to the cupid's bow, Roger cracked his lips and leaned in to suck gently on the tip of my thumb. The next thing I knew, the whole tip of my thumb was inside Roger's mouth, and his tongue was teasing it.

Roger started playing with the hem of my sweater. He rubbed his thumb over my flat stomach at the place where my pants and T-shirt hit. I slid from sitting next to him to lying underneath him on the couch with our legs interlaced. My pants rode low enough on my hips that he was less than an inch from the top of my cock, which was already grinding into his left leg.

I pulled at the back of his sweater until I finally touched the skin on his back. Roger was still bearing all his weight on his right arm. I placed my whole hand on his skin and pulled him closer to me, saying, "I won't break."

Roger ground his cock into my left leg as he placed his body weight on top of mine. His weight covered me like a warm blanket as I explored his back as much as I could reach from my position. I continued to pull out his shirt until it was completely untucked from his pants. I let my hand wander. Roger humped my leg. Every slight movement of his hips made me want to take him inside me. *Don't rush this.* I looked up at him, stared into his eyes and said, "Kiss me."

He lowered his head and traced the outlines of my lips with his tongue before pressing his mouth firmly against mine. We kissed deeply and passionately. I got utterly lost in his lips. When I finally came up for air, I said, "Let's take this somewhere more comfortable."

"I thought you'd never ask," Roger said. A playful glint in his eyes made me smile. He pushed himself backward on the couch. Once his weight was over his knees, he put one foot on the floor and pushed himself into a standing position. I lay on the sofa, taking him in, the outline of his cock pushing at his pants. He reached a hand down and I grasped it, letting him pull me off the couch. Without letting go of his hand, I pulled him toward Dylan's spare bedroom.

I opened the door and flipped on the lights. "Do you prefer to do it with the lights on or off?" I asked.

He responded by picking me up and launching me onto the bed playfully. I bounced twice and looked up at him, grinning. He lowered himself to his knees at the edge of the bed. I sat up, placing him between my legs. He wrapped his arms around my torso like he was holding onto a life preserver in a lonely sea. I stroked the side of his face. He looked up at me, smiled and placed a hand on my stomach as he pushed backward, encouraging me to lie down. I laid one arm behind my head to look down at Roger more easily as he knelt between my legs. He released my belt from my pants, then used his teeth to pop the button. He looked up at me as he took my zipper in his teeth and dragged it down.

He was soon exploring the skin right over the pair of boxer briefs I was wearing with his tongue. "No pink flamingos this time?" he asked.

"Huh?" I said absently.

"The first time I ever saw you, you were wearing a pair of boxer briefs with pink flamingos."

"How do you remember that?"

"Trust me… That image is etched permanently into my brain, like this one will be." He reached under me and gently helped nudge my pants out from beneath my hips. Then he lifted one of my feet to take the shoe off…then the other. He left my socks on. Then he smoothly slid my pants down and off my body.

With my pants removed, my cock was on full alert, trapped beneath my underwear, wanting to break free.

Roger leaned forward and nestled my crotch next to his cheek before using his tongue to trace the full length of it, still trapped. I reached down to free it, but Roger sprang forward, lifting himself off the ground and on top of me, pinning my arms above my head to the bed.

"Not yet," he whispered into my ear. "I want you to beg me to release it."

He slid a hand up under my sweater and found my left nipple, which he rolled in his fingers as he pressed his lips to mine. His right hand still held both of my arms to the bed. I let him stay in control for a second. I didn't want him to think I was an easy mark, so I bucked my hips, catching Roger off guard. Using more force than he had anticipated, I rolled Roger sideways off me and came up straddling his hips.

I reached back and undid his belt without needing to turn around. I popped the button on his pants and slid the zipper down. I reached behind me and slowly used my index finger to trace the outline of Roger's cock. There was a small wet spot at the tip. *God, I love pre-cum.* I rolled my thumb in it as it seeped through the underwear, then brought it up to my lips and tasted him.

"God, that's fucking hot," Roger said. "How do I taste?"

"Best dessert ever," I said as I lay down on top of him, resting my head beneath his chin. I ground myself into his crotch.

Beneath me, Roger shuffled his legs. There was the distinct sound of one, then two, shoes hitting the ground. "Wanna do me a favor and slip my pants off?" Roger said between kisses. I pushed myself off the bed, standing at the edge. Roger lifted his hips to help me finish taking his pants off. His cock was barely being held in his shorts.

I reached down and scooped up my cell phone from the floor. It must have slipped out of my pants pocket when Roger helped me out of them. "Mind if I put on some music?" I asked.

"Go right ahead," Roger watched as I walked to the front of the bed and fiddled with Dylan's equipment until I found the iPhone jack. The computer was already on, so soft music filled the air. "Who is this?" Roger asked.

"Sigur Rós' *Takk*. It was listed online as one of the best albums to fuck to," I said without turning around. I let my hips slowly groove to the music. Roger was suddenly sitting behind me on the edge of the bed, his legs on either side of me. He gently pulled me backward as I continued my little dance. I lowered my ass to his crotch and ground on him. I lifted my undershirt and sweater from my body and let them fall to a clump beside the bed. I turned around and helped Roger out of his.

The only thing between Roger's cock and me was now a pair of black boxer briefs, so I lowered myself to my knees. I mouthed his entire shaft up and down beneath the shorts before finally slipping a finger under the waistband and freeing just the head of Roger's dick. I used my tongue to explore the underside of his cock, licking it. While I let my tongue tease him, I pulled the rest of his cock out until the front part of his shorts slipped beneath his balls. I licked his shaft slowly from the head to his balls. I took one into my mouth and licked around it, then repeated the treatment with his other one. When I could tell Roger had enough of my playing around with his balls, I reached under his hips and pulled his underwear the rest of the way off. I leaned back and looked at the rod standing in front of me. He was maybe eight inches long, but he was damn thick.

I looked up from my position and saw Roger propped up on one arm, watching me. We made eye contact as I started at the base of his shaft, and I licked all the way up the underside until only the tip of my tongue lapped around the opening. Roger's cockhead had a nice, wide opening, so I let my tongue explore the hole, while I gently stroked up and down with my right hand as I pulled on his balls slightly with my other hand. Roger moaned but didn't break eye contact. When I thought he couldn't take any more teasing, I opened my mouth and started to take him down my throat.

I must have looked like an anaconda unhitching its jaws as I swallowed Roger's cock. When my nose hit his bone, I didn't stop. I needed to let my gag reflex get used to his cock tickling the back of my throat. *Swallow, don't fight it*, I reminded myself. The tip of Roger's cock moved quickly past my gag reflexes. I pumped him up and down at the base a few times before rising, taking a gulp of air and going down on Roger again. At some point, Roger stopped making eye contact. His head had rolled back on the bed, and he whimpered under me in pleasure.

I was tired of going down, but I didn't want to lose momentum. I stood, slipped my boxers off and put my knees on either side of Roger's pelvis, barely keeping my weight from toppling backward. I grabbed his cock and started rubbing it against my hole. I wanted to feel him buried inside me. Roger sat up and threw his arms around me.

"My turn," he said.

Flipping me over, he pinned me down on the bed and shifted himself to lie sideways as he licked from my pubic bone to my balls. In a swift move, Roger had both of my balls in his mouth and was licking around them while lightly pulling on them with his teeth. A moan escaped me, unlike none I had ever known.

I put one arm behind my head so I could watch. I caressed Roger's face with my free hand while he licked my cockhead. I lifted his face after a couple minutes to look into his eyes. He smiled, then sucked me all the way down—and did it again and again. I writhed in pleasure under him as he directed me to fuck his throat. At one point, I reached a hand down and held the back of Roger's head as he went up and down on me. I wasn't forcing him down. I just wanted to feel his head beneath my hand while he hungrily slurped.

Before long, I couldn't stand it. Seeing Roger's cock pointing toward me made me swing around to face it while he was still going down on me. Sixty-nining on the bed, I lost myself as wave after wave of pleasure rolled over me when we swallowed each other's cocks.

I slipped from Roger's lips. I looked down to see a string of pre-cum hanging from my tip to Roger's lips. He lapped hungrily after it. I swiveled around and kissed him. "God, you're gorgeous," I said, looking down on him.

"You ain't too bad yourself, Wes."

I rocked myself into position right over his pelvis. When I positioned his cock behind me, he didn't stop me. I was about to slip inside him, but he pulled me forward and kissed me one more time.

"You know, I don't have to fuck you unless you want me to. I want you to do what is comfortable. With that said, I'm on PrEP and passed my last STI test a week ago."

"I'm on PrEP, too, and the only person I've had sex with is Dylan, and he was tested earlier this week. So, if you want to fuck me, I want to feel you in me. I want you to come inside me and not stop until you finish shooting," I whispered back into his ear. I reached over to the nightstand and grabbed the lube. Before sliding a finger inside my ass, I squeezed out a healthy amount onto Roger's dick.

"Let me do that," Roger said. I handed him the lube and he squirted some on his hand. As Roger slid one finger inside me, I got on all fours. I took a deep breath and let it out as one then two fingers entered me. He angled his hand so he could easily stroke my prostate, which sent me into an ecstatic high.

"I want you in me."

Roger lay on his back and I grabbed his rock-hard shaft and angled it toward my ass. I poked the head against my hole and pushed back. Roger let out a sigh as he pushed past my first muscle. As I slowly let him slide into me, I let out a calming breath. I took my time going all the way down. When his head passed the internal sphincter, my insides opened to take all of him. I knew Roger was long, but I didn't realize he was that long.

I raised myself up, then slid down again. Roger reached out and grabbed both of my hands to help steady me as I went up and down. I looked into his intense gaze as he entered me repeatedly.

"Ready to switch positions?" Roger asked. "Your knees have got to be ready for a break."

I hadn't paid attention to anything but the sensation of him sliding in and out of me, but now that he mentioned it, my legs were stiffening a bit.

I nodded.

Roger sat up suddenly, keeping inside me. He wrapped his arms around me, and I instinctively wrapped my legs around him as he gently lowered me onto my back while he faced me. He bent down and kissed me as he pulled out and slammed back into me. Our kiss caught my sudden intake of breath as the power of Roger's abdominal muscles slammed his cock into my ass for the first time. He kept kissing as he pulled out and did it again. This time I was ready for the urgency in Roger's fucking.

I grabbed my dick and started beating on it. Roger looked down and added some spit to my jerking off to help me. He looked at me and asked, "How are you doing? Need more lube?"

"Maybe a bit. Not dry yet, but don't want it to get there."

Roger built up some spit in his mouth before letting it drop and fall on my ass as he gently guided the spit into me. He did it a second time, then went back to fucking me like a jackhammer.

"Oh fuck, I think I'm gonna co—" I didn't get the entire word out before streams of cum covered my stomach, chest and forehead. I quickly wiped at the drizzle on my brow to stop it from running down into my eye. Nothing kills the mood faster than 'cum eye'. That shit stings.

Roger leaned down and licked the cum off my chest before transferring a bit to me in a deep kiss. I could taste myself on Roger, which totally kept me standing at attention.

"Oh, fuck!"

I felt Roger's orgasm inside me before he warned me. He pumped and pumped for what felt like hours, emptying himself in me. My ass milked it out of him, enjoying every drop.

Roger finally let out a breath and eased his way out of me, catching his breath. "Holy shit," was all he said. When his breathing normalized, he added, "I haven't had an orgasm like that…ever. Whoa."

He pulled up next to me on the bed. Our naked bodies pressed into each other. We lay in silence, staring at each other. I reached up and caressed the stubble on his cheek. When I pulled my hand away, Roger followed it down to my lips and kissed me.

We kissed for a few minutes, then I flipped over and pushed my back into his chest, wanting to be the little spoon. Roger wrapped his arm around my stomach, and I interlaced my fingers with his.

Chapter Fourteen

Roger

I woke a few hours later. I swore I heard a dinging sound but thought I must be hearing things. The sun was poking through the blinds. Before I opened my eyes, I smelled him next to me…my little spoon. Wes fit so perfectly next to my chest. Feeling him there caused me to stir, but I didn't want to wake him with my raging hard-on pressing against his ass for more. As much fun as that could be, it was probably a bit much for a first date. Instead, I willed little Roger to take a breather and enjoyed feeling Wes next to me.

"I know you're awake." Wes' voice groggily broke through the silence. "Your breathing changed."

"Good morning, babe," I said, leaning in to kiss the back of his neck. Wes responded by rocking his pelvis backward toward my crotch. "Hey, if you keep that up, we'll have a repeat performance of last night."

Ding!

"What is that?" I asked.

"What was what?" Wes responded.

"I swear I heard a bell."

"Probably Dylan's computer," Wes mumbled through a yawn. "Go back to sleep."

Wes shivered next to me, so I nestled in against Wes' back, wrapping my arm around him to bring him closer. We were both still stark naked. Thankfully, Dylan's apartment had been warm enough that neither of us had felt the need to sleep under the covers. Once my body was firmly beside his, he relaxed into me and fell back to sleep.

I closed my eyes and wanted to enjoy the moment. Wes' little snores were adorable. I could get used to waking up like this every day. *Ding! Ignore it*, I told myself.

I lost track of time, and a little while later, Wes stirred next to me. He yawned and said, "You let me fall back to sleep."

"I didn't let you do anything. You fell asleep and were just too cute to wake back up. Besides, I don't even think you were awake the first time."

"True, but I know a way I could wake you up." His voice had a level of mischievousness to it that let me know our minds were thinking the same thing. My stomach growled. Nothing kills a sexy mood like a grumbling tummy.

"Guess someone is hungry," Wes said.

"You know, we could get up, go to breakfast and come back for round two," I said.

"I like your thinking." He pulled away from me and scooted over to the edge of the bed. The sun broke through in stripes across his pale back. He had perfectly flawless white skin. I stood, saw that amazing ass in front of me. My cock stood at attention.

Wes looked behind and said, "Are you coming," but looked down and saw my erection and said, "I thought you said you were hungry?"

"I am, but he," I said, gesturing to my dick, "has a mind of his own."

"Don't they always." He reached a hand down to me. I wanted to pull him back onto the bed for round two right then but let him pull me off the bed instead. He led me to a bathroom connected to the room, and I joined him for a shower.

Thirty minutes later, we climbed out. We took that long because we rubbed one out in the shower to keep things moving. Wes got out first and handed me a towel. I dried off and went back into the room. I found my underwear and slipped them on. When Wes stepped out of the bathroom, I threw his to him, which hit him in the chest and dropped to the ground in front of him.

"Sorry about that," I said, stifling a laugh.

Wes smiled, turned around and made a huge show of slipping his underwear past the curves of his ass cheeks. He jiggled them slightly in my direction.

"Unless you want me to rip them off you," I said, looking at Wes' backside, "I would recommend against doing that for now."

We quickly found the rest of our clothes and put them on. "We should probably run by my place and pick up clean clothes before going out in public," Wes said. "I'm a bit of a wrinkled mess."

"That makes two of us. And these pants are allegedly wrinkle-free."

We left the room, and I was surprised by the sudden scent of coffee filling the air.

"Dear God, it's about time you woke up. I thought I would have to go in and dump a bucket of cold water on you two."

I stopped in mid-step. It took me a second to recognize Jackson's voice...*err, Dylan. I think Wes told me his name was Dylan.*

"Uhh," was all Wes got out before we were both standing in the living room staring at Dylan over in the kitchen. He was already pouring two mugs of coffee.

"Don't be shy now. Come. Get your coffee. From what I can tell, you two didn't exactly get much sleep last night," Dylan said with a smirk. "I'm Dylan, by the way."

The young man took me in, then extended his hand for a shake. I grabbed it, saying, "Roger Havemeyer." Dylan gave my hand a solid squeeze. He reached around, grabbed a coffee mug and handed it to me.

"Got any cream?" I asked.

"But of course," Dylan said. He walked over to the refrigerator and pulled out a small carton of half and half. "Our boy, Wes here, drinks his black, just like my soul." Dylan reached around, grabbed the third cup of coffee and handed it to Wes. I'd already added my cream, so I handed the carton back to Dylan, who left it on the counter.

I glanced between Wes and Dylan, and Wes rolled his eyes and said, "Don't listen to this jackass. He's trying to be protective."

"It's good when you have friends who will look out for you in life. We all need someone watching our backs," I acknowledged. My hand rested on the small of Wes' back. I towered over Wes and Dylan, since both men were the same height and I had at least four inches on each of them.

"I take it you enjoyed watching Wes' back." Dylan smiled. "You two put on quite a little show last night. Even in my bedroom, I could hear Wes."

"We were not that loud," Wes cut in. He turned and looked at me. "Were we?"

"No," I said. I was still wary of Dylan. From his reaction, I wondered if he'd hidden his actual feelings about Wes.

"Speaking of last night, why are you here?" Wes asked. "You said you were going down to the city and would be there overnight."

Dylan motioned to a small kitchen table, and we sat down. Wes scooted his chair so he could be right next to me, with Dylan on the other side. Dylan took a drink of his coffee and watched us. I slunk one arm around Wes' shoulders, and Wes leaned into the nook of my arm.

"God, you two are disgustingly cute. They could make Hallmark Channel movies about you," Dylan said as he apparently decided I wasn't out to do Wes harm. "How'd you two meet?"

"Coffee shop," I said without hesitation. I saw Wes shoot me a quick glance from the corner of my eye, but I kept Dylan's gaze and continued. "I moved here right before the new year. When I met Wes, I had just purchased a house. I got a bit distracted looking at him and dumped a cup of coffee at his feet. Not my smoothest way of introducing myself."

"That was you?" Dylan asked. Clearly, he'd heard the story.

"That was me."

"Wes talked about you for over a week after that. I had to shove my cock down his throat to get him to shut up," Dylan joked.

Dylan watched to see if I would react. I turned my head and kissed Wes on the forehead.

"You never answered Wes' question about what happened to you last night," I said before lifting my coffee to my lips. I could tell immediately it was one of the house brews from Java Junkie. I was already getting a pretty good nose and taste of the blend.

"Well, I got out of here later than anticipated. I drove down into Kingston, but the snow was coming down too hard and fast, so I turned around and hightailed it home." Dylan lifted his mug in both hands and took a drink before setting it down and continuing. "I was a little surprised when I came home and the lights in the living room were on. Then I heard Wes moan — or maybe it was you, Roger. I don't remember. All I know is that it didn't take a genius to know what you two were up to in my spare bedroom."

"You told me I could bring a guy over here any time," Wes said.

"That I did. And despite the third degree, I don't mind."

"I'm surprised you didn't barge in and try to join us," Wes joked.

Dylan turned and looked at me before saying, "Sorry. I'm not into daddy types."

Wes' whole body tensed next to mine. I was afraid he was about to explode, but the tension eased out of him before he said, "I already told you, Dylan, that Roger is not my sugar daddy. He's a genuinely great guy and fucking fantastic lover."

"I know, I know. Trust me, I know. I'm being an ass. Ignore me." Dylan then turned his head and looked at me. "You'll find that Wes' inner circle friends are all a little protective of him."

"Are you talking about you and Autumn?" I asked. "Autumn was the one who practically threw us together when the two of us were playing googly eyes at each other."

"That's what Wes told me," Dylan said.

"Why act like you don't know who I am?" I questioned. "I mean, I'm trying to figure out your angle."

"I'm sorry. Just grouchy is all." Dylan stood suddenly and looked down at us. "Despite what you may think, I'm not pining after Wes."

"I didn't—"

"I know you didn't," Dylan said. "I want to make sure you know that I'm not trying to get in the middle of you two. I'm really not. I want to make sure Wes doesn't get hurt. He's already experienced too much of that." Dylan put his coffee mug in the sink and rinsed it out. "Anyway," he said, looking at Wes, "I'm glad you came here last night. Truly, I am. As for me, I'm either going back to bed or taking a shower. I haven't decided which yet." Dylan turned and walked away.

"Well, that was weird," Wes said once the door to Dylan's room closed. "He's not normally like…like…whatever that was."

"He's worried about you. If our roles were reversed, I probably would have made a much larger ass of myself than he did."

"That's sweet of you to say," Wes replied, "but we both know that isn't true." He reached up and patted me on the cheek, then lowered me down to kiss him.

Almost immediately, my cock sprang back to life. Wes let out a light moan as we kissed. He glanced down and saw my growing appendage then reached down and patted it gently. "I don't think you should fuck me on his kitchen table. Would serve him right, but I'm still hungry."

With that, he stood, reached out his arms and grabbed my hands. He leaned back using all his weight until I gave in and stood. I reached forward and threw my arms around him and drew him into me. With no coaxing, he threw his legs around me and I started walking both of us toward the front door while we continued our kiss. We only stopped because we couldn't put our coats on, clinging to each other. I pulled away from him, pulled down his coat and helped him into it. I shrugged into my own.

"Why didn't you let me help you with your coat?" he asked.

"I'm taller. That would be harder to pull off."

He squared off with me and looked me straight in the eyes. "I am not fragile, despite what Dylan may have said back there. I don't want you to treat me with kid gloves. If this" — he waved his index finger between us —"is going to work, you can't treat me like a kid."

"I don't want to treat you like a kid. I don't see you as a kid. Just don't call me daddy," I said with a smile. "If you do, I'll bend you over my knees and give you a spanking."

"Flirt!" Wes spun around, grabbed the door handle, twisted and pulled it open. "You never know, I might like it when you spank me...Daddy."

He leaped forward, laughing before I could grab him. "I warned you what would happen if you used that word," I joked as I made sure the door to the apartment was closed then ran after him.

Chapter Fifteen

I wanted Wes to like me. I felt like I was thirteen again, having my first boy crush on Ricky Garcia, a neighbor who lived down the street from me. Ricky had been two years older than me, and I'd always sensed there was something about him that made him like me. I know some of the other kids around the block made fun of Ricky for his less than masculine hobbies. Last I'd heard, Ricky had married a woman and lived out in Fresno with a litter of little ones.

But in my early teen years, I had been drawn to Ricky and wanted him to like me. In retrospect, I think Ricky represented a force of nature that I was enthralled by. Despite all the teasing he got from other guys, he was unabashedly himself and would kick anyone's ass who confronted him to his face. Sure, kids had talked about him behind his back, but no one was stupid enough to say it to his face. Me? I was everything the kids said Ricky was, but since I played sports, no one had pointed their fingers at me. I had wanted Ricky's 'go fuck yourself' attitude. I'd always been attracted to men who were sure of themselves. Even Wes, despite his past and age, was pretty sure what he wanted out of life and how he would get it.

Wes and I spent all Sunday together. After we escaped Dylan's interrogation, where he all but asked, 'what are your intentions toward my son?' he took me to his favorite place to have brunch. I followed him to his apartment so he could get a change of clothes. I opted to stay in the SUV this time under the pretense of keeping the heater going. In all reality, I wasn't ready to meet Pietro. Over breakfast, Wes had gushed about his brotherly love affair with the infamous Pietro. After the inquisition earlier that morning, I didn't feel like surviving a second one.

The door to the Pathfinder opened, and Wes hauled himself inside with a duffel bag. "I've got all the essentials in here," Wes told me. The plan was to go head out to my place where I could throw on a new pair of clothes, then we could spend the rest of the day lounging around my abode, just chilling and getting to know each other better. And by getting to know each other, we both knew what that meant, inside and out. By the end of the day, I planned to have licked, sucked, tweaked or nibbled on every inch of Wes' body. And I wanted to encourage Wes to explore mine like he was Sir Edmund Hillary exploring Mount Everest for the first time. The invite had been to spend the entire day, with the understanding that I'd bring him back early the next morning to make sure he got to work on time.

I drove out to my place. Wes commented on how 'in the country' I really lived. When I finally turned off the road to head up to my house, I was glad to see that my snowplow driver had already been up there and cleared the way for me.

"Holy shit," Wes exclaimed as I drove across my stone bridge. "You said you lived in a log cabin, but you failed to mention it was a fucking mansion."

"Technically, it's not a mansion, but it's admittedly a lot of house. It was owned by Gerry Greenwich," I told him.

"Should I know who that was?" Wes asked.

"Probably not. He was a music producer back in the sixties and seventies. Greenwich started as a music writer but switched over to producing when he realized there was a ton more money to be made on that end than as a writer. He founded Platinum Studios in the Brill Building in New York City, which occupied the space where my firm is today."

"Did you know him? Is that how you bought the place? Would I recognize any of the people, albums or songs he produced?" Wes asked in rapid succession.

I started with the last series of questions and gave him a brief history of the various artists Gerry Greenwich had worked with back in the day. "As for did I know him? Not at all. I didn't even know he was the owner until after I'd made an offer on the house. At that point, I got a bit more information about the history of the place and found out about Gerry. It's pure luck I bought this place."

"Luck…or divine intervention?" Wes mused.

I pulled up in the driveway. Wes jumped out of the SUV. I heard the light crunch sound as his feet hit the snow outside. I followed suit. Wes slung his duffel over his shoulder, holding it with one hand resting there. He looked like a knight ready to storm the castle, so I kept the keys out of my pocket, walked up to the front door, opened it and let him storm.

He dropped his bag just inside the front door and moved to take off his shoes and hang his coat on the coat rack that was standing in the foyer. I walked him through the place. I showed him the first floor, then the second and the third, where I had a spectacular view of the entire area.

"See that building out there?" I said, pointing off to the rectangular building on the other side of the lawn. "There's a nice firepit in there, and it's right next to the hot tub."

"Awesome," he said, mesmerized by everything. "Though, in the dead of winter, how do you get from the house to there?"

"Well, if you were planning on streaking there, I would highly recommend against it. It's best to grab a towel and keep your clothes on until you're out there."

"You sound like a man who has learned this from experience." Wes eyed me with a grin on his face.

"I may have tried running butt-ass naked through the snow once. All was great until I stepped on a twig, which hurt like a bitch, and I went sprawling face-first into the snow. Landing in a snowbank in the dead of winter with no clothes on made my dick crawl inside my body for protection. Talk about shrinkage. I was closer to the hot tub than to the house, so I pulled myself up and made the last dash there."

"And afterward?"

"Yeah, going from the hot tub back onto the frozen land was another experience I would rather forget. So, for your own edification, don't follow in my footsteps."

He laughed. I turned and looked at him. His smile brightened up the room. Hell, his presence brightened up my entire house. I couldn't stop myself. I pulled him closer and started nibbling on his neck. And that was probably the last time either of us wore clothes until I was driving him to work the next morning.

I'd set the alarm for five a.m., so Wes could run through the shower and get ready. I laid in bed snuggling in the warmth left from the combined heat of Wes' and my bodies until I heard the shower go off. I dragged myself out of bed, then threw on a pair of sweats and a sweatshirt. When Wes walked in, I was just tying my shoes.

"Give me just a couple minutes," I said as I headed into the bathroom. Wes followed me and watched as I peed then brushed my teeth. Not the sexiest image first thing in the morning, but he seemed to enjoy watching me, so I let him.

Once my breath was fresh, I reached over and pulled him in for a kiss. "Let's go," I said when I let him go. "I don't want to be the reason you're late for work."

We walked outside. I'd already hit the remote start on the Pathfinder, so it was toasty when we got inside. I drove Wes into Woodstock. We were a few minutes early, so Wes and I used those few extra minutes together to leave each other breathless and wanting more — a lot more.

I let out a sigh when Wes left the warmth of the car and headed into the coffee shop. I pulled out of the parking lot and headed back to my place, where I planned on catching a couple more hours of sleep before I had my first meeting of the morning.

* * * *

Monday and Tuesday had flown by in a haze of Zoom meetings and campaign approvals. I had to take the graphic design file from Richard Salzman and tweak it in a few places before I sent it out to the producer of a new musical getting launched later that spring. Half of my tweaking had been looking at font combinations to determine which ones I liked and which ones I didn't. I had once sat through a lecture from a font designer on the science of fonts. She had droned on and on about font pairings. I had thought I would never need to know such senseless information, but boy, had I been wrong.

Tuesday evening, I had hosted a small dinner out at my place. Wes couldn't make it because he had an evening class. I had cheated and had the meal catered. I'd finished with the catering van when Dale and Talgat pulled up in his black Pathfinder and parked next to my gay-ass blue one.

"I see you went to the same cooking school Dale did?" Talgat said, stepping down from the vehicle.

"Yep. Who needs the CIA when you have Yellow Pages," I joked as both men followed me into the house.

"Do they still make Yellow Pages?" Dale asked.

I had to think about it for a second, but I had never received a physical phone book since I moved in. "I honestly don't know. I don't think I have a phone book."

"Thank God for the Internet and apps," Dale quipped. "Speaking of which, can I get your password? I have no bars out here. I'm waiting on an email from my granddad."

"Not a problem. It's DaleSucksTalgatsCock69!" The best part was Dale typed that in as if that would be the most natural password in the world for me to have at my house. "I'm joking," I finally cut in.

"I wondered, but ya know... Whatever floats your boat. If you want to dream of me going down on my boyfriend, be my guest."

I glanced over at Talgat, who turned an interesting shade of red. "Sorry," I said to Talgat. "You know how the two of us get when we get together."

"I do. The two of you would make a gaggle of sex workers blush."

"Gaggle of sex workers?" Dale asked. "Where did that come from? I totally would have gone with a swarm of sex workers…just for the alliteration."

"I personally would have gone with a pride of sex workers," I said.

"So, what has you in such a cheery mood tonight?" Dale asked. "If I didn't know any better… Holy fuck! What's his name?"

My eyes must have hit my hairline. I tried to squeak out a "What do you mean?" but even Talgat could see through that ruse.

"What's his name?" Dale said again.

"His name is Wesley, well, Wes. And before I jump into this, let's get a round of cocktails." I walked over to the bar in the living room and prepared a round of grasshopper martinis. I thought the combination of green crème de menthe, white crème de cacao and heavy cream would make an excellent starter cocktail. It also was one of my favorites, so I hoped Dale and Talgat would enjoy it. I knew Talgat was more of a beer guy, but he was queer, for God's sake. He had to like at least one cocktail.

I finished making them and the doorbell rang. *Saved by the bell.* "Be right back," I said as I walked to the entryway. I opened the door and found Ruby and Stephanie on my doorstep. Stephanie held out a bottle of wine.

"I told her it wasn't necessary, but she insisted," Stephanie said, gesturing to Ruby.

"In the South, you never show up for a dinner party empty-handed. That's just not done."

"Well, thank you," I said, grabbing the bottle. It was a nice Argentinian Malbec that I recognized and found delectable. "I love this vineyard. Come on in. You can hang your coats on the coat rack, and Dale and Talgat are already drinking martinis in the living room. I figure we'll hang out for a while. Then we can move into the dining room where dinner is waiting."

"Did you cook?" Stephanie asked.

"Oh God, no. I wouldn't do that to anyone. I can burn water," I joked. "I had it catered. So much easier."

I walked into the living room and immediately made more cocktails for Ruby and Stephanie.

"Don't think you're off the hook," Dale said. "Tell us about your new man. So, who is this mysterious Wes?"

I turned and did my best to look at Dale, but I saw the slight smirk on Ruby's face and the hint of a judgmental one on Stephanie's face. *Well, fuck!*

"Where should I begin?" I asked.

"How about the fact that he's twenty?" Stephanie muttered.

"Yep. I had a date with someone half my age." I figured being blunt about it was easier. Kind of like ripping off a Band-Aid.

"Good for you," Dale said. "Train them when they're young."

"How did you two meet?" Ruby asked.

"Coffee shop," I said. I turned and looked at Ruby and added, "Actually, I guess I should thank you. After I signed the papers in your office and you'd given me my first taste of Java Junkie, I had gone inside. Wes made me a flat white, and I, being the clumsy goof I am sometimes, dropped it right at his feet. I hate to admit it, but I hadn't paid attention to him until I saw his eyes flash in shock as the cup and coffee tumbled to the floor."

"Ahh, yes," Dale said. "The age-old gay love story. Try to scald the guy first, then date him." There was a look of puzzlement on Dale's face for a second, and he asked, "What took you so long to go on a date? You signed those papers like weeks ago."

I sat down on a love seat and took a sip of my cocktail. As I watched Stephanie's face, I wish I had added vodka to mine...lots of it. "Well, I had a hard time getting over the age difference. I figured it was a simple crush, and it was only on my side, so I had no intentions of making a move. I was in there last week having coffee, and Wes' best friend, Autumn" — *Sorry, you're not here to defend yourself, so you're totally getting thrown under the bus* — "came up and was kind of like, '*He likes you. I think you like him. Go on a date already,*' so we did."

"That's...actually kind of cute," Dale said with a roll of his eyes. "More importantly, how did it go?"

"He's...charming — and a hell of a lot more mature for his age than he should have to be."

"Well, he's had a rough go of it," Stephanie said.

"You know him?" Dale asked, utterly oblivious to the tension in the room.

"Yes," Stephanie said coldly.

"My wife over here is a protective mama bear when it comes to Wes. Almost makes me want to have our own children...almost." The joke was an attempt at breaking the tension, but honestly, I thought it made everything seem more awkward.

"Well, shall we move into the dining room?" I asked, hoping that a change of scenery would at least put an end to this conversation.

"I'm starving," Ruby said. She lifted the corner of her lip to let me know that she understood.

I rose, and the rest of the group followed me into the dining room where the caterers had set up the spread, complete with the little tea lights to keep the food warm. It was buffet-style, so I encouraged everyone to fill their plates. As I watched them go through the line, I realized I'd ordered enough food to feed a small army. There would be leftovers for a week…if not longer.

Thankfully, the rest of dinner steered away from my love life. Stephanie seemed to cheer up a bit as the conversation about Wes and me turned into more mundane, less controversial topics like politics and religion. After dinner, I made coffee, which I had picked up that morning from Java Junkie. It gave me a reason to get up early and go see Wes at work. Thankfully, no one asked about the blend.

Before long, it was time to usher everyone out of the house. I walked all of them to the front door and turned on the outside lights.

"Thanks for coming," I told Dale and Talgat as they left.

"It was good seeing you," Talgat said as he leaned in for a quick hug.

Dale followed suit but whispered in my ear when he hugged me. "Have fun with the young'n. Don't worry about Stephanie." I smiled.

Ruby gave me a good, firm handshake on her way out. The last to leave was Stephanie, who still eyed me warily. Finally, she let out a slight huff and said, "Don't break his heart. He's already been through so much."

"I have no intention of doing that," I said. "I know it may be unconventional, but I do like him. The last thing I want to do is hurt him." Stephanie gave me a curt nod and left. Both couples got into their vehicles and drove away.

I looked at the time and realized that Wes would already be in the middle of his Tuesday night show. Even though I'd already tasted every inch of his body, I still got excited at the prospect of watching him perform online. I hurried upstairs and hoped I hadn't missed the climax.

Chapter Sixteen

Wes

Autumn's and my schedules didn't line up on Monday and Tuesday. Her slate of courses at the Culinary Institute had her running ragged this semester. She worked late afternoon and evening shifts while I was doing more of the early morning, which was a total reversal compared to what we had in the fall. Thankfully, our shifts overlapped on Wednesday, and we finally had time to catch up. Well, we would have caught up, but we were slammed.

I ran to Stefan's office because I needed another pair of hands. I knocked lightly on the door and heard, "Come in."

"Stefan, can we get your help for a bit? We're totally slammed."

"What? Three customers came in at once?" Stefan snarked.

"Hardy har har," I snarked back. "Actually, there's a line out of the door."

Stefan looked at me incredulously, but he came out to help me, anyway. As soon as he stepped out of his office, he asked, "Where did all these people come from?"

"Haven't a clue," I said, hurrying back to help Autumn catch up with the drink orders.

We spent the next ninety minutes running around like crazy people, trying to serve everyone who was there. During the morning, we found out that a tourist group was from Canada and heading over to the museum at Bethel Woods, but let the whole bus do some shopping in the actual town of Woodstock before heading over there for a late lunch.

It was obvious when the tour guide came in, because she was half the age of everyone else and wore an official polo shirt for the bus company. She ordered a mocha. While I made the drink, I asked her, "You realize that Bethel Woods is like almost ninety minutes from here? We're not on the way. We're not even in the same county."

That's one of those little tidbits of information you grow up learning about living in Woodstock. The actual town of Woodstock had little to do with the infamous outdoor concert. In fact, at no point was it ever going to be in Woodstock. The original idea was to have it up in Saugerties, north of Woodstock, but still in Ulster County. Then it got moved to Wallkill down in Orange County, but the concert quickly grew beyond what the town board in Wallkill would allow. Finally, a farmer in Sullivan County offered his farm for ten-thousand-dollars for the three-day event. And the rest, as they say, is history.

"Oh yeah, trust me," the tour guide said, "part of my explanation this morning was how the name

'Woodstock' came from the name of the people who financially backed the concert, 'Woodstock Ventures'. I'm always amazed at how few people actually realize this."

I finished with her mocha and handed it to her. "Well, if you're ever going to be coming through here again, please call and give us a heads up. I promise, there will be a free coffee in it for you." I knew I didn't technically have the authority to do this, but I'd pay for her mocha if it meant we could have called in a little backup.

"Will do," she said. "Depending on how this Music of America tour goes, we'll probably be back again this spring."

"Where do you go next?" I asked as Autumn handed me the next order, and I got to work.

"We're heading down to New York City for two days. We're going to hit a lot of historic places that made an impact on the development of American music."

"Such as?" I said, turning on the frother.

"Tin Pan Alley, Carnegie Hall, the Brill Building —"

"My boy —" I stopped myself from completing that sentence because I wasn't sure what we were yet. "The guy I started seeing works in the Brill Building. Well, he's up here now. He bought a home from some guy who was a music producer, Gerry Greenwich. Ever hear of him?"

I took it as an immediate yes from the excited look on the woman's face. "Wow, Gerry Greenwich was a musical genius. His company, Platinum Studios, put out a ton of hits in the sixties and seventies. That's *so* cool."

We chatted off and on for the next twenty minutes as I made drinks, and she told me about the awesome things the tour was doing. After New York, the bus would head over to Nashville, Tennessee, to see another of the major hotspots of the music industry in the United States before heading up to Detroit then back into Canada. All-in-all, it sounded like an exciting tour if you were into music history. I couldn't wait to get off work so I could tell Roger about my morning.

Thankfully, things slowed down eventually. I went through the place and cleaned because we hadn't had the chance when all the Canadians had been getting coffee. I was wiping off a table when Stefan approached me and asked, "Can you stay for a couple of extra hours? We're almost out of coffee. I need to do another roasting. I haven't had to do a second roasting since before Christmas."

"Not a problem," I said. "I don't have class on Wednesdays, so I'm good to go as long as I'm out of here by five. I have a hot date at six." As soon as the words were out of my mouth, I kind of regretted them.

"Oh really? Is this, by chance, with that older mystery guy I've seen you chummy in here?"

I didn't exactly dislike Stefan. He was my boss. And I didn't feel the need to go into my personal life with him.

"Yes, it is. His name is Roger."

"Well, you two seemed to *fit* together nicely. Anyway, I need to get roasting. I'll let you know once I'm done."

I eyed him warily as he spun and walked away.

"What was that about?" Autumn asked as she wiped off the table next to me.

"Stefan wanted to see if I could stay late while he roasted. Apparently, we're almost out of our reserves."

"Those Canadians loved our coffee. We sold out of our bags, and we burned through like ninety-five percent of our daily roast. If anyone comes in now hoping to buy a pound of coffee, they'll be out of luck. Hell, if Stefan doesn't get his roast on quickly, we won't have any coffee by mid-afternoon." She finished wiping the table and looked at me expectantly.

"Yes?" I said, not sure what she wanted.

"Your date? I haven't seen you since Saturday. Dish. I want all the details."

A new customer walked in, and I said, "It will have to wait. I need to go wash my hands before I make their coffee. Can you take their order?"

"On it." Autumn looked at the new customers and said, "I'll be right with you," as she headed behind the counter.

I made a beeline into the bathroom and washed my hands thoroughly before heading back out to make their coffees. These two wanted our fresh chai-tea lattes, which Autumn had to explain we had run out of that, too. Thankfully, the couple took it in stride and ordered caramel macchiatos instead. *How does one go from chai-tea to caramel macchiato? They're not even remotely in the same ballpark.* I didn't express my monologue, thankfully. If I questioned every strange order we received, I don't think we'd have very many repeat customers.

I had their drinks up in a jiffy, then leaned against the counter for the first time in a couple of hours to catch my breath. Autumn did the same thing.

"Well, this was a morning to remember," she said as she poured herself a cup of coffee. "Want one?" she asked.

"Yes. Dear Goddess, yes!"

She chuckled and poured me a large coffee before handing it off to me. "The date?" she asked, looking over the top of her lid.

"It was amazing. We went to dinner at Silvia's, then made out in the parking lot. It was snowing so hard, and he was worried about driving home with me following, so we ended up at Dylan's place."

"Why there?"

"Dylan was supposed to be out of town."

"*Supposed* to be?"

I quickly filled her in on all the details, including the grilling of Roger over coffee the next morning. As for what Roger and I did before sleeping, I left out the specific details other than to say we had a fantastic time together.

"We went back to his place—which is a fucking mansion, I might add—then spent the day there." Autumn arched an eyebrow but said nothing. "Okay, you got me. Let's just say our clothes came off, and I didn't put any on until the next morning when he brought me to work."

"That's almost domestic sounding," Autumn joked. "Good for you. Have you seen him again?"

"Our schedules haven't meshed, but I'm going out to his place tonight. He had a dinner party last night. Apparently, he has a ton of leftovers, so we're going to eat and chill."

"Why didn't you go to his dinner party last night?" Autumn asked.

"It wasn't like that. I was invited. I couldn't go because I have class on Tuesday evenings."

"I guess that's a good sign. It's not like he's trying to hide his *dirty little secret* from people.

"He's not like that. Well, not completely." I told Autumn about how he'd introduced me as a 'friend of the family' when we'd run into Ruby and Stephanie at Silvia's.

"Well, it was a first date, and he is twice your age. There's a lot of stigma among some people about older people dating younger people."

"Tell me about it. Dylan keeps calling Roger my sugar daddy, which is driving me fucking crazy."

"Have you talked to Dylan, since he basically caught you two having sex in his house?" Autumn asked.

"Just via texts. Since I didn't get to hang with him on Sunday because — well, you know — I was preoccupied. We haven't seen each other. I'm hoping to see him tomorrow evening."

Autumn rolled her eyes. "I know how Dylan can be. He hates to plan things too far in advance in case he has a better offer."

"It's not like that," I countered. "I mean, not really. Sure, if it's a hot guy he's going to have sex with or me, I will always take the backseat. But if I ever need him, he's always been there for me — just like you and just like Pietro."

"How is the roomie?"

"I haven't seen him much in the last few days. Between me hanging out with Roger and him hanging out with Valeria, we don't seem to be at the apartment much at the same time."

"If you want my advice... Well, I'm going to give it to you whether or not you want it. Make sure you keep your friendships close, even as you start dating Roger. I've seen too many friendships destroyed when one friend starts dating and has no time for their old friends. If you break up — and I hope you never do — but if you do, your friends will be there for you."

"I promise. Cross my heart and swear to God. Without you, Dylan and Pietro, I do not know where my life would be right now. You're not getting rid of me that easily."

She leaned in for a hug and another customer came strolling into the café.

"Welcome to Java Junkie Café & Roastery," Autumn said as she turned to greet our latest guest.

* * * *

After work, I went back to my apartment and took a quick shower before laying out a nice, casual, staying-in outfit. Okay, I wore the 'I'm going to Applebee's' outfit. I thought about pulling out the leather pants but decided I'd keep those for a special occasion.

When I was ready to go, I did a quick check in the mirror. I looked fucking hot. I'd totally do me in an Applebee's bathroom.

Pietro was at home for the first time in days, so I took a second to say hello and tell him I was heading to Roger's.

"When am I going to meet this mysterious Roger guy?" he asked, throwing a chip in his mouth while watching *SportsCenter* on television.

"Anytime. We'll get it set up. Maybe we can go on a double date," I said with mock excitement.

"Don't mock it. Valeria has already asked about that possibility."

"Really?"

"She wants to make sure this Roger guy is good enough for you."

"Ahh…that's sweet. Tell her I would love to go on a double date at some point. Maybe Valeria and I will even invite you and Roger. Anyway, I have to go. Have a good evening. Don't wait up."

Pietro smirked and threw another chip in his mouth as he refocused his attention on the television. What straight guys get out of watching *SportsCenter* for hours on end is beyond me.

The evening was chilly but not crazy cold. Thankfully, my weather app didn't have any sign of snow on the horizon for the evening, so I had that going for me tonight. I turned on the car and waited for the little monster to heat up.

* * * *

Roger

I hated admitting it, but I missed Wes. I was glad he'd not been at last night's little dinner party because he didn't need to see the looks Stephanie threw in my direction every ten minutes. Anyone with half a brain could tell that she did not like the idea of Wes dating me. I couldn't tell if she didn't like me, if she didn't like the idea of Wes dating *me* or if she didn't like the idea of Wes dating an older man.

I was hanging out in the kitchen when the doorbell rang. *Who could that be?* I asked, looking down at my watch. *Wes shouldn't be here for another thirty minutes at the earliest.* I threw a kitchen towel over my shoulder and headed to the front door.

I saw Chad standing on my front porch in his brown uniform when I looked through the peephole. I opened the door.

"I have a package for you, Roger," Chad said with all the sexual innuendo of a bad porn.

"Oh, hey, Chad." I tried to make my voice as noncommittal as possible. "Sadly, I'm waiting for someone to get here, so I can't accept any deliveries unless they come in an envelope or a box."

"Too bad," Chad said in his deep voice. "I've been hoping to make more deliveries here, but you're rarely home when I get to your place."

I may have dropped to the ground and hid behind a couch once or twice when he'd shown up at the house. I liked Chad and he was a great fuck, but I wanted to focus my attention on Wes. Even though Wes and I were not technically *dating*, I still didn't want to violate what we had...whatever it was. Even if I watched Wes get fucked by Dylan, I knew that was a job and not something Wes did to get his rocks off. Besides, I saw how he was with Dylan and how he was with me. I could tell the difference.

"Well, maybe another time. But do you have an actual package for me?"

"I do," Chad said. I could tell he was a little disappointed, but he kept his professional facade up. He whipped out an envelope that said 'priority' on it and handed it over to me after he scanned it. "Hope you have a great night. And I hope to see you again soon."

"Thanks, Chad," I said. He turned around and walked back to the delivery van.

I closed the door and opened the package. It was nothing special. Some contracts needed my signature. I'd sign them then drop them off tomorrow. I set them on the table next to the front door and went back to heating food.

The next time the doorbell rang, I knew it would be Wes, because he'd called me when he left his apartment to let me know he was on his way. I'd finished what I was doing and hurried toward the door. Part of me wanted to ditch my clothes along the way and greet him in the buff, but I refrained. I had hot food, and I didn't want it to go to waste.

I swung open the door and said, "Good evening, gorgeous." There was a beat before my brain took in who was standing in front of me and I said, "What the fuck are you doing here?"

Chapter Seventeen

Jeremy Wertheimer stood on my front porch, bundled up and looking at me with hopeful eyes.

"No, whatever it is... just no. *Fuck* no!" I said as I started to close the door.

Jeremy stuck his foot in the door and stopped me from slamming it in his face. "Hear me out. If you want me gone after that, I will turn around and head back to New York City, and you will never hear from me again."

I narrowed my eyes. "You have two minutes before I call the cops to let them know there's an intruder on my property."

"I know what I did with Avery was inexcusable."

I barked out a dismissive laugh. "You're down to one minute and thirty seconds." I didn't know the actual time, but I figured this would move things along.

"I wouldn't have gotten a rental car and driven to bum-fuck Egypt if I wasn't worried. Or maybe I've come to gloat and take your sanctimonious ass down a peg or two in person. When I learned about the video,"

Jeremy let out a slight chuckle that unnerved me, "I wanted to see you in person to let you know I watched it."

"What video? What are you talking about?"

"*The* video," Jeremy said as he stared at me, looking for some kind of recognition. "Holy fuck, you don't know." The surprised look on Jeremy's face caught me off guard, but the gleeful look that crossed it worried me more.

"What are you talking about?" I asked. "I don't have time for your games."

"Oh, honey," Jeremy said, a look of pity in his eyes. "I may have fucked Avery, but you fucked a prostitute on camera. *You* don't get to take the high road anymore."

"I've never been with a prostitute. Not once in my life have I paid for sex."

"Oh, so you fucked a prostitute on the Internet for free. I don't know if that makes it better or worse."

It hit me like a sledgehammer to my gut. "Show me." Jeremy scrunched up his face in confusion. "The video. Show me the video."

Jeremy quirked his lips up in a menacing smile. He pulled out his cell phone and played through a video.

"I enjoyed the part where you cuddled and went to sleep afterward. Apparently, a lot of guys are into watching people sleep together, because you two rolled in the money." I wrinkled my forehead. "Your tip jar," Jeremy said. "You know, all that money you made fucking on camera for the world to see." I tried to mask the shock and betrayal on my face, but I couldn't. "Oh, this gets even better. Mr. High and Mighty got rolled by a rent boy and didn't even know it. I don't know if I should laugh or pity you."

"Go… Just go."

"I mean… Oh, how the mighty have fallen."

"*Go!*" I screamed with all the fury I had burning in me. "Get the fuck off my property and never come back. If I see you again, Jeremy, I will have you forcibly removed," I said through clenched teeth.

Jeremy turned around and started walking back to the rental car he'd driven up to Woodstock in. He left one parting shot of information as he stood next to his car. "Since you don't have the video, I'll make sure you get it. In fact, I've already sent it to your work email."

"How the fuck? You shouldn't have cell service out here."

"True. But then maybe you shouldn't have used the same password up here for your Wi-Fi system."

I stood there dumbfounded and watched as he backed out. Thanks to the outdoor lights, I could still see the smug look on his face through the windshield. When his taillights headed down the driveway, I closed the door. I spun and raced up the stairs to my office on the second floor. I opened my browser and loaded my email. Sure enough, Jeremy had sent me a video…and copied it to my boss, Colleen.

Fuck! I felt numb. I couldn't feel my feet or my hands. I didn't know what to do. My heart raced, and my breath caught in my chest. *I think I'm having a heart attack.* Sharp pain in my chest made me wince. I tried to call nine-one-one but hit Dale's number instead.

"Hey, Roger," Dale said. It only took him a second to realize something was wrong. "Roger, are you there? Do you need me to call someone for help?"

"Can't…breathe. Think I'm dying."

"Roger, listen to me. Do you feel like a pressure or a stabbing in your chest?"

"Stabbing. It hurts."

"Talgat's calling nine-one-one, and we're on our way over. Listen to my voice. Do you have a spare key outside hidden somewhere? I don't want the EMTs to have to break down your house to get to you."

"Door's unlocked," I got out before the world around me dimmed, and I lost focus. I slumped to the floor. The carpet felt nice against my face.

* * * *

"What happened?" I heard Dale's voice ask. Someone held my hand tightly.

"Well, his EKG is reading normal. He's tachycardic, but no indications it was a heart attack. I shouldn't be telling you this. You're not technically family."

"We're the family he's got here. What happened?" It took my brain a moment to realize the second voice was Talgat's.

"He probably had a serious panic attack. Again, the doctor will want to run some tests to be sure, but it looks like that's what happened. Do either of you know of any specific trauma that would have caused this kind of massive panic attack?"

"No," Talgat said immediately. "You?"

"Me neither," Dale responded.

"Well, we gave him a sedative. Hopefully, he'll sleep through the night, and we can figure out what happened when the doctor finishes her tests."

"Thank you…"

"Cody, Cody Benton."

My eyes fluttered open and I blinked them a few times. "Where am I?" I croaked out, my mouth feeling like a desert.

"Drink this," a voice said.

Suddenly, there was a straw between my lips. I instinctively sucked in water. The cooling sensation helped to lubricate my mouth. I wrinkled my forehead and fluttered my eyes trying to wake up.

"Are you with me, Roger?"

I looked over and saw Dale sitting in the chair next to me. "Hey, Dale. What's happening?" I said with a half-smile.

"Thank God you're awake. You tell me. What do you remember?"

"Things are a bit foggy," I admitted. I blinked a few more times. Then suddenly, like an avalanche, the memories of Jeremy and the video flooded my mind. I started to have trouble breathing and suddenly had a stabbing sensation in my chest.

"Nurse!" I heard Dale yell.

I closed my eyes and tried to block out the world. The sound of rubber soles squeaked on the floor as someone ran into the room.

"Mr. Havemeyer, my name is Nurse Benton. You're having a panic attack. I need you to listen to my voice."

The back part of the bed started moving, and I found myself in a seated position.

"Don't try to fight it. I need you to concentrate on my voice. Are you listening to me?" A guttural sound escaped me. "I'm going to take that as a 'yes'. I'm going to walk you through this. I want you to start by focusing on your breathing. It's going to be hard, but I want you to focus on breathing in through your nose, then out through your mouth. In through your nose, out through your mouth."

The nurse continued this mantra for what felt like forever but was probably only a minute, maybe two.

But I did as he said. I breathed in through my nose and let it out of my mouth. The longer I did this, the slower my heart rate became. Eventually, I was just breathing.

"Okay, well, that definitely solidifies the diagnosis," Nurse Benton said. "He had a panic attack. Any idea what triggered it?"

I kept breathing.

"He was waking up. I asked him what he remembered, then all hell broke loose."

"Video," I mumbled.

"What was that?" Dale asked. I turned and looked at Dale. Dale clearly saw I didn't want to speak in front of the nurse. "I think we may need a bit of privacy."

The nurse narrowed his eyes. "You saw what I did. If he starts to have another attack, you start doing that and get me immediately."

Dale nodded.

The nurse left the room, I took a deep breath and it all came spilling out of me, every last horrible detail, from getting the email inviting me to visit CammBate, to seeing Wes at the coffee shop, to our date, to Jeremy's visit.

"Holy fuck," Dale said and let out a low whistle to add emphasis. "Wow, just wow. I'm going to admit, I'm completely surprised. Wes has shown up twice already to check on you. He got there right before the ambulance."

I groaned. "I'm a grown-ass adult. How the hell did I get taken in by a twenty-year-old? I should have known better. I remember hearing the dinging sound of the tip jar. I knew I recognized that sound but didn't think about it because music was also playing."

"Any chance Wes didn't know what happened?"

"How could he not? I mean, it was his idea to take us to Dylan's apartment, then dragged us into the room where he and Dylan *performed*." I bit out the last word with as much venom as I could manage. "I'm such a fool." The tears welled in the corners of my eyes. Still, I refused to cry again for another guy, so I blinked them back and shoved the emotions that caused them down into the pit of my stomach. "I think I'm more embarrassed about the fact that I'm here. That little punk sent me to the hospital. What the actual fuck?"

"You did nothing wrong. Well, maybe you shouldn't have started a relationship with a guy you originally saw on CammBate. Still, we've all made disastrous relationship decisions."

"Thanks," I said, shaking my head.

"You know what I mean. If anything, the kid probably broke the law when he didn't inform you that you were being filmed during your sexual encounter."

"Maybe, but that's going to be tough to argue. I mean, I knew he was a CammBoy. I knew he worked with Dylan. I knew the room I had sex in was used for their shows together. It will be hard to argue I 'didn't know' with all that stacked against me."

"What are you going to do now?" Dale asked.

"Piece my life back together. I hope I'm not fired after my boss watched the video. I can't believe that fucker Jeremy sent the video to Colleen. I think that may have been what sent me over the edge."

"Only one way to find out," Dale said. "I brought my charger in earlier to make sure your phone was charged. You can check your email...if you want — or not, zero pressure. I don't want you to have another panic attack."

"I have to face the music sooner or later. At least here, they can drug me and haul me off if I lose it again."

Dale handed me my phone. I stared at the device sitting in my hand. I didn't want to look at it, but I didn't know what else to do. I touched the screen and checked out my work emails. I had a ton of them. I scrolled through and looked, but nothing seemed out of the ordinary. *What the fuck?* I had expected to see at least one email from my boss about this. Sure, there were a few of them from her, but nothing out of the normal. I called her office.

"Tristate Marketing Technologies. Colleen Dunham's office. This is Stephen. How can I help you?"

"Hey Stephen, it's Roger. Is Colleen available?"

"Oh hey, Roger. Long time. We miss you here in the office. Hope you like living upstate? Anyway, I'll patch you right through."

There was a sudden pause, and the hits of the sixties and seventies played in my ear. We really did take this whole Brill Building thing seriously in my office.

"Roger, did you get my email earlier?"

"Hey, Colleen. I know you received an email from Jeremy last night...."

"Deleted it. I figured anything he was sending would be up to no good. Should I ask?"

"No. In fact, I'm glad you deleted it." I shook my head. "Not that there was anything illegal, immoral or unethical about the contents. Let's say Jeremy had a video of me and wanted to share the video with you as a way to...tarnish my reputation."

"Revenge porn," Colleen said flatly. "Happened to a cousin of mine. Don't worry. I didn't watch it. Now I'm glad I didn't. And even if I had, I wouldn't have thought anything of it. What two grown people do in their private lives is not of my concern."

"Thanks. I needed to hear that."

"About my other email."

"I will look at it, ASAP. I didn't get to look at any other emails yet. I had a bit of a panic attack when I found out what Jeremy did."

"Understandable. Anyway, we need your approval for a new logo on the Hart Productions new show."

"I thought we already approved that logo...like three times."

"Yep. And the lead producer keeps changing his mind. I have half a mind to fire him as a client."

"But you won't."

"You're damn right I won't. He brings in a ton of money for the firm. And each time we create a new logo, I send him another bill."

"I'll take a look at the mockup as soon as I can."

"Perfect. And again, don't worry about that little...awfulness. I think you could probably have sex on my desk and I would still respect the hell out of you. I'd have to have the desk burned and my office sanitized, but I'd still respect you."

I laughed. "Such a way with words... How did you get in the marketing business?"

"Luck... Pure. Dumb. Luck."

"Anyway, I need to get back to what I'm doing here. I'll get that approval to you today."

"Take care." And with that, Colleen disconnected the phone.

"I take it that went better than expected?" Dale asked.

I'd forgotten Dale was still in the room the whole time I'd been on the phone with Colleen. I breathed through my nose and out through my mouth. "My boss deleted the email. She never looked at it. When she saw it was from Jeremy, she got rid of it. Apparently, everyone at TMT is well aware of the state of my relationship with Jeremy. Colleen assumed it was some kind of revenge tactic on Jeremy's part. Thank God for small mercies."

The knocking sound caused my head to twist toward the door.

"Hey Dale, has Roger woken up yet?"

I immediately focused on my breathing. *In through the nose, out through the mouth.*

"He's not awake at the moment," Dale lied. "In fact, I can tell you that he very much doesn't want to see you…ever again."

"What did I do?" Wes asked.

"Don't play games with me, kid. I'm not that much older than you. Let's just say that little video stunt of yours almost killed Roger when he found out."

"What vide — ?"

"Don't lie to me. I spent a good deal of my life lying to people. I can recognize it from a mile away. I don't think Roger is vindictive enough to take this to the District Attorney's Office, because he's too fucking nice. Personally, I would want to see your ass locked up in jail. So do the world a favor and never get within a half-mile of Roger."

I could hear Wes trying to say something, but Dale closed the door on him.

"Sorry you had to hear that," Dale said. "I figured it was easier coming from an asshole like me. I know how to be blunt."

"Thanks. I don't think I could have done it." A single tear streaked down my cheek. I turned my head so Dale couldn't see it.

Chapter Eighteen

Wes

I drove away from the hospital bawling. I didn't know what happened. I had to pull over to the side of the road and let my emotions pour out of me. I was in no shape to be behind the wheel of a car. I looked down at my phone and wasn't sure who I should call. I scrolled through the numbers and hit Pietro's name.

"Hey, Wes, what's up?"

"I need you," I whispered into the phone.

I heard the quick intake of breath. "Wes, tell me where you are."

I swiveled my head around because I wasn't sure where I was. Thankfully, I recognized a building across the road. "You know that place where you took your car last year to get fixed?"

"Down on Twenty-Eight toward Kingston?"

"I'm across the road."

"I'm on my way."

I hung up the phone and burst into more tears. *What did I do? Why did Roger not want to see me? Why did he have that guy do it for him?* I'd broken up with guys before, but this was different. I'd never felt like this before. I thought everything had gone so smoothly. I saw the four-door sedan pull up behind me. I unlocked the passenger side door.

Pietro opened the door and slid in beside me. "What happened?" I watched as Pietro's car sped off. "I brought Valeria. She's taking my car back. I didn't think you should be driving from the way you sounded. Can we switch?"

I didn't say anything, but I opened the door, looked to make sure there was no oncoming traffic and walked to the back of the car. Pietro met me in the middle. He reached out to grab me, and I lost it again. I tried to slide to the ground, but Pietro held me up. I let him take me to the car's passenger side, and he buckled me in. I leaned against the glass and stared out of the window, trying to figure out what I had done wrong.

I didn't hear Pietro get into the car with me. I felt the car's movement as the scenery started passing by. I tried to start talking a couple of times, but the sounds that came out of me were garbled nonsense. Pietro reached across the center console and grabbed my hand at some point. I could hear him trying to coax the story out of me, telling me it would be all right. I stared into space.

When we got back to the apartment, Pietro practically dragged me into the place. He helped me into my bedroom, took off my shoes and covered me with a blanket. I lay there in the dark for what seemed like forever. Eventually, the door to my room opened.

A human form lay down on the bed next to me. I could smell the combination of Pietro's body odor mixed with his favorite brand of cologne.

"I'm here," he said quietly. "When you're ready to talk, I'm here."

"But Valeria?" I managed to croak out.

"She understands. You're… You're family. If you're breaking, I'm breaking. You need me now. She gets that." He rolled over and wrapped an arm around me. "You're safe. Go to sleep. We'll deal with whatever this is in the morning."

* * * *

The next morning's first hint of light came through the blinds, and I looked at the clock. I was already late to work. I looked for my phone and found that Pietro had placed it on the charger next to my bed. I pulled it off and read through a slate of text messages, the first from Autumn.

Pietro called. What's going on?

The next was from Dylan.

Dude, what happened? Autumn's totally freaked. Call me.

Next, Autumn texted again.

Don't worry about your shift. I've got it covered. Txt when you can?

I rolled back over, trying not to wake Pietro. He was lying facing away from me, but he was still wearing the same clothes he'd picked me up in yesterday. I let myself close my eyes and listen to the sound of Pietro's breathing next to me.

A couple of hours later, I rolled out of bed. I wasn't going anywhere today. I took a quick shower and put on a pair of pajamas. I headed to the kitchen because I needed coffee and something to eat.

"There he is," Valeria said as I walked in. "Pietro had to go to class. He didn't want to leave you here alone, so he asked me to stick around."

"I don't need a babysitter," I quipped. Immediately, I regretted that. "I'm sorry. I'm just…" The waterworks began to flow again. I collapsed into a sitting position in the middle of the floor.

I was looking down at the ground when a box of Kleenex appeared below me on the floor. Valeria sat down next to me. She reached out an arm and placed it around my shoulders.

"What's wrong with me? Tell me what's wrong with me," I implored.

"How about you tell me what happened first? What did this guy do to you?"

"I didn't say anything about a guy."

"You didn't need to. I've seen this type of emotional breakdown before. There's always a guy involved. So, what happened?"

"I… I don't even know." I laid out everything that had happened.

When I finished with my story. Valeria said, "Fuck him!"

"That's not—"

"No," she said flatly. "Fuck him," she repeated, drawing out each word slowly. "As my older sister once told me, *'two tears in a bucket, motherfuckit.'* You've shed plenty of tears over this guy already. If he can't see why you're amazing, then that's on him. Not you."

We sat on the floor for a while longer. I finally pushed myself up and made it into the kitchen.

"What can I get for you?" Valeria asked.

"Coffee and a Pop-Tart."

"You man-children and your Pop-Tarts. You do realize they are not food? They're pastries, not an actual meal."

I shrugged. "They're tasty."

She rolled her eyes but headed right to the cabinet where we kept the boxes of Pop-Tarts. "Toasted?" she asked. I nodded. I felt like a little kid again.

In a couple minutes, she had a cup of coffee and a Pop-Tart sitting in front of me. By the time Pietro came home, I had started to dig myself out of my funk a little bit—at least enough to tell him what had happened. He didn't try to patronize me and tell me it would be all right. That's one thing I liked about Pietro. Even when my parents died, he'd never said, "They're in a better place," or "Snap out of it." He'd let me grieve…in my own time.

The next few days were the roughest. I tried texting Roger a couple of times, but I didn't get a response. I hadn't expected one. I kind of went through the motions at work and school. I didn't do anything else. I would come home, crawl into bed, only to wake up and do it all over again. I figured each day I woke back up was a small victory.

Dylan checked on me a couple of times, but he didn't know how to handle depressed me. *No one* knew how to handle depressed me. I dropped a coffee one day, sat down in the hot mess and cried. Stefan had called Pietro to come get me. The last words I heard were Stefan saying, "That boy needs professional help. I can't have him back working when he's like this," so I didn't go back.

I was beginning to get out of my head when I realized my financial situation would be coming to a head again soon. I had rent that was going to be due. I had some money in the bank, but only enough to cover one month. The last time I'd gotten depressed like this, it had taken me almost six months, therapy and good drugs to help me pull through. Thinking about it made me curl up into a ball and fall asleep.

On the one-week anniversary of my breakup with Roger, I pulled myself together enough to go back to work. I promised Stefan I wouldn't break down again. The look he gave me let me know that he wasn't too convinced, but he let me back in the door. I went through the motions and even plastered on a smiling face to make the customers feel better about their lives.

"Dude, I've been trying to get ahold of you. Where have you been?" I looked up to see Dylan standing in front of me.

"I've been trying to keep it together. All I can do is put one foot in front of the other." I glanced over and saw Stefan watching me from the other side of the store. "What do you want to drink? The boss is watching."

"The usual."

"One bold roast coffee coming right up." I turned around, grabbed a cup and sleeve then poured Dylan his coffee. When I finished the pour, I turned around and gave the coffee to Dylan. "If you want to talk, I think I have a break coming in like five minutes."

I went back to my work. I looked at my watch and informed Stefan that I was going on break. I grabbed a coffee and headed over to the table in the corner of the café where Dylan sat reading something on his phone.

I sat down across from him and took a sip.

"You look like crap," Dylan said.

"Well, hello to you, too," I mumbled.

"Well, you do. What do you want me to say? 'Why, Wes, you look like sunshine and daffodils are fluttering out of your ass'?" I smiled at his attempt to infuse our conversation with humor. He finally looked at me and asked, "What happened?"

I took a deep breath, and with the least amount of emotion possible, I told Dylan the story. When I was done, he had a pitying look I saw from everyone these days.

"Well," Dylan started, "at least you made some money off him. Speaking of which, I have the four grand I owe you two. Guess it all goes to you now. Fuck him." The befuddled look on my face caused Dylan to stop talking. "Let me ask you one question."

"Okay."

"Did you know you were streaming yourself and Roger the night you slept with him at my apartment?"

My jaw dropped in shock.

"You recorded us?" I asked. The fire started to flame deep in my belly.

"Not me. I wasn't there. Remember? But I think you may have turned the system on accidentally. I honestly thought you knew you'd let him fuck you on camera. Hell, I thought you did it for the fun of it. I even said something like, '*you two put on a good show last night*,' or something like that. Maybe I should have been more specific — something like, 'I spanked my own meat watching you fuck on camera.'"

I sat there running through the night with Roger in my head. I remember going into the bedroom and turning on the lights. I tried to skip over the sexy parts. "Fuck, I plugged my iPhone into the charger connected to the computer so we could have music."

"That probably turned everything on. I had set it up to make it start faster and the volume on the tip jar lower. I hadn't thought anyone else would be in there messing with the computer." Dylan looked down at his coffee cup before meeting my eyes. "I feel like I'm responsible for this."

I tuned Dylan out for a second as I ran back through my own memories. The words Roger's friend had said now made perfect sense. *"That little video stunt of yours… I don't think Roger is vindictive enough to take this to the District Attorney's Office… See your ass locked up in jail."*

"He thinks I did this on purpose," I realized out loud. "And why wouldn't he? I take him to the apartment where he first saw me have sex with you, then suddenly there's a sex video of him and me out floating around in cyberspace." I leveled my gaze at Dylan. "We both know those videos don't stay on CammBate, no matter what the end-user licensing agreement says. Once we've filmed a video, anyone can find it."

"That's why we don't use our real names," Dylan said.

"True, but Roger and I didn't bother with fake names because we didn't know anyone was watching."

"But it's not your fault," Dylan tried to reassure me.

"I don't think it matters who or what is at fault here. The fact is…it happened. I have no idea what kind of fallout this could have caused Roger."

Dylan let out a sigh. "That's one of the things I love about you, Wes. Even when you been tossed to the ground and kicked, you still worry about the man kicking you."

"He's not kicking me…at least not intentionally. Admittedly, this is based on one-hundred-percent conjecture. He could have decided he didn't like me after all. Hell, the guy in the hospital room could have been his old lover, for all I know."

"Do you think that's what happened? Honestly?"

I hesitated and shook my head, "No."

"If there's a way to make this right," Dylan said, holding eye contact, "I'm going to find it."

With that, he pushed himself away from the table and walked out of the café. I turned and watched him leave.

Chapter Nineteen

Roger

After getting out of the hospital, I had spent the next week walking through the motions of life. I had found every copy of the video I could and asked websites to pull it. If they hadn't responded, my lawyer sent them a letter warning them that I would sue them if they didn't. It was easy to threaten websites based in the US, Canada and most of Europe. The laws became much more complicated once we got to Africa, the Middle East or Asia. I had never guessed I would have a sex video on the Internet. I had made Dale and Talgat swear to me on the apple orchard's crops for the next one hundred years that they wouldn't try to find the vid. I didn't need them to watch my shame.

At work, I had tried to pretend nothing was wrong, but everyone had noticed I was a bit distant. I had confided in Mitzi, who was less shocked about me dating a twenty-year-old or having a sex tape than she was about Jeremy showing up at my house.

"If he shows up again, can't you just shoot him?" she asked me during a Zoom call.

I looked sternly at her. "For the record, since this call is being recorded, I have no intent of causing Jeremy harm today, tomorrow or any day in the future. Also, New York is not a 'stand your ground' state, so I can't just shoot anyone I want if they're on my property. I have a legal obligation to get away from any criminal first."

"Well, that sucks," Mitzi grumbled on my behalf. "Too bad. I wanted to see you shoot him. That's a video I'd pay good money to watch."

She had at least made me laugh. I said goodbye, and there was a knock on my front door. "I'll see you later, Mitzi. I think the UPS guy is here."

"See you tomorrow." I clicked on the 'leave' button.

I walked downstairs and opened the door.

I really do need to learn to look through the peephole. "What do you want?" I growled.

"Down, boy," Dylan Holland said, standing on my doorstep. "I have some information you may want to have. You may not care, but I think you should hear it anyway."

I glared at him for a second. I had to admit that it took a lot of balls to come out here to my place. And I'd seen Dylan's balls and knew he had some low-hanging ones.

"You're over twenty-one?"

"Yes, I am… Why?"

"You might as well come in. We can have a drink."

I held the door open for Dylan, and he walked in. I didn't think he'd be here that long, so I didn't bother telling him to take off his jacket.

"Follow me," I said and led him into the living room. "So, what's your poison?" I said, gesturing to the bar.

He walked over and let out an appreciative whistle. "Damn! You are stocked."

"I take it you've seen the video," I said, making a somewhat perverted gesture to my crotch.

Dylan rolled his eyes. "Whiskey…neat," he said.

"Let's make that two," I said. I pulled the most expensive bottle I owned.

"What are you serving?"

"Macallan M Single Malt Scotch Whiskey," I said as I poured out one finger for him and two for me. I handed him the glass, "Sip, don't chug. At two-hundred-and-forty dollars an ounce, you want to make sure you take your time with alcohol like this."

"Holy fuck!"

I didn't respond, but the price tag had gotten the response I wanted from the kid. I wasn't feeling overly generous at the moment, so making it clear that we lived in two very different worlds was entertaining.

I took a seat in my usual recliner and looked at Dylan. "Why are you here?" I wanted to add the word 'boy' at the end, but I figured I wasn't in the South and couldn't get away with that.

"I think I know what happened between you and Wes, and it's my fault."

I didn't respond immediately. Instead, I took a sip and rolled it around in my mouth. "If you smell this whiskey, you should get a hint of oak, vanilla and spice. When you taste it, you should recognize the spice burst with the vanilla, dried fruit, ginger and clove. It makes for a potent experience—or so the salesperson told me when I bought the bottle a few years ago. I bought it because I wanted to say I purchased a six-thousand-dollar bottle of whiskey. I wondered if I could distinguish between a genuine article or a lesser brand. I want to think I could, but I'm not sure." I turned my head to look Dylan in the eyes before asking, "So, what makes you think I'll believe anything you have to say?"

"Easy, because I don't care if you believe me or not. I do believe you still care about Wes. If you didn't, you wouldn't be this much of an ass."

I chuckled. I almost felt like an evil Bond villain. But Dylan had interrogated me once, and the shoe had flipped. So, I would let him squirm for all it was worth. I took another sip and gestured for him to continue.

"I didn't know you were coming to my place. That was one hundred percent by accident, so I couldn't have known that you'd broadcast yourselves using my account."

"That lets you off the hook legally. You can plead ignorance—"

"But that's just it. Wes didn't know about my new setup. He hadn't cammed with me in days, so I hadn't shown it to him. When he plugged his iPhone into my system so you could listen to music, he inadvertently booted the entire system. I had it designed to do that. It was just faster. There's no way he knew that I'd done it."

I took a sip.

"Now, I know you're sitting there all high and mighty judging me, but ultimately, I have no skin in this game, other than my best friend is hurting. I know I'm not his best friend. The hierarchy of Wes' friendships goes Pietro, Autumn, then me. It's been that way for years, and I'm okay with that."

I took a sip.

"But I care about Wes, and you shoving him out of your life like this is eating him up from the inside. Normally, I'd tell him to get some dick and move on, but he's hurting. And I'm not talking like kiddie-crush hurting. I've seen Wes go through a crushing breakup. This is different."

A ping of guilt hit me. I'd never even given Wes the chance to explain himself. I took another sip.

"If you don't believe me, I don't blame you. If you don't like me, I don't give a fuck. I really don't. But when you hurt Wes, I care. I care a lot." He took a sip, then gulped the rest down. "That's what I've come here to tell you. Believe me or not, I don't care. But I can tell you're hurting, and I know Wes is. Can't you two hurt together?" Dylan set the glass down on the coffee table. "Oh," he said as he stood. He reached into his pocket and pulled out a round wad of cash. "Here's two-thousand dollars." He tossed me the rolled-up bills. "I wanted to make sure you got paid. If you're going to look down your nose at us for doing what we do, the least you can do is get paid for the time you spent on camera...like the rest of us." He started to leave. "Don't bother showing me the way out. I know it already." He turned and faced me one more time. "Unlike Wes, I did sell my body for sex. Trust me, I know every nook and cranny in this place. Mr. Gerry was one of my best clients, and not once did he ever treat me like you've treated Wes — and I actually was his whore."

I rolled the ball of bills around in my hand and listened for the front door to close. I let out a breath.

Part of me wanted to run screaming from the house, but another part needed to digest the conversation. I went upstairs and lay down.

* * * *

Wes

Pietro and Valeria were out on the town enjoying their Valentine's Day evening. Me? I was still hating life, but it got a little easier every day. I was going to curl up in a ball and watch a serial killer plow his way through college coeds but decided I should probably make a little money instead. The world was full of guys and the occasional gal who would be home on Valentine's Day looking for an online boyfriend experience.

I took a shower and got myself ready. Can't take a dildo on camera if you don't douche properly. Once I was ready, I put a sock on my door handle — just in case — and turned on my webcam. I was wearing my usual outfit — a pair of shorts and a tank top with a jockstrap underneath. I quickly realized that showing them my ass before taking off my jockstrap earned me higher tips. And I was all about the tips.

"Hey there, ChristopherTree69. Haven't seen you in a while. Glad you're here."

"Oh really, CarlyBear117? You want to see me without my tank top? It's going to take some tips to inspire me."

"GorgeousCock10. Hmm…that sounds like a lot of fun. I'm sure feeling you inside me tonight would be nice. I have something that's about that size around here somewhere." I pulled out my twelve-inch dildo and held it up. "If we're lucky, I'll totally get to take this tonight for you."

I worked my way down to my jockstrap over time. I talked with the people watching, got myself hard, tweaked my nipples and my tips started coming in very slowly. Basically, I felt like I was doing CammBate by numbers. I think the crowd could tell that I wasn't into it.

Suddenly, the jackpot exploded on the screen, letting me know I had a new high tipper. *Holy shit! Someone tipped me five-thousand-dollars.* "Thank you, 40sCammGent." As soon as the screenname was out of my mouth, I took a deep breath and tried not to think about the man behind that screenname. My cell phone buzzed. I looked over and saw Roger's phone number show up. It's not like I could lie and say I wasn't here. He obviously was watching.

"What? I'm a little busy."

"Don't hang up. Please hear me out," Roger said rapidly.

"I'm listening," I said coolly. I looked at the screen and said, "Hey, viewers. You all remember the hot older guy who fucked me on camera? Well, he dumped me, and now he tipped me a huge tip and called my phone. What should I do? Do I hear him out or hang up on his ass?" *The wisdom of crowds.*

I watched as the responses came into the chat box. There was definitely a mixture of reactions. Some were like 'Kick him to the curb', while others said, 'Take him back'. I didn't know if he wanted me to take him back, since I had put the phone down and stopped listening to him. After a minute, the responses slowed down. I picked up the phone. "Well, it looks like my audience says I should at least talk to you."

There was a knock on the front door of my apartment. I threw on my shorts and grabbed my shirt, casually leaving my room and walking to the front door. I looked through the peephole. Sure enough,

Richie Rich stood on my front porch with a bouquet, chocolates and a bottle of wine.

I opened the door. I didn't say anything. I let him follow me down the hall to the living room. I spun and sat down on the couch.

"Speak. You already know I'm busy."

The look that crossed Roger's face was not what I expected. He looked remorseful, shameful even. I had been ready for pissed off or even begging, but shame I wasn't ready for.

"Dylan came by my house yesterday."

"Oh?"

"He told me everything."

"Okay." This wouldn't be a very long conversation if I kept up with the one-word responses.

"You may hate me, but until Dylan told me what had happened, I felt like I had been in the right to be such an asshole. I thought you had tricked me into being on camera with you."

"I would never have done that," I spat out. "I thought you knew me better."

"I do. I fucked up, okay? I freaked out. Jeremy showed up on my doorstep with the video then he sent it to my boss. I had a full-on panic attack and went to the hospital because I'd stopped breathing and passed out. And I let Dale turn you away, thinking it was the easiest thing for me while I lay in the hospital. I shouldn't have done that. Don't blame Dale. Let's face it. Woodstock is a small town. You're probably going to run into him at some time. Don't blame him. He's actually a nice guy. I'm the one you should blame."

I sat there for a second looking at Roger. I wanted to have a snappy comeback and put him in his place. Really, I wanted to hurt him as much as I'd been hurting. I closed my eyes and took a breath in through my nose. As I let out the breath, I opened my eyes and looked into Roger's face. The hurt and venom I had disappeared in one cleansing breath. "I'm sorry, too. Even though I didn't intentionally send your video over the Internet, I should have known something was up with the computer. In retrospect, I've looked at the times when I should have known it happened. From dismissing the dinging sound on Dylan's computer to not picking up on Dylan telling us that he'd watched and enjoyed the show."

"Well, that part he left out yesterday when he was at my place," I said with a laugh. "Not the 'having seen it' part, but the 'enjoying it' part."

"Yeah, he totally spanked off watching us go at it."

"Apparently, him and a ton of other guys across the world."

Roger placed the Valentine's Day items on the coffee table, then came and kneeled before me on the ground.

"I am so sorry. I have no right to ask you to give me another chance."

I looked down into his pleading eyes and could tell he was completely genuine. My heart melted. I grabbed both sides of his face and drew myself down to his mouth. I desperately needed to feel his lips against mine. He wrapped his arms around me and pulled me closer to him, my legs on either side as he held me. I didn't care that he'd destroyed me over the past week. I knew I needed him.

"Well, this is awkward," Pietro's voice thundered from the entryway. "And you are?"

Roger turned and stood up. He extended his hand and said, "I'm Roger Havemeyer. You must be Piet—"

"Pietro, why are you standing in the hallway?" Valeria poked her head around. She looked at me and mouthed, *He's hot*, before saying, "This ought to be good."

"Pietro, let me introduce you to the guy I've been seeing," I said, standing from the couch.

"This is the motherfucker who hurt you," Pietro said.

"And from the looks of it, he ain't hurting anymore," Valeria said as she noticed the giant bulge in my pants. I shifted behind Roger and used him as a shield to hide my growing erection. I tried to will the blasted thing down, but he wouldn't cooperate.

"Oh," Pietro said, his face turning red as he tried to divert his eyes from looking in my general direction. "Well, umm…"

"He's not usually speechless," I said. "I think we broke him."

"Yeah, probably not the best way for us to meet. Would love to have you and Valeria out to the house for dinner sometime. If that's okay with Wes and both of you?"

Pietro was about to say something, but Valeria cut him off. "That sounds lovely. Pietro and I are going to head into his bedroom…on the other side of the apartment." She gently pushed Pietro in the direction of his room before she added, "From the looks of things, we'll see you two in the morning."

"What?" Pietro got out before she shoved him into his room and closed the door.

I couldn't help myself. I busted out laughing. "Well, that was fucking awkward."

"Understatement of the year."

Roger turned around, gripped both sides of my face, leaned down and kissed me. When we pulled away for air, he said, "I am so sorry. I can't say that enough. After Jeremy, I was immediately ready to assume the worst. Admittedly, learning about the video from him on my doorstep didn't help, but I should have called you immediately."

"Yeah, but like you said, he sent it to your boss. If Stefan had been sent the video, I think I would have freaked out and never left the apartment. Did she watch it?"

"Huh?"

"Did your boss watch the video?"

"Thank God, no. She saw it was from Jeremy and deleted it. I did tell her what it was...generally speaking. I didn't think Colleen could handle all the juicy details."

"Hmm..." I said, leaning my cock into Roger. "I like juicy details."

"I like how you think."

I grabbed Roger's hand and pulled him into my bedroom. I got into the room and realized I was still broadcasting. "Oh, sorry about that," I said as Roger sat down on my bed. "I had been... Well, you know, you sent me the giant tip to get my attention, which totally worked. I should turn this off. I'm totally talking too much. Am I talking too much?"

"No need. This is who you are, and I'm not ashamed of who we are together. Let 'em watch."

"Are you sure?" I asked. "I don't want you having regrets later."

"I don't regret having sex with you. I don't regret that people watched us. I regret learning about it the way I did and how I handled it."

I turned to the camera. "Well, everyone," I said, "this is my boy toy…" I looked around the room. The first book I saw had the last name 'Archer' on the cover, so I went with it, "Archer."

"I'm Archer," Roger said, utterly unfazed. "And we're going to have some fun together tonight. We hope you enjoy watching us as much as we enjoy being us."

"I don't want you to distract us, though, so I'm turning off the tip menu," I said. Roger shot me a look, but I continued, "It's Valentine's Day. For all you guys who don't have someone tonight, you have Archer and Erik. We're a slightly dysfunctional but incredibly passionate gay couple who like to fuck. And trust me, this time, I'm going to pound the hell out of Archer's ass."

Roger shot me a slight grin. I knew he was game. I straddled him and started kissing him. He wrapped his arms around me. I could feel him growing through his suit pants. Without a doubt, this was going to be a CammBate show people talked about for ages.

Chapter Twenty

Roger

I woke up the following day, and I could still feel the emptiness left by Wes' cock from the past night. He may not have been as big as me, but I hadn't taken a cock in me in a long time. I won't lie. It had stung like a bitch at first. Then he hit my prostate, and I remembered why I'd enjoyed getting fucked in the first place.

Wes was tucked against me. I know I had two orgasms, and I think Wes had three, maybe four, before we finally called it a night, showered, changed the sheets and crashed. I reached over to Wes' nightstand and grabbed my cell phone to ensure I wasn't missing anything. The first message was from Dale.

So, Talgat and I checked out a little website last night out of curiosity. We were a bit surprised by what we saw... I guess it's clear you have mended fences.

Hope you enjoyed and learned a thing or two, I sent back with a winky face. *I can't wait for you two to meet him in person.*

The next text was from Jeremy. I didn't bother reading it. I deleted it. I hope his friends watched me getting fucked by a guy half my age. Since Christmas Eve, I truly felt free of him for the first time. I didn't love him anymore. I didn't even like him anymore. I didn't hate him, either, though. I wasted a lot of emotional energy hating Jeremy. Now, I didn't care.

"What are you doing?" a voice nestled against my chest asked.

"Responding to some texts."

"Is it time to get up?"

"What time do you need to get up?" I countered.

"I think I already missed going to work."

"I texted Autumn when you went to sleep last night and told her we made up and that you probably wouldn't get to the coffee shop on time this morning. She agreed to switch shifts today. You'll go in later this morning and still have plenty of time to get in your hours at work before heading to class this evening."

"Wow, you know my schedule," Wes said, finally propping himself up next to me.

"That I do. I like knowing where you are." I reached forward and pressed my lips against his.

"Ugg…" Wes said when he pulled away. "I have morning breath."

"You taste amazing."

"I'm sure you tell that to all the boys."

"You know what would taste even better?" I asked.

"Coffee?" Wes said jokingly.

"Well, that, too, but I think I should get some protein in me first." I lowered myself down to Wes' crotch and licked under the top of his waistband. My teasing sure got something poking into my chin quickly. I pulled back his pajama bottoms and let his gorgeous cock spring free. I started at the bottom and licked all the way up, then all the way down. I teased it with my tongue and hands. Wes moved beneath my control, wanting to push into me. When I knew he couldn't stand it anymore, I opened my jaw and took him all the way down to his base. I got up off him and kneeled on the bed.

"Fuck my face," I said.

Wes stood up on the bed in front of me, reached up to the ceiling to steady himself, aimed his cock at my lips and started pumping my throat. At some point, he stopped using the ceiling to balance himself and instead used the back of my head. I concentrated on my breathing and used my tongue to explore his cock as it slid in and out of my mouth.

"Fuck!" I heard him say as the first splurge of cum hit the back of my throat. He tried to pull out, but I kept going until I had milked every last drop from him and swallowed.

Wes lowered himself down to the bed. "Whoa, that was unexpected."

"I hope in a good way," I said, narrowing my eyes at him questioningly.

"Oh, it was perfect. Who would have guessed a guy your age could have such amazing cock-sucking skills?"

"Oh, don't you start in on that. You know I have no problem bending you over my lap and spanking you."

"Promises, promises," Wes said with the largest smile I'd ever seen on his face.

* * * *

Wes and I spent the rest of the week either at my place or at his. I never needed to do a repeat performance as Archer, but I let Wes know that I would be happy to jump in whenever he needed Archer's cock or ass for a show.

By the time the weekend rolled around, I was ready for a big party at my place. I invited everyone—my friends and Wes'. I wanted everyone to see us as a couple, and I didn't care who knew.

Ruby and Stephanie couldn't make it because they were out of town at a women's only retreat up in Vermont. Wes tried to cajole Pietro and Valeria into coming. Valeria had them locked into seeing her parents down in the city that weekend. That left Dylan and Autumn on Wes' side and Dale and Talgat from mine.

The front door rang. "Hey, Wes, can you grab that?"

"On it," his voice called from downstairs. I had just gotten out of the shower. I didn't know who was there, but they were early.

I threw on my underwear, a pair of jeans and a sweatshirt. I wanted to be as casual as humanly possible tonight. Introducing our friends would be a massive step for Wes and me, so I wanted it to be natural.

Wes came walking into the bedroom, "UPS Guy was here."

"What did Chad want?" I asked.

"Mr. Powell had a package from your office."

Jason Wrench

"Wait a second?" I said suddenly. "Mr. Powell?"

"Yeah, his name is Chad Powell, though most of the gays around Woodstock just call him UPS Guy. I swear that guy has delivered more packages to gay men than Santa."

I turned my head to not look at Wes, but he was too bright. "You totally fucked Mr. Powell," Wes said, a mischievous glint in his eyes.

"I may have partaken of his delivery service a few times when I first moved here."

Wes laughed. "He really does fuck everyone who moves here."

"I guess his van helps him get around," I said, finally looking at Wes. As soon as I did, I saw it written across his face. "You've totally fucked him, too."

"Why do you think I call him Mr. Powell? He totally loved it when I talked like that to him," Wes said. "Oh, and Dylan has fucked him dozens of times."

"Dale and Talgat have both made that mistake, as well. Talgat actually dated Chad at one point."

"Wow, I didn't know Mr. — Chad — dated anyone. I assumed he was the town slut."

"Ugh, I hate that term. It's so demeaning and makes people feel shamed for expressing their sexuality. What about town hussy?"

"Skank?" Wes suggested.

"Strumpet?" I offered.

"*Strumpet*? Wow, that's not a word you hear very often. But Chad is definitely one of a kind. I think 'town strumpet' is a term I can totally get behind."

"I'm sure you could. I already know you've gotten behind Chad before," I said, trying to suppress my smile.

281

"Uh-huh," Wes said, rolling his eyes. "And I'm going to call you the Woodstock wanker."

"I can live with that. And you can be 'the town tart'."

"That makes me sound like you're going to eat me."

"Come here, little boy," I said in my best wolfish way.

"What a big...cock you have?"

The doorbell rang.

I looked at Wes. "You ready for this?"

"I am. You?"

"We've got this. And we have great friends, so I think everyone should get along swimmingly."

We bounded down the stairs together and walked to the front entrance. I grabbed the handle, twisted and opened the door to the next chapter in our lives.

Want to see more from this author? Here's a taster for you to enjoy!

Up on the Farm: Sanctuary for a Surgeon
Jason Wrench

Coming January 2023

Excerpt

I've seen a lot of things in my emergency department before but staring down at my latest patient had me stumped. I was waiting for the computerized tomography or CT scan to get sent to my laptop before transferring my patient to the plastic surgeon on call. I hadn't told my patient yet, but the surgical team was already prepping the operating room. She was still in good humor, so I opted not to stress her out. Some people hear the word 'surgery' and immediately freak.

"Good afternoon, Dr. Betancourt," my boss and best friend, Dr. Bryce Camden-Thompson, said, coming into the patient bay. "For those of you who are new to this rotation, Dr. Betancourt is one of our trauma surgeons on staff." He then turned to me and asked, "Doctor, what do we have this afternoon?"

I looked up to see why he was being so formal and noticed the string of medical students he had in tow. "Well, Dr. Camden-Thompson, there's a metal rod through the patient's left orbit media inferior quadrant."

"Dr. Chauncy," Bryce said, turning to one of his residents, "do you agree with Dr. Betancourt's diagnosis?"

The resident's eyes grew as he tried to refocus on his attending physician. I stifled a snicker. I could tell the resident had been staring at the patient and not listening to what I was saying. Let's face it... It's not every day you see a stiletto heel sticking out of someone's eye socket.

"Yes, uh, of course, Dr. Camden-Thompson. Dr. Betancourt's diagnosis is accurate."

I tuned them out as I looked down at my patient. "How are you holding up, Ms. Albariño?"

"I just want this thing out of my eye," the six-foot-three-inch individual said.

"You okay with the medical students and residents being here?"

"I already told you, doctor. Let the children see me in all my glory and idiocy."

The Lady Albariño was a bit of a frequent flyer in the emergency room. The legendary queen had been around the West Village for decades, performing and hosting. Her current attire was a sparkly dress that looked inspired by *Priscilla, Queen of the Desert*.

"Ms....?" Bryce asked the patient.

"I'm The Lady Albariño," she replied. "I would shake your hand, but I'm just as likely to shake your" — glancing down at Bryce's crotch — "since my vision isn't great...for some reason."

There were a few nervous chuckles from the medical students. Still, the residents were doing their best to appear completely affectless. One thing we explain to new students, interns and residents is that you can never look shocked when dealing with a patient. No matter how mangled or gory a patient looks, they're looking to you to be competent and in charge—even if you want to freak out.

"Yes, Ms. Albariño," Bryce continued. "Will you please explain how you ended up with the object in your eye?"

I patted Albariño's shoulder as she began her story for probably the thousandth time since entering the ED. "I was at a gig getting ready when another queen accused me of having an affair with her man—which I most assuredly would *not* be having sex with that beast. That hairy monstrosity would give a Wookie a run for their money. Well, there was a little altercation, and I ended up with Bellatrix Bordello's heel sticking out of my eye."

"Thankfully," I interjected, "the patient can still see out of her left eye, and it responds to light."

Bryce conferred with his group. My cellphone vibrated in my pocket as the ping of an email wanted my attention. I pulled out my phone, looked down and saw it was from radiology. The radiologist summarized, *"We have a left infraorbital canal-orbital floor and posterior wall of the left maxillary sinus fracture with a left maxillary hemosinus. CT scan showed no injury to the optic nerve, superior or medial rectus."*

"Well, Ms. Albariño," I interrupted Bryce's mini-lecture. "I got the CT scans back, and we will get you up to surgery now. The good news is that your eye is in good condition, so you shouldn't lose any visual function. There is a fracture in your eye socket that will need to be repaired surgically."

"Is that your way of saying you'll have to drug me, doctor?" The Lady Albariño said seductively. "You could have simply invited me over to your place for cocktails."

"As much fun as I'm sure that would be, I'm afraid my husband would have a problem with it."

The Lady Albariño sighed and threw her hand over her heart like a leading lady from the old silent films. "All the good men are either married or straight,"

I smiled and patted her on the shoulder, "Before you go on any dates, we need to have a plastic surgeon get that blasted heel out of your eye. It's not your best accessory."

I left the patient bay and watched as Bryce took the students over to a computer terminal where he could go over The Lady Albariño's CT scans with them in more detail. I got surgery on the line and let them know The Lady Albariño was being transferred into their capable hands. A minute later, she was wheeled out of the ED.

I went back to the physician's desk area and started my dictation of the case for the hospital chart. I was so lost in my work that I didn't even see Bryce sit down as he slid a cup of fresh coffee over for me.

"Well, that was a first," Bryce said. "I mean... I've read about a heel in an eye socket before in medical journals but never expected to see a drag queen with a scarlet stiletto embedded in her."

"Do you know The Lady Albariño?" I asked.

"Not personally. Richard and I have seen her show a few times over the years."

Richard was Bryce's husband and the other half of Camden-Thompson. I've always known them as the Camden-Thompson's, so I don't really know who was Camden and who was Thompson before they were married.

My husband, Chance Mercer, is an infectious disease physician at New York University. Even though we both worked for NYU, it had taken a disaster in Mexico City to bring us together. I was finishing my Surgical Critical Care Fellowship at New York University when there was a giant earthquake right outside Mexico City. I agreed to fly down with a team from NYU to help Doctors Without Borders in the aftermath. Even though Chance was almost thirty years my senior, we had fallen in love. One and a half years later, we were married, when I had been in my early thirties.

"What's Chance up to today?" Bryce asked. "Attending the vigil this evening?" What Bryce had asked about was the annual NYC AIDS vigil that took place every September twenty-seventh for National Gay Men's HIV/AIDS Awareness Day.

"He's attending but not presenting this year. I may walk over to the NYC AIDS Memorial Park at St. Vincent's Triangle on break if things are quiet around here."

The Greenwich Village Emergency Department entrance was less than a block from the NYC AIDS Memorial Park, so this was entirely doable. In fact, I could worm my way through the bowels of the facility and take a side exit that opened right across the street from the park.

"Doctors!" a voice cut through the ED. I looked up to see one of the ED nurses taking a call. "A car drove into a crowd of pedestrians at St. Vincent's Triangle. There was a gathering. Multiple injuries are heading our way. We're the closest ED, so this is an all-hands-on-deck emergency."

Without thinking, I stopped my dictation, downed the cup of coffee and went to the supply closet to put on emergency personal protective equipment. I took a deep, centering breath as I prepared myself for what was about to enter the ED. Out of the corner of my eye, I saw Bryce organizing his medical students, interns and residents into triage teams. The ED was a flurry of activity around me. When the sliding doors opened and the first victim was rolled in, I approached.

"We have a twelve-year-old male who was hit by a motor vehicle. The victim is unconscious..." The EMT read off the vital statistics of the patient.

Without waiting for more information, I said to the closest nurse, "I want a full work-up, including a whole-body CT."

"Yes, doctor," the nurse said and took over.

The following patient had a bone sticking out of her leg. I told the next nurse to get orthopedics on the phone because we had an emergency surgery. That was what my life was like for the next hour. I quickly evaluated patients, then turfed them to their next destination. Because of our proximity to the accident, we had around twenty victims come through our ED.

After helping Bryce organize surgical teams, I scrubbed in for a two-and-a-half-hour surgery. My patient had internal bleeding from blunt force trauma. Thankfully, I was able to open him up and get the bleeding stopped. The patient would have to undergo a couple of more surgeries before he was on the road to recovery, but we had him stable, and that was all that mattered.

By the time I pulled off my last set of bloodied PPE, I was exhausted. As a trauma surgeon, you learn to turn off your emotions during a crisis. If I let all the carnage get to me, I would be paralyzed in a situation like this. Instead, I took each case as it came. I had to always think three or four steps ahead in my treatment plan to keep on top of my patients. I headed back down to the

ED to see if there was anything else I could do to help. I should have been tired but I always had this buzz of energy after I finished surgery. *Probably adrenaline.*

I looked across the ED and everyone looked haggard. Thankfully, emergency medical services had diverted any non-critical cases away from our facility.

"How are you holding up?" Bryce asked as he came to stand next to me.

"I'm good. You?"

"Same."

"What about your posse?" I joked.

"They performed well. The students and interns did as they were told, and the residents stepped up. I had to order one medical student to leave the ED because he froze. I think this may have been his first or second rotation."

"Talk about being thrown into the deep end."

"Have you talked to Chance yet?"

"No," I said, the sudden realization hitting me. "I haven't thought about him and not even checked my phone." I reached into my scrubs and pulled out my cell. I was surprised that I didn't have any messages, but sometimes, in the basement of the ED and the operating room, cell reception could be spotty. I hit Chance's number and waited for the call to connect.

He didn't pick up.

I dialed again.

I heard Raul Esparza's rendition of *Being Alive* from the musical *Company* playing lightly. It took my brain a second to register the song...*our* song, the one Chance used for my ringtone on his phone. My heart plummeted as I hit redial and searched for the source. I found a colleague in a back patient bay pulling the sheet over the top of one of the victims. Absently, I hit redial again. When I heard Raul's voice break through the silence, I took three steps forward and lifted the sheet.

"What are you—?"

I ignored the physician.

Chance's blank eyes stared up at me. I don't know what happened next. The guttural sound that escaped my throat was primal.

About the Author

Jason Wrench is a professor in the Department of Communication at SUNY New Paltz and has authored/edited 15+ books and over 35 academic research articles. He is also an avid reader and regularly reviews books for publishers in a wide number of genres. This book marks his first full-length work of fiction.

Jason loves to hear from readers. You can find his contact information, website details and author profile page at https://www.pride-publishing.com

P U B L I S H I N G

Sign up for our newsletter and find out about all our romance book releases, eBook sales and promotions, sneak peeks and FREE romance books!